ALSO BY IAN MCGUIRE

Incredible Bodies
The North Water

THE
ABSTAINER

THE
ABSTAINER
Ian McGuire

A NOVEL

RANDOM HOUSE
NEW YORK

Published in the United States by Random House, a division
of Penguin Random House LLC, New York.

RANDOM HOUSE and the Random House colophon
are registered trademarks of Penguin Random House LLC.

LIBRARY OF CONGRESS CATALOGING-IN-PUBLICATION DATA
Names: McGuire, Ian, author.
Title: The abstainer : a novel / Ian McGuire.
Description: First edition. | New York : Random House, [2020]
Identifiers: LCCN 2019040115 (print) | LCCN 2019040116 (ebook) |
ISBN 9780593133873 (hardcover : acid-free paper) |
ISBN 9780593133897 (ebook)
Classification: LCC PR6113.C4832 A63 2020 (print) | LCC PR6113.C4832
(ebook) | DDC 823/.92—dc23
LC record available at https://lccn.loc.gov/2019040115
LC ebook record available at https://lccn.loc.gov/2019040116

Printed in the United States of America on acid-free paper

randomhousebooks.com

2 4 6 8 9 7 5 3 1

Book design by Diane Hobbing

First Edition

To Abigail, Grace, and Eve

———⟫•◦•⟪———

And in memory of my mother,
Joan McGuire (1925–2018)

THE
ABSTAINER

CHAPTER 1

Manchester, November 22, 1867

Midnight. There are field guns on Stanley Street, and timber barricades at every bridge and junction. Bright flames from a dozen watch fires glint orange off the black and boatless Irwell. Inside the Town Hall on King Street, James O'Connor knocks the rain from his bowler, unbuttons his top coat, and hangs them both on the iron hooks by the recreation room door. Sanders and Malone, and four or five others, are sleeping on palliasses in one corner. The rest are sitting about at tables, playing whist, gabbing, or reading the *Courier*. The place has the homely barracks-tang of stewed tea and Navy Cut; there is a rack of Indian clubs and medicine balls gathering dust by the left-hand wall, and a billiard table covered over with planking in the center. Fazackerley, the duty sergeant, notices him and nods.

"Anything?"

O'Connor shakes his head.

"There'll be someone shows himself eventually," Fazackerley says. "Some daft bastard full of ale. There's always one. You wait and see."

O'Connor pulls a chair across and sits himself down. Fazackerley half-fills a dented metal teapot with scalding water from the urn and swirls it twice.

"I'm the only Irishman awake this side of Kingstown,"
O'Connor tells him. "All the others are safe in their beds,
doing as the priests advised and staying well away."

"I thought your Fenian boys didn't pay too much attention to the monsignors."

"They pay attention when it suits them," he says. "Much
like the rest of us."

Fazackerley nods, allows himself a smile. His face is a
bristled mass of lines and planes, his eyebrows are un-
kempt, and his graying hair is scant and greasy. If it wasn't
for the incongruent brightness of his pale blue eyes—more
like the eyes of a newborn babe or a china doll than of a
man past fifty—he might look exhausted, gone-to-seed, but,
as it is, he presents, even at rest, an impression of half-
amused readiness, vigor even.

"They've seen the cavalry trotting up and down Deansgate," O'Connor goes on. "They've seen the cannons and the
barricades. They're not as stupid as you think."

"There are three of 'em who won't look so very clever
come eight o'clock, I'd say."

Fazackerley tilts his head to one side and makes a bog-
eyed, strangulated face, but O'Connor takes no notice. It's
been nine months now since he arrived on secondment from
Dublin and he's become used to the ways of his English colleagues. Always joking with him, striving to get a rise, always prodding and poking about to see what he will say or
do in answer. Friendly enough at first sight, but beneath
the smiles and laughter he senses their mistrust. Who is he
anyway, they wonder, this sudden Irishman, come to tell
them how to do their jobs? Even Fazackerley, who is the
best by far, treats him, most of the time, as an amusing
oddity, some kind of strange exception to the rule, like a
visiting Apache or a dancing bear. Other men would feel
insulted, but O'Connor lets it pass. He has no desire to ex-

plain himself. *It is much simpler and easier, sometimes,* he thinks, *to be misunderstood.*

"Maybury asked to see you as soon as you got back," Fazackerley says, straightening himself. "He's up with Palin now."

"Maybury and Palin together? What do they want with me?"

Fazackerley laughs.

"You're the true fucking oracle, Head Constable O'Connor. Didn't you know that? They want you to tell them what the future holds."

"If they'd paid me any heed before, then Charley Brett might still be living."

"That could be true, but it'll do you not the slightest good to point it out. Our great lords and masters don't generally enjoy being reminded of their missteps."

"I hear Palin's out on his arse anyway after all this dies down. Pensioned off."

"Policemen do love to gossip, don't they?" Fazackerley says. "Do you fancy your chances of taking over if he goes, Jimmy? Chief Constable O'Connor, is it?"

Fazackerley snorts at the idea as if he has just made a great joke. O'Connor finishes his tea, tugs down his waistcoat, and politely advises the duty sergeant to bugger off.

Upstairs, he listens for a moment at the office door. He knows Maybury well enough, but he has seen the chief constable only at a distance on official occasions—standing on a dais or seated on a charger. Palin is a short, soldierly-looking man. And, in public at least, rigid and a little twitchy. The day of the ambush he was away somewhere, unreachable, and the various clear warnings went unheeded as a consequence. A clerk in the Head Office has already been dismissed for it, but now the rumors are that the Home Secretary, Mr. Gathorne Hardy, has intervened and Palin will eventually be made to step down, forced retirement to the country and an afterlife of ease and plenty being about as rough as it ever gets for a fellow like him.

O'Connor hears them talking through the door, Palin's low voice, Maybury's occasional interruptions, but can't make out the words. He knocks, the conversation pauses, and Maybury calls him to come in. Neither man smiles or rises from his chair. Maybury, who is of medium height, stout with muttonchop whiskers and a port wine stain on one cheek, nods once. Palin gazes suspiciously at O'Connor as if he has seen him before but can't remember where. Both men are in their shirtsleeves and Palin is smoking a cigar. There is a jar of mustard and a bottle of vinegar on the table; a smell of sausage lingers in the blueish air.

"The sergeant told me you wanted to see me, sir," he says to Maybury.

Maybury glances at Palin, offering him the chance to speak first, but Palin shakes his head.

"Give us your report, please, Head Constable O'Connor," Maybury says. He makes it sound as if this is a normal everyday duty, as if reporting directly to the chief constable of Manchester in the middle of the night is part of his job.

O'Connor takes his notebook from his inside pocket and thumbs its pages.

"I've been walking the town all day," he says. "And I've spoken with some of my informers. I'm confident we have nothing to fear tonight. The hangings will go off smoothly, I'm sure of it. If the reprisals come, they will come later on, when things have quieted down a little. After the troops have all left town."

"So you have heard some talk of reprisals?"

"Oh, there's plenty of talking, sir, as there always is, but it's nothing we need to take too seriously for now."

"The Fenians are frightened of us, then," Palin says lightly, as if the conclusion is obvious. "Our show of force has worked as we expected."

"For now, sir, yes," O'Connor agrees, "but in a month or two I expect the situation will be different."

"Different how?" Maybury asks.

"The executions will provoke anger. There is already a strong belief that the sentences are unjust, that Sergeant Brett's death was manslaughter at worst, not murder. When the three men are hanged, then others who were on the outskirts of the Brotherhood will likely be drawn closer in. The Manchester circles may end up larger and stronger than they were before."

Palin frowns at this and sits up straighter in his chair.

"I don't follow that reasoning," he says. "You seem to be suggesting that a severe punishment might actually serve as an encouragement to others to commit a similar crime. How could that ever be the case? What is the sense?"

O'Connor glances at Maybury for help, but Maybury merely raises his eyebrows and smiles blandly back.

"If you create martyrs, sir, then that is a powerful thing."

"*Martyrs?*" Palin says. "These men are not martyrs, they are common criminals. They killed a policeman in cold blood."

"I agree, sir, of course, but that's not the general opinion in the Irish parts of town."

"Then the general opinion makes little sense to me. Are your countrymen really as foolish as all that?" he says. "Will they never learn their lessons?"

O'Connor doesn't answer straightaway. He still remembers when they brought the old rebel Terence MacManus back from California in '61, and half of Dublin turned out in the brown fog and pelting rain to watch the funeral parade. They were leaning out of windows and standing six deep in Mountjoy Square that day. When the column reached the

gates of Glasnevin Cemetery it was near-enough two miles
long. Twenty thousand Dubliners and barely even a whisper when they laid him in the tomb. If you give the Fenians
a corpse, then you'd better believe they'll know what to do
with it, he thinks. Before they brought Terence Bellew Mac-
Manus home, the Fenians were nothing to speak about, but
the next day they were the anointed successors to the men
of '48. Heroes all in-waiting. A clever man will never under-
estimate the motive power of dust and bones, but Palin isn't
clever. None of them are.

"Most of my countrymen are poor and untutored, sir,"
O'Connor explains. "The Fenians take advantage of their
ignorance. They promise them freedom and an end to all
their sufferings."

"The Fenians are fanatics."

"Quite true, sir, but fanatics are not easily discouraged."

"Neither are *we* easily discouraged," Palin says. "That's
my point, Constable. The British Empire is not a weak or
fragile thing; it has survived worse mutinies than this one.
Perhaps you should ask your friends to pass that message
along. Let our enemies know they are sacrificing themselves in a hopeless cause."

"That's not quite—"

O'Connor starts to answer, but Maybury interrupts him.

"His friends are not in a position to pass on messages,
sir," Maybury explains. "Their lives would be in danger."

"Of course," Palin says, "of course. I forgot."

There is a pause. Coal crumbles in the grate. Palin sniffs
twice and rubs the tip of his cigar into an empty coffee cup.

"Where do we get these informers from anyway?" he asks,
turning to Maybury. "And how do we know they can be
trusted?"

"Generally they make themselves known to us," Maybury
explains. "It's money that they're after. We treat what they
tell us with caution, but it sometimes proves useful. If we

understand what the Fenians are planning, we can usually nip it in the bud."

Palin scratches his chin and frowns.

"Men like that are parasites. I wonder sometimes that we lower ourselves."

"To get to the treasure you must sometimes swim through the shite, sir," Maybury says cheerfully, as if quoting an old proverb. "That's why we have Constable O'Connor here."

Palin nods, smiles, then looks across.

"I see. Is that what you do for us, O'Connor?" he asks, twitching a little at the indelicacy of the phrase. "Swim through the shite?"

"In a manner of speaking, sir, yes I suppose you could say it is."

"And you enjoy this work? You find it suits you?"

O'Connor recognizes that he is being mocked now, that Palin is letting him know where he stands. He is well used to being goaded by his English colleagues, but he is still surprised that the Chief Constable himself should feel the need.

"I do my duty, sir," he says. "As best I can. I trust that the work I do is of some small value."

Palin shrugs.

"We are waging a tiresome battle against a puny and irrational foe. None of us will be getting any medals for it, Constable, I can promise you that."

O'Connor nods at this but doesn't answer. He gazes down at his toe caps: scuffed black leather against the swirling reds and greens of Palin's Persian carpet. He feels the warmth of the fire against his calves and backside. He has learned to keep his own counsel at times like this. There is nothing much to be gained by speaking out, he knows, but plenty to be lost.

"You should get back to your work now," Maybury tells him. "Let us know if you hear anything more of interest."

"And tell Harris to bring us more coffee," Palin says, stretching forward for the evening paper. "This pot's already dead."

Downstairs in the recreation room, O'Connor plays whist instead of sleeping. He loses a shilling, then wins it back, then loses it again. At first light, he settles up with Fazackerley, puts his hat and overcoat on, and goes back outside. Soot-black buildings stand clenched beneath a marbled sky. He crosses Deansgate and follows Bridge Street down toward the Irwell. Ragged groups of red-eyed men, disgorged from the beer houses, blink and look quizzically about as if trying to remember exactly where and who they are. Shawl-clad women clustering in doorways laugh together, shake their heads, and hug themselves against the cold. The shop windows are boarded in case of trouble, but there are hand barrows selling coffee and pies, and ragamuffin boys crying halfpenny broadsides. O'Connor pauses on the Albert Bridge and watches the crowd gradually assemble.

They come in twos and threes, in sixes and sevens. From Knott Mill and Ancoats, from Salford and Shude Hill. Dark bulky figures dressed in wool and fustian. Their skin is yellowed and grimy. They smell, as they brush past him, chattering and jokey, of sawdust and pipe smoke and the acrid ingrained sweat of endless mill work. There is grandeur in a hanging, O'Connor admits; it's like watching a fine house burn down, or a great ship come to wreck. Seeing such a sight you feel, just for a moment, that you have glanced into the heart of something, that all the coyness of this world has briefly dropped away, and you are left with the nub.

Special constables, youthful irregulars, brought in from Rochdale and Preston, are massed below the gibbet to guard against sudden attack. They smoke, laugh, wrestle, sing songs; occasionally they are brought to order and made to drill. They have staves as weapons and white badges on their sleeves to indicate their status. There is much light-hearted toing and froing across the wooden barricades, much raucousness and taunting. As the sky lightens to the east, the crowd thickens and O'Connor feels an excitement growing inside him, in his chest and belly, down into his balls. He cannot help it. He is human like the rest. As he walks over the bridge toward the prison, the crowd warms and rubs against him. He tastes their beery breath, breathes it in, and feels, for a moment, part of something greater than himself—a shared desire, a sharp but indefinite urge. Up on the railway viaduct overlooking the prison's north wall, there are lines of red-coated infantry with rifles and bayonets. Blue-uniformed policemen stand in silent groups at every junction. The prison clock strikes out the half hour.

The soldiers are a mistake, O'Connor thinks—brute force won't resolve the Fenian problem, and the sight of troops makes people imagine we are at war. Such displays of might serve no good purpose, they only add more fuel to the fire. It is hard detective work and good judgment that will win this fight, he believes, not exhibitions of bombast or cruelty. Yet cruelty and bombast are what the English prefer. He has expressed this opinion, in more measured tones, in reports to Maybury and letters back to Dublin Castle, but he could be writing them in Chinese or Hebrew, for all the difference it makes.

As the clock strikes eight, the people around him stop talking and look upward. A door at the rear of the scaffold opens and a tall priest in full canonicals steps onto the platform followed by one of the condemned men—William Allen. The priest is reciting the liturgy, and Allen, who appears frail and weak-kneed, is responding. *Christ have mercy on us. Lord have mercy on us.* Their entwined voices are faint but clear. Allen glances out at the crowd, then looks away again. Calcraft the hangman appears next on the platform, followed by the other two prisoners, O'Brien and Larkin, each with a warden and an intoning priest in tow. Allen's eyes are closed and his pinioned hands are raised up in clumsy prayer. The priest is whispering into his ear. Calcraft fits and tightens the nooses, binds their ankles, and puts a white cotton bag over each man's head. O'Brien edges sideways and kisses Allen clumsily on the cheek. Larkin's legs buckle and there is a small commotion as one of the priests and a warden struggle to keep him upright. Calcraft, unperturbed, moves back and forth along the platform, checking and readjusting the fastenings with the quick, fidgety expertness of a tailor sizing suits. He gazes briefly at his work, nods in satisfaction, then steps away. O'Connor hears the caw of a crow like a dry cork being pulled from a bottle and, from over near the river, a clatter of cartwheels and the whinny of a horse. For a long moment, the three men stand side by side beneath the heavy oak crossbeam, separate but conjoined, like rough-hewn caryatids, and then with a startling suddenness they are gone. Instead of their breathing, living bodies, there are only the three taut lines of rope like long vertical scratches on the prison wall. The crowd inhales, then gives up a long guttural sigh like a wave slowly pulling back from a beach. O'Connor shudders, swallows, feels a pulse of nausea sweep up from his stomach into his mouth.

There is a pause, a silent gap, the crucial moment seems to have passed, then one of the ropes starts to twitch and swing and there are grunts of exertion from the fenced-off compartment below the platform. Boos ring out, then catcalls. The priests break off their prayers and peer downward. The rope continues its twitching, and Larkin's bagged head bobs up and down like a half-hooked fish as Armstrong the apprentice executioner lifts the body up and tugs it down again to finish the job. *Sweet Jesus, is it really so com-*

plicated to kill a man? O'Connor wonders. *The rope,* he thinks, *the fucking drop. How difficult can it be?*

He turns and starts shouldering his way back through the dense and shifting crowd. Out of habit, he looks around as he moves, checking for familiar faces. Off to the left, thirty feet away, he notices Tommy Flanagan standing alone, wearing a greasy beaver hat and smoking a meerschaum. Of course, O'Connor thinks, if any man is going to ignore all dictates of wisdom and good sense, it will likely be Thomas Flanagan. He stands awhile and looks at him. Flanagan sucks his pipe, blows out the gray smoke, blinks, and glances upward. He is a short, scrappy-looking fellow, with thick black eyebrows, sucked-in cheeks, and a nose too large for his narrow face. He looks, as he always does, much too pleased with himself. You might think he had just won at the horses, not witnessed three of his countrymen being hanged by their necks until dead. O'Connor moves closer in and tries to catch his eye. When Flanagan finally notices him, he frowns, then smiles quickly and nods his head in the direction of Worsley Street.

Ten minutes later, the two men are sitting together at a small table in the rearmost private room of the White Lion. Flanagan is dribbling hot water into his brandy and O'Connor is watching. He has his notebook out on the table and a pencil in his hand.

"You're wondering what I'm doing here, I'll bet," Flanagan says. "Wondering why I didn't stay in my nice warm bed, or go along to mass with all the others."

"Someone sent you, I expect. Told you to report back."

Flanagan sniffs and shakes his head.

"Not so," he says. "I'm here under my own recognizance. I'm not a man to be bound by the rules, you know that, Mr. O'Connor. I like to blaze my own particular path, don't I?"

O'Connor nods. That is how Flanagan likes to justify his various betrayals, so it is best not to quibble. He is a vain and trivial fellow, but he is well trusted by the Manchester Fenians and in among the general nonsense he talks, there is sometimes a gobbet or two of useable truth.

"So a sightseeing trip, then, is it?"

Flanagan frowns and looks suddenly solemn, as if the quip is in poor taste.

"I wanted to be near them at the very end," he says, "or as near as I could be. I've known Michael Larkin for a good long time. I know his wife too—Sarah she's called. The others, Allen and O'Brien, were a little hotheaded, a little bit wild, I'll grant you that, but Michael was a good family man. His four poor children orphaned and all for what?"

"They're not the only orphans hereabouts," O'Connor says.

"What happened with that prison van was just an accident. Everyone knows it. They tried to shoot the lock off the door and the poor bugger Brett got himself in the way, that's all. It was never murder. It never was."

"It hardly matters now. What's done is done."

Flanagan shakes his head.

"It matters to the fellows I know," he says. "Oh, it matters very much indeed to them fellows."

He pauses, blows the steam off his brandy, and takes a delicate sip.

"It's a nice wee drop, that one," he says, "and I thank you for it, Mr. O'Connor."

"So they're angered," O'Connor says. "But is the anger likely to lead to anything else?"

"It'll lead to plenty, to plenty. I hear there are grand plans afoot."

"What plans are they?"

"That I don't know, but I know they're fucken big."

O'Connor doesn't answer. The plans he hears about from men like Flanagan are always big, yet it's rare that anything much comes of them.

"There's a man being brought over specially from America, I hear," Flanagan says. "A soldier from the war."

"What's this man's name?"

"I don't know his name. I just know he's being brought over specially from America."

"Where's he coming from in America, New York?"

Flanagan shrugs.

"Could be New York. Could be Chicago. He's here to wreak some havoc, that's what they say."

"I've not heard of anyone coming over from America. No one else has mentioned it to me."

"That's because they don't know about it. He's a secret."

"Without a name, that's not worth anything," O'Connor says.

"I'm telling you what I know. He's sent here to take revenge for the hangings, show the world that we're not weakened or afraid."

"If you don't know his name, it's most likely he doesn't exist. He's just an idea in someone's head."

"He exists all right. They're being extra careful with it, that's all. They're wary of spies."

O'Connor nods, then licks his pencil and writes a sentence in his notebook.

"So you better watch yourself," he says.

Flanagan shrugs again. O'Connor stands up and puts a coin on the table.

"Get yourself another brandy," he says. "If you learn that name or anything else of value, you know whereabouts to find me."

Flanagan pockets the coin and nods his thanks.

"Did you see poor Michael wriggling there at the end, Mr. O'Connor?" he asks. "Did you see it? Wasn't that a terrible fucken sight? Just terrible. Can you imagine what the man was going through dangling half dead and half alive on the end of that rope with his wrists and ankles all bound? It's a shame and disgrace, if you ask me. No one deserves to die like that. To have the very life dragged out of them in public, for all to see."

"Calcraft doesn't know his trade. He's an oaf. They'd replace him tomorrow if they could, but no one wants to be a hangman these days. Who would?"

Flanagan thinks on this a moment.

"I'd consider the job myself if they ever asked," he says. "Why not? If the money was right."

O'Connor looks down at him quickly, then shakes his head.

"It's the bottom end of the rope I'd worry about most if I were you, Tommy Flanagan," he says, "not the top."

CHAPTER 2

A t the Liverpool docks, Stephen Doyle asks a porter for directions, then walks up the long hill to Lime Street Station with his knapsack slung across his shoulder and his legs still quaking from the eight-day voyage. Empty-eyed beggars call and hold out their broken billycocks to him as he passes, but he pays them no mind. He buys a ticket at the window, checks the times to Manchester, then takes a seat in the second-class waiting room. Through the wide windows, beyond the iron barricades, he watches the massive engines come and go. He counts them, then looks at his watch. Thirty trains an hour, he calculates, five hundred a day, or possibly more. The old man sitting beside him is eating plums out of a paper bag. The juices dribble pinkly into his white beard. On the platform, a guard in a neat blue uniform blows a tin whistle twice and raises a red flag.

When the train halts at St. Helens Station, a young man dressed like a farmhand comes into the compartment and looks at Doyle carefully.

"Are you the Yank?" he asks.

"Who are you?"

"I have a message."

He gives him a note and Doyle unfolds and reads it. It is

signed by Peter Rice, the Manchester Center, and it warns
him that there are detectives waiting at London Road Station with orders to stop and question any Americans arriving on the train from Liverpool.

"Do I get off here?" Doyle says.

"Next one. There'll be someone waiting. I'll show you."

Doyle nods and puts the note in his pocket. The young
man sits down in a corner seat and stares out of the carriage window at the empty platform. He has fawn-colored
down on his lip and cheeks, and his skin is greasy and pus-
tulated. The train hisses twice, then starts to clatter forward. At Collins Green, they get off together and the young
man leads him outside and points to a waiting hansom.

"This is Skelly. He'll take you where you're going," he says.

"Do you know who I am?" Doyle asks him. "What did they
tell you about me?"

"They told me I'd know you by the scars on your face," he
says.

"And what else?"

He shrugs.

"They say you've come to cause trouble."

Farms give way to quarries and brickfields, then to mills
and lime works and rows of soot-stained terraces. Doyle
can smell smoke and see the factory chimneys ahead, clus-
tered against the rain-dark sky like scorched remnants of a
ruined forest. They pass by the Exchange and follow an omnibus onto Corporation Street, then they turn again onto a
narrower side street and come to a stop. Skelly leans down
and tells him they've arrived. Another man appears, and
Doyle is led through an unpaved passageway and into a
shadowy courtyard crisscrossed with lines of dripping laundry. There is a pig rooting in the ash heap and a low, hot
smell of rot and urine. The man knocks on a door, and Doyle
hears the brief squeal of a bolt being pulled back.

The room within is small and bare, two worm-eaten

chairs and a table in the center, but nothing else. The light through the dusty windows is halfhearted and gauzy. Peter Rice gestures to one of the chairs, then sits down himself. He is a heavyset man, thick-shouldered. His grizzled hair is cut tight to his square skull and his features are fleshy and broad.

"This is where you'll stay," he tells Doyle. "There's a bed upstairs. I'll have a woman come in to build you a fire."

Doyle looks about the room.

"What about the neighbors? Do they know who I am?"

"They know to keep quiet. You don't need to worry about them."

"The boy gave me your note on the train. It's not what I expected."

Rice shifts a little and rubs his nose.

"It pays to be cautious," he says. "It might have been nothing."

"There were police waiting at the station?"

"That's what we heard from the porters. That they were asking about any Americans coming in from Liverpool. That's what we heard, but it might have been nothing."

"How many people here knew I was coming?"

"Three or four."

"Can you give me the names?"

Rice shakes his head, shifts his elbows, leans forward a little. His skin is pitted and grimy; the stubble on his jaw is thick and black as iron filings.

"That's not the way we do it," he says. "You don't come here and start asking us questions, suspicioning."

"How else would the police know I'm coming?"

"They don't know you're coming. It's guesswork, rumor, that's all. They don't even have a name."

"Who starts the rumor?"

"Mebbe someone in New York. Ever think of that? From what I hear, New York is full of traitors."

Doyle breathes twice, then shrugs. Kelly has already warned him about Peter Rice: He is loyal to the cause but jealous of his authority and mistrustful of strangers.

"I need to be sure before I start off," Doyle says. "I can't take any risk."

"Before we attacked the van no one talked. Twenty-five men and not a whisper. You should remember that, before you start thinking about finding any spies in Manchester."

"Men change—get scared or greedy. I've seen it happen." Rice shakes his head.

"In America they might but not around here."

Doyle nods.

"Colonel Kelly told me you were your own man," he says. "That you might not like taking orders."

"His letter don't mention taking any orders. It says I should offer you my help when required and that's what I'll do."

Doyle takes a pouch from his pocket and fills his pipe. He offers the pouch to Rice, but Rice shakes his head.

"If a Manchester man were to get an urge to talk to the police, how would he do it?"

"There's a detective office in the Town Hall on King Street."

"Do you keep a watch outside?"

"Most of the time."

"But not always?"

Rice gives him back a sharp, skeptical look. Doyle reminds himself to be careful. If he treads too hard he will lose him completely and it's much too soon for that.

"We have a boy watching in the daytime," Rice says, "but there's no one there at night."

Doyle nods.

"And if someone goes to the Town Hall intending to talk, which detective do they ask for?"

Rice shakes his head and sniffs.

"No one goes to the Town Hall," he says. "No one talks."

"But if they ever did?"

Rice pauses before answering. The pig snorts in the courtyard. A baby begins to wail.

"There's a head constable named James O'Connor," he says. "They brought him over from Dublin six or seven months ago. He likes to put himself about, ask questions."

"Do you know where he lodges? His address?"

Rice shakes his head.

"But I could find it out easy enough."

"I want to be sure, that's all," Doyle says. "You understand. I can't start this until I'm sure."

"Take your time," Rice says. "Wait if you want to. No need to rush in."

Doyle nods and looks around the empty room.

"When that woman comes, I need an oil lamp and a bottle of whiskey," he says.

"I'll pass the message on."

Rice has a ragged crêpe band tied around his right arm. Doyle looks at it and nods.

"How were they captured in the end? Kelly didn't tell me."

"The peelers got them on the Gorton brickfield. Larkin was too sick to run quick, and the other two stayed back to help him."

"The British did us a service with the hanging," Doyle says. "If they were locked in jail the names'd be forgotten next year."

"They died for their country," Rice says. "I don't call it a service. I call it murder. Them boys are martyrs."

"At Gettysburg, I saw a thousand killed in a single afternoon. They stacked the bodies up like cords of firewood. You could say those men were martyrs too, except no one's making songs about them."

Rice narrows his eyes and tilts his head back.

"Why would a white man risk his life fighting for the Negro? I always wondered that."

"I didn't join the Union army to free any Negroes. I joined because a man with waxed mustaches and shiny brass buttons on his coat offered me twenty-five dollars and a glass of beer. I wasn't a soldier when the fighting started, but I turned into one quick enough. I had to. Then afterward I found I had a taste for it."

"And now you fight for Ireland."

It is not a question, but it nearly is. As though there are degrees of loyalty and conviction, Doyle thinks, and Rice is wanting to show him where he stands.

"I was born in Sligo; I left there when I was thirteen. Do you doubt me, Peter?"

Rice shakes his head and frowns as if he doesn't understand the implication.

"Why would I ever doubt you?" he says.

After they finish talking, Doyle takes his knapsack upstairs and lies down on the bed to rest. The mattress is damp and smells of semen and hair oil. An hour later, a young woman arrives with a box of candles, a loaf of bread, three eggs, a twist of tea, and a bucket of coal. When he asks about the whiskey, she says she hasn't heard anything about whiskey. While she is kneeling down making the fire, a boy comes with O'Connor's address. Doyle takes the note and tells the boy to wait outside. After he's eaten his supper, they go to George Street and the boy points to number seven. Doyle loiters on the corner for a while, walks about, then comes back again. There is a faint light in the downstairs window but no sign of any movement in or out. It is dark and cold now and a grimy rain is coming down in gusts. The starless sky is the same flat color as the roofs and the walls, and the roofs and walls are the same flat color as the muddy pavement beneath his feet, as if all the world has been inked in the same grim and deathly hue. He walks onto Oxford Road and asks directions to King Street. It would be quicker to take a cab or omnibus, he knows, but he needs to learn the ways himself. When he reaches the Town Hall, he waits, then goes inside and looks for a sign to the detective office. When he finds it, he sits on a bench in the corridor and watches the policemen coming and going. They look calm, unconcerned, as if nothing could possibly go wrong. No one talks to him or gives him even a second glance. He thinks about asking for James O'Connor, making something up, but decides against it. After half an hour of sitting there, he takes out his notebook and pencil, and draws a diagram of the corridor and the rooms coming off it, then he stands up and leaves.

The next morning, Doyle waits by the cab stand on King Street and when James O'Connor emerges from the Town Hall, Rice's boy, Seamus, who knows him by sight, makes the sign as agreed. The two men walk along Piccadilly past the infirmary and lunatic asylum, then on up the hill: O'Connor ahead, hunched, oblivious, and Doyle following thirty feet behind. Black smoke leaks from the high factory chimneys into a cloud-packed sky; the morning light is weak, recessional, as if the day is ending before it has even begun. When they arrive at the London Road Station, there are five constables and a sergeant already there. O'Connor joins the group; they talk for a while, then, when the train arrives from Liverpool, the constables spread along the platform and start questioning the male passengers as they disembark. Doyle sits on a bench near the ticket windows and watches. It is a clumsy method, he thinks. The platforms are too crowded; a man with any kind of sense could easily await his moment and slip past unnoticed. The Liverpool trains arrive every half hour and Doyle watches them repeat the process seven times. On two occasions, one of the constables waves to O'Connor and O'Connor comes over and talks to the passenger himself, asking him more questions and writing down the answers in his notebook, but both times, after ten or fifteen minutes of talk, they let the fellow go.

At noon, a new group of six constables arrives. The two groups mingle for a while, talking and joking, then, when the train comes in, the first group leaves and the new men start questioning the passengers. O'Connor stays on the platform to make sure they know what to do, then goes into the station cafeteria and sits down at a table by the window. Doyle watches. O'Connor orders a cup of tea and drinks it slowly, blowing first, and putting the cup back down on the saucer between each sip. When he's finished the tea, he grimaces, rubs his eyes, then takes his notebook out of his pocket and leafs through it. His face is pale, the eyes shadowed and sunken. There is something about the way he sits and moves, a stiffness and hesitancy, that makes Doyle wonder if he is sick or has suffered some injury. A waiter asks him a question, and O'Connor nods, then looks back at the notebook. A few minutes later, he pays the bill, counts the change, and puts it in his waistcoat pocket. He leaves the cafeteria and walks back past the bench where Doyle is still seated. Doyle waits until he has passed, then stands up and follows. The two men, separated but together, move, in Indian file, across the bustling concourse, then back out into the cold, gray largeness of the day.

It is after midnight when Doyle finds what he's been searching for. He is sitting alone in a dram shop on one of the narrow lanes off Deansgate. He has a glass of rum untouched on the table in front of him and is listening carefully, without appearing to listen at all, to the conversation of the two men seated at his right. The men are discussing the price of a silver pocket watch and chain. The one selling is younger. He talks quickly, and shifts about in the chair, as if he is not used to staying seated in one place for long. He has a scanty mustache and his skin in the gaslight is damp and grainy. The other man is fat with a long brown beard spread out like a dirty napkin across his chest. His manner is coy, satirical, querulous. As he listens, he prods the watch back and forth across the table with his fingertip and shrugs or rolls his eyes. When the seller names his price, he chortles and then shakes his head, as though charmed and appalled in equal measure by the outlandishness of the sum invoked. The younger man persists nonetheless. He recalls, again, the watch's many virtues, calls loud attention to its weight and luster. They approach another price, much smaller than the first one, then back away, then approach again, and finally, with great displays of reluctance and reckless generosity on both sides, arrive at a concord. Doyle estimates that the man has paid less than a quarter of what the watch is worth, but for something so obviously filched it is a reasonable bargain. He waits until the purchaser has left, then turns to the younger man and nods.

"Would you happen to have another watch like that for sale?" he asks.

The man glances at him then looks away, as if he is not sure the question is worth the energy of a response.

"And what if I did?" he says.

"Then I'd give you a fair price for it," Doyle says. "More than that other fellow just gave."

The young man sniffs and looks him up and down.

"What are you anyway," he says. "American?"

"Irish. From New York."

"One of them," he says.

"I'd have given you a good deal more for that watch. A good deal more."

The young man shrugs.

"I decided to let him have it on the cheap," he says. "He's an old friend of mine, that's why."

"It was a fine-looking watch. I'd say a watch like that one's not so easy to come by. A man needs to know where to look."

The young man nods, then smiles.

"Oh, I know where to look," he says. "If anyone around here knows where to look, then it's me."

"You're the expert, are you?" Doyle says.

The young man shakes his head and straightens as if remembering who he is.

"I'm not a boaster," he says. "I keep my business to myself."

"You're a capable fellow, though: brave, quick-witted, resourceful. That's what I mean. I can tell it just by looking at you."

"Maybe so. I wouldn't disagree with that."

"And if a person had a particular need, a requirement? If there was something I wanted, for instance, that I couldn't get in the normal way?"

"What requirement would that be?"

Doyle picks up his glass of rum and moves across to where the young man is sitting. He holds out his hand.

"My name is Byrne," he says.

"Dixon."

Doyle looks down at the chair and Dixon nods.

"Help yourself," he says.

Doyle stacks the empty glasses already on the table, pushes them to one side, then puts his own glass down and sits.

"I can get you a watch like that other one easy enough," Dixon tells him. "You meet me here tomorrow night."

"It's not just a watch I'm talking about now, it's something else besides."

"What is it?"

Doyle shrugs, then leans forward and lowers his voice.

"It's nothing at all," he says, "for a brave, quick-thinking fellow like you at least. A minute's work, that's all."

CHAPTER 3

The day of the Fenian funeral parade—a week since the hangings. Three thousand Irish gather in Stevenson Square in the noonday damp: men, women, and children sporting green neckties and ribbons and rosettes and, at the head of it all, a fife-and-drum band playing the "Dead March in Saul" and three priests holding framed portraits of the recently departed. O'Connor waits in a side street until the procession begins, then joins in at the tail. They walk through Piccadilly, black umbrellas upraised like Roman shields against the afternoon drizzle, then by the infirmary and lunatic asylum, past clots of curious onlookers, and on up London Road. They cross the Medlock by the printworks and turn right onto Grosvenor Street. O'Connor makes his way gradually forward through the crowd, looking and listening all the time. Apart from the scrape and shuffle of footsteps and the strains of music from the front, there is a churchlike quietness about it all. People speak to each other in undertones, and if a child laughs or shouts out, they turn around to look. The parade is a show of strength, a reminder that the hangings haven't cowed them. Something else will follow after, O'Connor is sure of it, a gesture, or more than a gesture. He wonders again about Flanagan's American. They would only send someone across from New York if there was a plan. And it won't be an uprising again, not so soon after that last debacle; it will be something much smaller, something designed to scare and unsettle their enemies and give their supporters new hope—gunpowder perhaps, or arson, an assassination at the worst, although these things are always much more boasted about than achieved.

The rain stops and the umbrellas are taken down and furled. They pass the All Saints Church on the right and the Chorlton Town Hall on the left. The sky is the color of wet mortar, and the air tastes of soot and also faintly of ammonia from the chemical works nearby. There is no wind to speak of, and the dark smoke rises in shattered columns from the chimney pots. In Hulme, more people join, and when they get to Deansgate the phalanx of mourners is nine or ten wide and three-quarters of a mile long. The cabs and omnibuses pull onto the pavement to let them past. Before they cross the river, O'Connor notices Tommy Flanagan up ahead. He has a green ribbon wrapped around the crown of his brown bowler and a black mourning band on his arm; he is deep in conversation with a man O'Connor doesn't recognize. Over the bridge, the march pauses in front of the prison and the priests offer up some inaudible prayers. The gibbet has gone from the top of the wall, he notices—dismantled already—but the fenced-off place below the drop where Michael Larkin was finished off is still extant. O'Connor stays back until the other man moves away, then he positions himself by Flanagan's shoulder and speaks without turning his head.

"Who was that fellow you were talking to just now?"

Flanagan looks to see who it is, then quickly looks away again.

"Not here!" he says. "Good Christ. Have you no sense at all?"

"It's a simple enough question."

"He's no one you need to know about."

Flanagan sounds nervy, O'Connor thinks, much less cocksure than usual.

"Did he say something to upset you, Tommy?"

"It doesn't matter what he said."

"It wasn't your famous American, was it? Is he arrived already?"

"What American?"

"The one you told me about last week."

"There is no fucken American. That was just stupid talk is all. You should move away now. This is not the place or time."

"So that's not him, then?"

"Course not."

O'Connor tries to see where the other man has gone to. He only glimpsed him quickly from the side. He had long dark hair, what looked like a scar on one cheek, but more than that he couldn't say. He checks the time by his pocket watch and makes a note in his book so he won't forget the details in his next report to Maybury. There is something wrong with Flanagan, but it might not be important. Most likely the man is just a creditor.

The parade curves back across the river and into Shude Hill. It has lost some of its earlier somberness, voices are raised, there is laughter, and, now and then, a group bursts into song. When they reach New Cross, the band put down their instruments and someone comes out of the Crown Hotel with a crate of ale; the three priests say their farewells and get into a cab. O'Connor stands in the doorway of a pawnbroker's and watches the crowd disperse. There has been no trouble, but then he didn't expect any—Manchester isn't Liverpool or Glasgow where the Orangemen are bellicose and thick on the ground. He wonders whether to go directly back to the Town Hall now to write out his report but decides against it. It is getting dark and he is hungry. He will have his dinner at the Commercial coffeehouse, he thinks, then stop at the detective office on the way back.

He steps out of the doorway and walks across the cobbled junction toward Oldham Street. Groups of people from the parade are still chattering and killing time. He sees someone take a dented pewter flask from his pocket, have a sip, and pass it. He feels the usual pang, the inner tremble, but nothing worse. He will have a good plate of hot pot, he decides, and a ginger ale; he will smoke his pipe and read all the magazines.

O'Connor has not taken a drink since he arrived in Manchester, although the temptation is still strong sometimes. Instead of whiskey, now, he drinks lime cordial, gingerette, sarsaparilla, black coffee, and mugs of sugared tea. He smokes a half ounce of cheap tobacco every day and works more hours than he is paid for. The weight in his chest is smaller than it was, but he can still sense its pressure when he moves about. He feels, most days, like a man making his way across a tightrope, reaching out with his stockinged feet for each new step and never daring once to look down. He knows he is better off here in England, where no one knows or cares about him, where he is free alike from history and expectation, but he wonders too how long this balancing act can last and how it will end. Will he really spend the rest of his life here in solitude and exile, playing bagatelle in temperance coffeehouses?

He folds up the magazine and pushes it to one side. When he is reduced to reading the airy pieties of the *British Workman* he knows it is time to go home. The clock on the wall shows it is past ten already. He is not yet tired enough to sleep, but if he stops on the way to write his report, by the time he gets to his bed he might be. He pays the bill and says goodbye to Olson, the manager. Outside, it is raining again and the flagstones quiver blackly in the gaslight. He buttons his overcoat high and tugs up the collar for protection. The streets are still busy—bent-over women cowled in shawls and aprons make their way home from the Newton Street Mill, broad-hipped carts grumble past carrying barrels of pork and fish to the Smithfield market. He passes the cab stand on Piccadilly and nods to a porter taking shelter under the glazed awning of the Royal Hotel. In the detective office he has only Fazackerley and Malone for company. They talk for a while about the Fenian funeral parade, which, in Fazackerley's opinion, being a week late and three corpses short, was not very much of a funeral parade at all, and then O'Connor writes out his report, signs it, and leaves.

As he walks back toward George Street, O'Connor thinks of Catherine, his wife who died: her shape and her smell, and the sound of her voice whispering in his ear as they danced one Christmas Eve in the Finnegans' parlor with Patrick Mooney playing the fiddle and the others laughing and clapping along. It is painful to remember her still so alive, the press of her hand on his shoulder and the pale part of her coal black hair, but the thought that one day that pain might fade or disappear completely is worse. Forgetting is the final betrayal, he thinks. The pain is what is left of the love, and when that pain is gone there is nothing.

He was thirty-three when they met. She worked in the grocers on Bishop Street; he went in there one day to buy matches and they fell to talking. She told him she liked to read, but she could hardly afford to buy books, so the next day he came back into the shop with a copy of Tennyson's *Poems* wrapped up in brown paper and gave it to her as a gift. He told her he had other books just like it she could borrow if she ever wanted to, and she smiled and thanked him. He wasn't usually so bold, his years in the police had taught him to think twice and move slowly, but once it had begun with Catherine, he couldn't help himself. Afterward, when they were married and living together on Kennedy's Lane, he wondered whether he had been lonely back then without even realizing it. After so long living in barracks, he had thought he was happy being alone, but perhaps the truth was that he had just grown used to the flavor of his own suffering.

Their son, David, was born in '63 but died of pleurisy, and two years after that Catherine became ill herself. She complained of headaches and tiredness at first, then she noticed the swelling one Sunday after mass. O'Connor was a head constable in G division working with the Fenian informers. He spent all the money he had saved on doctors, then borrowed more and spent that too, but nothing they did made a difference. After she died, he started drinking whiskey every day. It felt like a means of survival, a way of fending off the future. He would drink in the mornings before he left for work, and in the afternoons, if he was alone, he would find a quiet pub and drink some more. He should have been dismissed half a dozen times. It was only Pat Hurley, the inspector, who shielded him, made excuses, but in the end even Hurley lost patience. He called him in one day and told him that it was Manchester or nothing. He said he would write the reference for Maybury without making any mention of the drinking, but that was the very last lie he would tell.

He has just crossed the Gaythorn Bridge and is approaching the railway viaduct with a high brick wall on his left when a man walking the other way stops him and asks for the time of day. The man is young and sallow-skinned and dressed in laboring clothes. He smells of potted meat and cheap spirits. O'Connor tells him it is close to midnight, and when the man asks how close exactly, he reaches for his pocket watch to check. It is too dark to see the dial, so he walks over to a lamppost nearby and, as he does so, another man, taller and broader than the first, carrying a truncheon, steps out from a doorway and strikes him a fierce blow across the back of the head. O'Connor gasps, then drops to his knees and slumps forward. His cheek and forehead, unprotected, slap down onto the wet pavement like a side of beef slipped from a butcher's hook.

CHAPTER 4

The next day, a young man knocks on the door of number seven George Street and waits. His head is still sore from the previous night, and his feet ache from the walking. He tries to remember what his mother used to tell him about James O'Connor, but he can only remember some of it. He has so many aunts and uncles that they get mixed up in his mind. He has seen a photograph from their wedding day, he is almost sure of that. He remembers Catherine looking surprised and serious in her lace veil, and Jimmy with a white rosebud in his buttonhole smiling as if he had just had a grand stroke of luck.

The door is opened finally by a small plump woman with gray-black hair pulled back in a bun and a shawl around her shoulders.

"And are you the doctor?" she says.

"I'm here to see Jimmy O'Connor. I'm his nephew off the boat from New York."

She looks him up and down.

"He didn't mention any nephew from New York to me."

"He doesn't know I'm here yet."

"A surprise, then, is it?"

"A surprise," he says, "yes, you could call it that."

The woman shrugs.

"He needs a doctor looking at him. You should see the state of his face."

"What's wrong with his face?"

The woman rolls her eyes, then steps backward and gestures him inside.

"You can go up and look for yourself. He thinks it'll heal on its own, but I told him he needs a poultice or at least a plaster put on it, so it don't get poisoned."

The young man leaves his suitcase in the hallway and starts to climb the stairs.

"You have a visitor, Mr. O'Connor," the woman shouts out, "your nephew from New York." Then she says to the young man, in a quieter voice, "It's the door on the left there."

He knocks. There is a long cough and then a voice calls him in.

O'Connor's face is lumpy and discolored—the skin is a pale, chicken-fat yellow around the cheekbone and jawline, a dull black and shiny purple about the blood-streaked eyes. He is sitting up in bed with a book open on his knee, although it is hard to believe he is able to read it.

"Christ alive, what happened to you?" the young man says.

"I was robbed last night. Two men attacked me."

It is hard for him to tell from his distended features whether O'Connor recognizes him or not.

"It's me, Michael Sullivan," he says, "your nephew. Edna's boy. I'm just off the boat from New York. I thought I'd try my luck over here in England for a while. Do you remember me from Ash Street, Danny's little brother?"

O'Connor frowns and looks at him more carefully.

"I remember," he says. "When did you go over to New York? Ten years ago, was it?"

"Eleven. I was eight, Danny was fourteen."

"And your da was dead by then, so it was just you two boys and Edna."

"That's right."

O'Connor pushes the blankets away from his legs, rolls sideways a little, and, with a gasp and a wince, swings his feet onto the rugless floor. He is wearing an ancient blue cardigan over his pajama top and gray bed socks. His hair is skewed sideways. He scrapes something green from the corner of one eye and looks at Sullivan more carefully.

"Eleven years—you were just a child last time I saw you and now you're here in England, no letter or warning even, knocking on my bedroom door?"

Sullivan glances around the room. There is an old wardrobe painted brown, an iron washstand, and a chest of drawers piled high with books and papers. On the floor beside the bed there is a papier-mâché tray with a cheese rind, an apple core, and an empty teacup on it.

"Family is family in the end," he says. "The years don't matter much. That's my belief."

O'Connor sniffs and nods his head.

"And it's a convenient belief to have in the circumstances," he says.

"I would have written you before to say I was coming, but I had to leave in a rush."

"Are you in some trouble? Is that why you're here?"

Sullivan smiles, then changes his mind and tries to look somber. He remembers one of his uncles telling him that, before he started up drinking, Jimmy O'Connor was about the smartest man he knew in Dublin. Sharp as a pin. But the grief and the whiskey together had softened his brain. The story going around was that they had sent him off to England because the English wouldn't know the difference.

"I can tell you're a policeman. Not much gets past you."

"So what was it? Debts? A woman?"

"A woman," he says, "a woman named Katie Dolan. We

got a little too friendly, you could say. They wanted me to marry her, and the brothers were threatening all kinds of mayhem if I didn't agree."

He pauses to see if O'Connor believes him. It is the kind of story, he thinks, that upright men pretend to be appalled by but never really are, since running away like that is what most of them would do themselves if they ever got the chance. And he is an excellent liar, he knows that. He has lied to plenty of people and none of them could ever tell.

"What are you using for money?" O'Connor asks him.

"I borrowed enough to pay my passage to Liverpool and to feed myself on the voyage, but now I need to find work. I'm a bank clerk by trade, I can tally figures and write a good, clean hand. If you know an opening in that line, or can tell me where to look for one, I'd be grateful for it."

"There's no shortage of banks in this city. If you have a letter of introduction from your place in New York, it should be easy enough to find work here."

Sullivan picks one of the books off the chest of drawers and looks at it for a while.

"Or I could try some different line, I suppose," he says with a sudden smile. "I could even become a policeman like you are. What would you say to that?"

"I'd say it's hard work and it doesn't pay so well. You should stick with what you know already."

Sullivan shrugs and puts the book back down.

"Can I sleep here tonight? If you can find me a blanket to lie on, I'll be fine right there on the floor." He nods down at the space between the bed end and the fire. "I'm a quiet sleeper. I won't trouble you any."

"So you really have no money left? Nothing at all?"

Sullivan shakes his head.

"But I'll be looking for work tomorrow," he says. "I'll start off early, and I won't stop until I find something."

O'Connor stands up slowly, waits for the pain to lessen,

and then walks over to the wardrobe. He stretches up and takes a metal box from the top.

"Here," he says. "I'll lend you half a crown. Go along to the Kings Arms and get yourself something to eat. You can sleep on the floor for two nights, but no more than that or Mrs. Walker will start complaining."

"The landlady? What difference does it make to her how long I stay?"

"She won't like a stranger sleeping on the floor. She runs a tidy house here."

Sullivan takes the coin, looks at it a moment, then puts it in his pocket.

"I'm sorry about Catherine," he says. "From what I hear she was a good woman."

O'Connor looks at him blankly for a moment, and he wonders if he has made a mistake in mentioning it at all. Perhaps he finds it too painful to be reminded of what he's lost, even now.

"Who do you hear that from?" O'Connor asks.

"From my ma and Danny. They remember her from the old days when she worked at Callaghan's. Before you two were married."

"You don't remember her yourself, though, do you?"

"No, I can't say I do. I was too small. But I've seen the pictures."

O'Connor nods.

"The Kings Arms is over on Clarendon Street," he says. "You go left at the end, and you'll see it on the corner."

When Sullivan is gone, O'Connor goes downstairs to explain things to Mrs. Walker. He tells her it will be for two nights only, and if it is any longer than that he will pay her something extra. She waves away the offer but reminds him tartly that he should properly be looking after himself before he looks after any long-lost nephew arriving from America without a penny to his name, or even the decency to tell anyone they're coming. If you marry into a family you must put up with the consequences, he tells her. And Mrs. Walker looks back at him and nods in a way that makes it clear she thinks he is wrongheaded but is too well-mannered to say so.

Two hours later, there is another knock and Mrs. Walker answers again. O'Connor, back in bed, listens carefully for a minute, then, cursing under his breath, levers himself up. He steps out onto the upstairs landing and bends down to look. Sullivan is slumped against the wall, holding forth in a slurred, singsongy voice about the pleasures of New York, while Mrs. Walker, who is Methodist and teetotal, but has lived on George Street long enough not to be surprised by much, has her arms folded tight across her chest and is nodding. O'Connor, moving slowly and wincing with each step, is almost at the bottom of the stairs before Sullivan even sees him.

"*Jimmy,*" he exclaims. "Christ, look at you. Those fellows really gave you a good pounding, didn't they? Have you ever seen anything like that face, Mrs. Walker? I can't say I have. I really can't."

Mrs. Walker doesn't answer him. She looks over at O'Connor and shakes her head.

"I'll make you two some tea," she says. "And there's bread and beef dripping in the kitchen. Then I'm up to my bed."

"Bread and beef dripping!" Sullivan shouts. "Christ, I could slaughter some bread and beef dripping right now."

"I gave you that money for food, not whiskey," O'Connor says.

Sullivan turns and smiles loosely at him. He seems pleased with himself, as if getting drunk on someone else's shilling is a rare achievement.

"I didn't like the look of what they had. Honestly. The chops were coated with grease. Just seeing them fairly killed my appetite, so I thought I'd just have a pint or two instead. I'll pay you back, I promise, just as soon as I get somewhere."

Mrs. Walker calls them into the kitchen. She puts a pot of tea and half a loaf on the table with a knife, and says her good nights. There is an oil lamp burning on a shelf near the door, but the rest of the room is dark apart from the pulse of the fire in the blackened range. O'Connor slides a finger into his mouth and feels his loosened molars. The pain is always worse at night. He stirs the pot with the knife handle, then pours.

"What will you do to them fellows when you catch up with them?" Sullivan asks. "What kind of lesson will you teach them for what they did to you?"

"They'll be tried before a magistrate like anyone else. Although I doubt I'll catch anyone unless I get a good slice of luck."

"You remember what they look like, don't you?"

"I remember one of them, but it's a big town and there's no reason to think I'll ever see him again."

Sullivan blinks and rubs his eyes like a child waking up from a long nap. For a moment, O'Connor wishes he was young again like that, young and foolish, with his mistakes all ahead of him, and no one to think of but himself.

"I meant that about becoming a constable, you know," Sullivan tells him. "I've thought about it more. I've had enough of sitting on a stool all day long. I'd rather be outside, stretching my legs, meeting new people."

He cuts off a piece of the bread and looks around for the dripping. O'Connor pushes the bowl across and watches him gobble.

"You wouldn't like it," he says. "Day in, day out. It wouldn't suit you."

"I'd look fine in that uniform, though, wouldn't I?" He

raises his eyebrows and grins at the thought. "Big shiny black topper, big fucking truncheon like that—just imagine me."

"You'd look like a great fool," O'Connor tells him.

Sullivan laughs.

"Oh, you're a hard man," he says. "To say such a thing to your own sweet nephew. Hard and cruel, that's what you are."

O'Connor spoons the sugar into his tea and stirs it.

"Is that what Edna told you about me?" he says. "That I'm hard and cruel?"

"Edna?" Sullivan shakes his head. "Oh no. Edna loves you. They all do. Jesus, they think you're just the best."

O'Connor nods. He still remembers Edna Brice when she was seventeen and lived on Flag Alley—tall and handsome, always full of the gossip. After she married Robbie Sullivan, she would take Catherine aside now and then and offer her advice about the wedded state. When Jimmy O'Connor's name came up one time, Edna said she could do a lot better than a sour-faced police constable from Armagh with no people to speak of. *Sour-faced.* He'd laughed about that when Catherine told him. None of the Brices had liked him much. They were a lively family, noisy and boisterous, and they didn't trust his quietness. They thought he must be keeping secrets from them, holding something back. They thought he was proud but proud of what? When he married Catherine and they moved a mile away to Kennedy's Lane, they believed he was taking her away from them, and perhaps he was. Five years after that, when Catherine got sick, and he had to ask the Brices for help to nurse her, he could sense even beneath their concern a cool current of self-satisfaction as if they had been shown to be right at long last.

"Edna's keeping well, I trust," he says.

"Ah, she's right as rain. She's a grandma now, you know.

Danny married an Italian girl, Antonella, and they have a little clapboard house in Brooklyn and two baby daughters. He works himself ragged on those streetcars. Up before dawn every single day."

O'Connor nods. He remembers Danny Sullivan outside the house on Ash Street playing rounders with an old broom handle and a ball made of rags and twine, short britches on him, and his grubby knees like knots in a piece of string, and now suddenly, in an instant it seems, he has a clapboard house in Brooklyn and a wife and two daughters.

"Is that so?" he says. "I didn't know."

"Danny says it suits him to the ground. I wouldn't want it for myself, though. I'm not cut out for family life. I'm more like you are."

"More like me? And what am I like?"

Sullivan grins for a moment, as if he is about to tell a sly joke.

"Free and easy," he says. "You answer to yourself alone."

O'Connor feels a spike of anger at the foolishness of it, a sudden hardening in his chest.

"I'm not free and easy," he says. "No one is. You'll learn that soon enough."

Even through the fug of drunkenness, Sullivan understands that he is being rebuked. He frowns, then blinks and looks up at the ceiling.

"Ah, I'm just playing around," he says. "I don't mean anything by it."

His words are slurred, as if his tongue has grown too big for his mouth. O'Connor stands up.

"I'm getting tired now," he says. "We should finish."

"I didn't mean anything by it," Sullivan says again. "I talk without thinking sometimes. Danny always chides me for it."

"It doesn't matter."

Sullivan shrugs, then rubs his chin. He is disheartened

by this sudden change of mood. He wants things to go back to how they were before.

"You keep an eye on the Fenians, don't you?" he asks O'Connor. "That's what I heard in New York."

O'Connor nods.

"More or less," he says.

"I met one on the boat coming over here. He told me he was a draper from Harrisburg, Pennsylvania, but I could tell straightaway he wasn't any such thing. We'd play poker in the evenings just to pass the time away, four or five of us, all Irishmen. We kept the conversation playful as a rule, but one time, someone mentioned the Brotherhood. This fellow said, in his opinion, they were nothing but a dreamy rabble led on by men who cared more for their own pocketbooks than for the poor men of Ireland. Well, the rest of us didn't get too exercised about it, we just nodded or shrugged and picked up the next card, but this fellow Byrne—Daniel Byrne was what he called himself—you should have seen the furious fucking look that came over him. He stiffened up like he was all ready for a fight right then and there. He looked this other fellow in the eye and started on about the difference between those who like to talk about liberty but are too fearful and womanly to ever act, and those others who keep quiet as a rule but are bold and manly enough to take up arms against their oppressors when required. Take up arms against their oppressors—that's what he said, I swear."

He waits for O'Connor to sit down again, but O'Connor stays where he is.

"If he told you he was a draper from Harrisburg," O'Connor says, "that's most likely all he was."

Sullivan shakes his head. The sweet fumes rise off him in waves. His cheeks are bright red and his lips are still shiny from the dripping.

"If you ask me, he was an old Union soldier. He looked

the part—long hair down to his collar nearly and scars on his face."

"What kind of scars?"

"Bad-looking ones," he says, pointing at himself. "Here and here. Could have been a musket ball or bayonet. I've seen men come back from that war looking like they've been passed through a threshing machine. Arms and legs and hands missing. Holes where holes shouldn't rightly be. Fucking gruesome."

O'Connor remembers the man talking to Flanagan at the parade, the thick mustaches, the long dark hair, and the deep clefts gouged into his cheek and jaw like half-formed eyes or lips. A coincidence, he thinks, but not impossible.

"What day did your ship get in?"

"Wednesday. I've been staying on in Liverpool with a fellow I met. He thought he might have a job for me, but that didn't come to anything."

"And was this Byrne coming here to Manchester? Did he tell you that?"

"He said he might, but he wasn't sure when. When we tallied up the winnings at the end of the voyage I owed him a few dollars, but I had nothing left, so I gave him my note of hand and he wrote down an address I could send it on to."

"Show me."

Sullivan goes through his pockets and finds the piece of paper. O'Connor reads it, looks at the other side, which is blank, then gives it back.

"Jack Riley's alehouse, it's one of the places they gather," he says.

"So I was right?"

"Tell me more about this taking up arms. What did he say?"

"He said the milk-and-water men would talk and talk, but it was only bloodshed that ever changed the world. He said the war had already started, but the point was to make everyone in England realize it. I don't remember all the rest. But I could go to that address he gave me if you'd like. I could ask for him there."

"No," he says. "You leave this with me. I'll see about it tomorrow."

"Those Fenians are just blatherskites and rabble-rousers, if you ask me. To be truthful, I don't care for politics much at all. I'm too young and what does it matter anyway? The way I see it, some bastard or other will always be in charge, and whoever it is they will be looking after themselves first of all. Isn't that right?"

O'Connor looks at Sullivan again, sitting there at the table, dazed with drink, talking just for the sake of talking, to fill up the emptiness. There is something about the eyes that reminds him of Catherine—the width between them perhaps, or the particular shade of green, he's not sure exactly what, but it pains him to see it, this blood-borne echo of the dead. He wishes it wasn't there, or that he could deny or ignore it.

"It's time to sleep now," he says. "I'll take you over to the Town Hall in the morning and you can tell your story there."

CHAPTER 5

Tommy Flanagan sits at a splintery corner table in the parlor of the Pier Head Inn on Albert Street with his best bull terrier, Victor, panting like a hot little engine at his feet. Tonight is the night of the monthly rat-match and the place is already filling up with dog fanciers and sporting men of all types and classes—coachmen out of livery and unbuttoned soldiers, shopkeepers and costermongers, gentleman gamblers, cabmen, and clerks. The waiters are shouting out orders for beer and battered fish, and the nervier dogs are growling at each other across the room, scratching the wooden floor and straining at their collars. Flanagan has owned some good-looking ratters in his time, but Victor is the finest yet. It is not strength, size, or stamina that counts with the ratting but eagerness, and Victor is deadly eager. Some dogs will kill a rat quickly, then pause and mope over the bloodied corpse awhile, sniffing or licking it like a child with a rag doll, and in that way precious seconds can easily be lost, but Victor doesn't ever pause or mope, he presses on to the next rat and then the next one after that, as if he knows in his head that a clock is ticking. Such eagerness, in Flanagan's opinion, is a rare gift of Mother Nature that can't be trained in or bred for. He paid five shillings for Victor as a pup, and if he wins the match tonight he won't sell him for a penny less than ten pounds, which will be a sweet profit, but also a just reward. For there are many who proudly claim to know a ratter when they see one, but there are precious few like him who have the living, panting proof to back that judgment up.

It will pain him to sell such a dog, but he needs the cash for his escape. This new man Doyle, the Yankee incomer, is already making ructions, nosing. He tells everyone he meets that his first appointed task is to root out all the spies in Manchester. When he first sees you, he shakes you firmly by the hand, gives you that fierce cockeyed look of his, with that wound set into his face for all the world like an extra arsehole, and whispers hotly in your ear that if you know anything at all, *anything,* however small, about the spies, then his door is open. Tommy Flanagan has always been careful about his business, he has covered his tracks well enough, but he's not sure he has been careful enough to evade the concerted shrewdness of a loon like Doyle. Much better then, he thinks, much safer all in all, to take a little trip abroad, at least until the present situation calms itself. Let the bloodthirsty Yank find another man's throat to cut.

Around nine o'clock, the landlord rings a brass bell behind the bar and calls the patrons upstairs to begin the contest. They enter a large, brightly lit room, with high, shuttered windows on both sides. The floor and walls are dusty and unadorned, and in the center is a circular wooden pit, ten feet wide and four feet high, painted white on the inside to improve the view. On a pitch pine table at the far end of the room, watched over by one of the waiters, are two large wire cages both crammed with a squealing mass of river rats, their dark pelts twisting and roiling about inside like the quickened surface of a peat stream in flood. When the dogs smell the keen, cloacal reek of the caged rats, they start up howling and barking and the large room is suddenly filled with a hectic, sharp-edged raucousness. On a signal from the umpire, the waiter carries one of the cages up to the edge of the ring and empties it out. Fifty or sixty newly released rats swirl and scurry around the floor like scalded tea leaves in a pot, then pile together into three separate twitching clusters at the perimeter as if for safety. The landlord calls for his stopwatch and the first dog is made ready.

Flanagan leans against the ring's edge to watch the match proceed. The man standing beside him is making bets on every dog that comes into the ring. Five shillings here, ten shillings there. Every bet he makes he loses.

Flanagan looks at him. He's surprised a man like that has such money to squander. His hands are calloused and his black jacket is cheap and threadbare. A laborer, he thinks, or possibly a journeyman. He must have won the money somehow, either that or stolen it. Whatever he is, he knows fuck-all about dogs.

"Let me give you a tip," Flanagan says to him.

The man, who is holding a pewter mug of ale, turns and peers back at Flanagan as if he has done something peculiar or as if the very fact of his speaking is somehow untoward.

"What *tip* might that be?" he says.

"Put all your money on this one." He nods down at Victor. "If you do it now, you could get double or treble what you lay."

The man looks unconvinced. He is young, but his bottom teeth are sparse and carious.

"I don't see you making too many bets on him," he says.

"If I had money I would. I'm short today, is all."

The man thinks about this, then nods and kneels down to look more carefully at Victor. He squeezes his hind legs and peers into his mouth, as if he knows what he's looking for.

"He's a strong little bugger," the man admits.

"Ah, he's strong enough, but it's not the strength that matters most with the ratting, it's the eagerness."

"The eagerness, you say?"

"That's right." Flanagan looks around a moment, then points over to the other side of the room. "You see that bulldog over there. The white one, Hercules. That's a nice dog. He goes about his work in the right kind of way, neat and tidy, doesn't dawdle or leave too many twitchers lying around the ring. He'll kill you fifteen or twenty rats every time with no fuss or commotion. That's what I call a decent, reliable ratter, but is he truly eager? Eager like Victor here is?" He looks at the man to let the question sink in, then shakes his head. "He don't even come close."

The man stands up, finishes his ale, and waves to the waiter for another.

"Everyone's the expert," he says.

Flanagan shrugs.

The next dog in the ring is a ragged-looking Airedale. It twists and writhes around in its owner's arms, yipping and growling, as they wait for the signal to begin. Bets are being taken and the man next to Flanagan has his money out again. He puts five shillings on the Airedale to kill fifteen or more. Flanagan sniffs and shakes his head.

"I'd go low with a dog like that one," he says. "Too much fizz in him, I'd say. Not smart enough. He'll chase the rats about instead of taking out the easy ones."

"If I'm ever short of a smart opinion, I'll know where to go looking," the man says.

"Good money after bad, that's all I'm saying."

They watch the Airedale go to work. It starts off well but then becomes distracted by the noise and commotion of the ring. By the end, there are ten dead rats and six others that are bloodied but still moving.

Flanagan puffs on his pipe and feeds titbits of tripe to

Victor to keep him calm. He can hear the man cursing beside him, but he keeps his own counsel. The next dog up is
a bow-legged Staffy, grizzled around the nose with a scat-
tering of bite scars across his face and chest like moth holes
in a blanket.

"How about this one?" the man asks him. "Too old?"

Flanagan shakes his head.

"What the fuck do I know?" he says.

"I'll give you half the profit if I win it. Half is fair enough."

"He'll do better than the Airedale but not by much."

"They're offering ten."

"Go higher and keep your fingers crossed."

The Staffy is slower than the Airedale but fiercer and less
flighty. After he kills a rat, he gnaws and shakes the stricken
corpse awhile, then tosses it aside and looks around for the
next. With a minute to go, there are nine black bodies curled
up like fat commas on the whitewashed floor, and the dog's
short muzzle is dark red and dripping.

"Go on, you little beauty," the man shouts out. "Go on
now, you vicious bugger."

"He's got some pepper in him that one," Flanagan agrees.
"He's not so quick about the ring, but he's plenty cruel."

The Staffy kills two more rats, then, just before the umpire blows the final whistle, kills a third to make twelve
dead in all. The man roars out with laughter, dances a jig,
and slaps Flanagan hard on the back. They have a drink
together with their winnings and then another drink for
luck. The man, who says his name is Henry Dixon, agrees
that he will bet all the money he has left on Victor at eight-
to-one to win the rat match outright. He reaches into his
pocket to check how much he has, and pulls out a folded-up
five-pound note and some coins.

"Someone remember you in their will, did they?" Flanagan asks.

"I had a bit of luck," Dixon says. "You know how that goes."

He must have stolen it all, Flanagan thinks. Clubbed or garroted some unexpecting bastard in a back alley, then rifled his pockets. A man like Henry Dixon, with his grubby hands and staring eyes, doesn't come by that amount of money in any lawful fashion.

"Some men drop things, others pick them up," Flanagan says. "You have to keep your eyes peeled, that's all. You never know what you might find lying in the gutter."

"Oh, I keep my eyes peeled right enough," Dixon agrees. "Not much gets past me, I swear."

"You found a nice fat wallet somewhere, by the look of it," Flanagan says, nodding at the money. He can tell that Dixon is drunk enough to want to boast about his crimes. All he needs to do is egg him on a little more.

Dixon laughs.

"There was a wallet involved, true enough," he says. "But that wasn't the half of it."

"Pocket watch?"

Dixon shakes his head.

"I can't tell you all what happened. There are other parties involved and I've been sworn to secrecy."

Before Flanagan can press him any further, the umpire calls out for Victor to enter the ring. Flanagan picks him up, and the two men push their way through the dense crowd. The seconds, who are speckled with rat blood and have their trouser bottoms cinched with twine, take a minute to clear out the maimed and dead rats and then restock from the rusted wire cages. When Victor sees the fresh rats skittering around and sniffing and biting at themselves, he starts to rant and kick out in his urge to get to them. Flanagan grips the hot, shuddering body like a sack of treasure and waits. The umpire counts down from ten, then blows the whistle, and Flanagan tosses Victor forward. His claws scramble on the deal floor as he lands, and the screaming rats explode outward in a burst. He kills eight in the first minute, ten in the second, and ten more in the third. When the time runs out, there are only six rats left alive in the ring and the onlooking fancy are hooting and hollering and banging their fists on the side panels. Flanagan has seen better ratters than Victor, he knows it, but not many, and not around these parts. After a showing like that, he will get ten pounds for him now, he is sure of it, and if Henry Dixon can be enticed to make a bid, it might be a good deal more.

There are two more dogs to try before the prize can be given, but everyone knows that Victor has won it. Flanagan enjoys his triumph for a while, then looks around for Dixon. He finds him downstairs in the parlor, drinking whiskey and looking gleeful.

"That's a fine dog right there," he says, pointing at Victor, "and no lie. Forty rats, was it, in the end?"

"Forty-four."

"Forty-four!" Dixon shakes his head and whistles. "Would that be a record for the Pier Head?"

"Close enough, I'd say."

Dixon is so full of drink now that he barely needs any prompting. All Flanagan needs to do is keep his nerve and stay patient.

"So, what will you take for him?" Dixon bangs his hand down on the tabletop. "Give me your price."

Flanagan tries his best to look amazed.

"He's not for sale," he says. "I couldn't part with him."

"Come on now. He's not a lapdog, he's a ratter. A good one, I'll give you that, but don't try to tell me he's not for sale because you're soft on him."

Flanagan shakes his head and winces, as if the very conversation pains him.

"A fellow upstairs offered me fifteen pounds just now, but I told him the exact same thing I just told you."

"*Fifteen?* You wouldn't be telling tales, would you? You Irish can be slippery bastards. I know that."

"I'll take you up there to meet him if you like. He's a smart fellow who knows his dogs, but I told him just what I told you. The dog's not for sale."

Dixon scratches his chin and shifts about in his chair. They hear some cheering from upstairs and then the long blast of a whistle. Flanagan gets up from the table and offers Dixon his hand.

"I'll pick up the prize now," he says, "and then I'll be away."

Dixon stands up too. His eyes look off-kilter and he sways a little before finding his balance again.

"Oh no, you don't," he says. "You wait here. Just give me a minute and I'll be back with my winnings. You can finish off my whiskey while I'm gone."

Dixon points him back down into his chair and, after a measured pause, Flanagan sits.

When Dixon comes back, he is patting his waistcoat pocket and smiling like a goon.

"Nothing like winning a nice fat wager," he says. "Best feeling in the world."

He slumps down, picks up the empty whiskey glass, peers into it like a telescope, sighs, then waves for another.

"So, the fellow upstairs offered you fifteen pounds, did he? And you told him the dog wasn't for sale, whatever the price?"

Flanagan nods.

"That's right."

Dixon leans forward until their noses are almost touching.

"I know what you're up to," he says, "don't think I don't know. But I can't blame you for it. A man has a dog to sell, he wants the best price, I understand."

"I don't want to sell him. I told you that."

Dixon snorts derisively.

"Listen," he says. "I could offer you seventeen pounds or

eighteen, and you might take it and you might not, but let's not bugger about. I want that dog and this is what I'll give you for him."

He takes his bundled winnings from his jacket pocket, deals out twenty pounds on the table between them, and leans back in his chair.

Flanagan waits a moment, then takes the money and hands Dixon the leash.

"He's a good dog," Flanagan says. "I wouldn't part with him for a penny less."

Dixon smiles and half-hitches Victor's leash around the leg of his chair.

"If I set my mind on something, I'll get it done," he says. "One way or t'other, I'll get it done. No bugger stops me. That's how I am."

The parlor is filling up now. Waiters are taking final orders, the landlord is shaking hands and making promises for next time. Flanagan puts the money in his pocket and starts to stand up, but Dixon puts a hand on his shoulder and pushes him down again.

"Have another drink," he says. "Don't be rushing off like that."

"I'll have one more, then I'll be on my way."

"One more my arse."

Dixon calls for the waiter, and the waiter brings them two more whiskies and two pints of ale on top. Victor growls at him then barks, and Flanagan reaches down to scratch between his ears.

"Do you want to know where I got that money from?" Dixon says. "I'll tell you the story if you'd like."

"I thought you didn't dare."

Dixon leans forward across the table and whispers.

"I can't give you the fellow's name, but I'll tell you what he looked like. Big American, he was, nasty scar on his face right there."

Dixon jabs a forefinger into his cheek and smiles. Flanagan puts down his glass.

"You robbed him?" he says. "You robbed the American fellow?"

"Christ no. That's not a man you'd ever want to rob. Try to rob a man like that and you'll end up the worse for it. I partnered with him, that's all. He needed something and I helped him get it, and he paid me nicely for my troubles. Very nicely indeed."

Dixon is swaying a little in his seat, twitching occasionally and licking his lips now, like a dog tangled up in a dream. Flanagan finishes his ale and wipes his mouth with his sleeve. He knows very well there can only be one American of that description in Manchester. The fucker Doyle is everywhere, he thinks bitterly, everywhere at the same time. The man's like the holy fucken ghost.

"What did he need?" he asks.

Dixon squints at him for a while, then wrinkles his nose and holds out his right hand, finger and thumb an inch or two apart.

"A little piece of paper," he says. "A little piece of paper with some writing on it."

"Writing?

"Names. Dates. Don't ask me what it all means, that's no business of mine, but let me tell you one thing." He leans forward again and lowers his voice to a growl. "Some poor bastard's going to catch it soon enough, and I'm fucking glad it's not me."

Flanagan picks up his glass and drinks from it, then realizes it is empty and puts it back down. His head is spinning. He can't think what paper Stephen Doyle could possibly need that a man like Dixon could help him find, but if Doyle already has a plan of action, it must mean that things are further along than he feared. He shakes Dixon's hand, ignoring his pleas to stay, and pushes his way through the crowd to the front door.

Outside, on Albert Street, he looks quickly left then right, but there is no one else about. He pushes Dixon's money deeper into his pocket, pulls down the brim of his hat, and sets off walking. When he reaches King Street, he loiters for five minutes in a doorway until he is sure no one is watching for him, then crosses the road and goes into the Town Hall. He asks for Head Constable James O'Connor, and they write down his name and tell him to wait on a bench in the corridor. Nearly an hour passes, and then another policeman named Rogers comes out. Rogers, who is bald and portly and has a careless, cynical manner encouraged by years of being lied to by criminals, explains that Constable O'Connor is not on duty tonight.

"Then I'll need to get a message to him," Flanagan says.

"If you tell me, I'll pass it on when I see him next."

"When will that be?"

"Tomorrow or the day after, most likely. He had an accident. He's resting up at home."

"Give me the address. I'll go there myself."

Rogers sighs, as if Flanagan is a fool to even suggest such a thing.

"I can't give you his address," he says. "What's this about?"

"I need help," Flanagan says. "There's a man named Stephen Doyle who's intending to kill me."

Rogers looks blandly unsurprised by this suggestion.

"I see, and has this fellow Doyle made any actual threats on your life? What has he said to you exactly?"

"It's not what he's said."

"Then what is it?"

There is an aproned porter coming toward them from the far end of the corridor pushing a barrowful of papers. Every now and then the street door swings open and someone enters or leaves. Flanagan rubs his face and groans softly. He is not about to tell a man he has never seen before that he is a Fenian spy.

"I need to talk to O'Connor in person. He's the one who'll understand what's going on."

"If this Stephen Doyle hasn't made any threats, then we can't help you," Rogers says. "We can't arrest people on just anyone's say-so."

"I'm not just anyone," Flanagan says. "I've been talking with O'Connor for months. I've been telling him things. Important things."

"There's plenty of people who tell us things," Rogers says. "I've never heard O'Connor make special mention of any Thomas Flanagan."

"Because it's a secret, that's why. Because no one else must know my name."

Rogers shakes his head as if he has heard this kind of specious reasoning too many times before.

"You should come back tomorrow," he says. "He'll most likely be here tomorrow."

"I can't come in here again. It's too dangerous for me. Tell him to meet me at the White Lion on Worsley Street near the jail. Tell him to meet me there at noon."

"The White Lion," Rogers says, nodding and turning away. "I'll tell him that."

Flanagan finds a cheap hotel near Piccadilly and takes a room under the name of Brierley. He explains to the proprietor that his luggage was stolen at the railway station and asks him for writing paper and ink. He needs to get a message to his sister to tell her that he is in trouble, that it will blow over eventually, but until it does he will be safest elsewhere. Rose will not be pleased with him, he knows that, but she will understand, and when he gets to wherever he is going he will send money back. Perhaps if he covers his tracks carefully enough, Rose and his mother could even

join him eventually? It occurs to him that to have a policeman like O'Connor under a sense of obligation might not be
such a bad thing after all—that so long as he escapes from
this intact, he might end up better off than he was before. A
brand-new life, he thinks, and why not? He writes the note
to Rose and gives the night porter a shilling to have it delivered for him immediately. He smokes a pipe, then un-
laces his boots and takes off his jacket. The room is warm
and clean; the brass coal scuttle is full and the bedsheets
look almost new. Perhaps he is not doing so badly after all.

At two o'clock, he is woken by the night porter with a
note marked urgent. The note is signed James O'Connor,
and it asks him to come immediately to the detective office
in the Town Hall. Rogers must have seen sense in the end,
Flanagan thinks. Most likely, he told his superiors about
the visit, and they gave him a kick up the arse. He pulls his
boots back on, laces them up, and tugs a comb through his
tangled hair. It is raining outside, and he is still half asleep,
but the walk will clear his head. He decides he will tell
O'Connor that he wishes to live in Canada, and that he
needs his sister and mother with him there. Manchester
has never suited them much anyway. It's a dirty, cramped,
money-grubbing sort of place and he is sure they'll be glad
for the chance to get away.

Aside from the reeking, sloshing carts of the night soil
men and the slumped forms of sleeping indigents, the
streets are empty. Flanagan walks past an abandoned
warehouse, its windows smashed to pieces and its lower
walls covered over with the tattered remnants of fly posters
hawking spring overcoats and beef extract. He can hear a
dog barking in the distance and, closer to hand, the clacking
of his own boot heels on the wet cobblestone. Rain is dripping off the brim of his hat and he smells coal gas and horse
manure on the dampened wind. Five more minutes, and
he will be there. He wonders for a moment how O'Connor

knew where to send the message. Did Rogers have someone follow him over from the Town Hall? Strange if he did, he thinks, but how else?

He hears a sudden noise behind him and turns around. There is a man standing there wearing a long, dark over-coat and a discolored bowler. He has thick gingerish whiskers and a bent nose.

"Patrick," Flanagan says. "What the fuck are you doing here?"

"You need to come with me now, Tommy," the man says. "We need to have a talk."

"Have a talk about what?"

"I think you know very well about what."

Patrick Neary is one of Peter Rice's men. He works dipping hides all day in the tannery by the boneworks.

"I don't know what you've heard," Flanagan says, "but there's none of it's true."

"It's not what I've heard that counts most here."

"You don't believe what Doyle tells you? You can't believe all that shite."

"I've got Skelly's hansom cab waiting around that corner there. When we get you back to Ancoats, you can say your piece to Doyle direct."

Flanagan doesn't move. He could run, but he knows he wouldn't get far.

"How did you know where to look for me?"

"We read the letter you sent to Rose. That was a stupid fucking move, I must say."

"That letter was private between the two of us. You had no right."

Neary snorts.

"Do you believe this is a game, Tommy?" he asks. "Is that what you believe?"

Flanagan stares back at him a moment. This is not the way it finishes, he thinks, it can't be. Not here.

"You know what I'm like, Patrick," he says. "I may be a fucken idiot sometimes, but I wouldn't ever do anything to harm the cause. I'm loyal to a fault."

The other man shakes his head.

"You were always a little bit too pleased with yourself, Tommy. I do know that for a fact."

Flanagan nods. He holds himself steady a moment, then looks behind and sees Skelly's ancient hansom cab, palled with horse steam and slickened with rainwater, creaking out from a side street like a hearse.

CHAPTER 6

———————➤•◀———————

Next morning, O'Connor takes Michael Sullivan into the Town Hall to tell his story. They wait outside in the corridor and then, when Maybury is ready for them, they go in together and Sullivan, who still looks pale and clammy from last night's drink, tells about the man he met on the boat coming over. He talks too long and stumbles and repeats himself more than once, but Maybury hears him out. When he is finished, Maybury nods and looks at O'Connor.

"We just hanged three of the bastards and now they're sending us over a fresh one. Should I be worried?"

"If it's the same man Flanagan told me about, then they've sent him here to stir up trouble. It sounds like he's a soldier and that means that whatever he gets up to, it's liable to be more than just talk. If I knew his real name, I could find out more."

"So arrest him on suspicion of something or other. Bring him in."

"We'll have to find him first. I believe I saw him at the funeral parade on Sunday, but aside from that all we have is the address on Rochdale Road, which is an alehouse the Fenians use. They have lookouts on every corner."

"Send the lad Michael here. Why not? They won't know

he's your nephew. He could get you the real name at least, I'd bet."

O'Connor can see that this makes some sense, but the thought of being beholden to Michael Sullivan makes him wary.

"I'd rather not do that," he says. "Not yet, anyway. Michael's just a young fellow, not a policeman. If he goes in there and looks at them wrong or speaks out of turn, it could get dangerous. For now, I think we should get this man's description out to every constable, and send telegrams to Liverpool and London to see if they know anything about him there. And I'll talk to my informers today to find out if they have anything fresh."

Maybury nods.

"Agreed. I'll see to the telegrams myself and I'll write to Dublin Castle too. Let me see: goes by the alias of Daniel Byrne; calls himself a draper; five foot ten or eleven; long dark hair, mustache, and scars on the right cheek. Is that the full description?"

"Yes, sir."

Maybury slowly writes a note to himself, then puts down his pen and takes off his spectacles. He tilts his head to one side and gives O'Connor's face a careful look.

"So you were robbed by two men. Robbed and beaten. That's what I heard."

"Yes, sir. Out near the Gaythorn Bridge night before last."

"What did they take?"

"Some money, a pocket watch. The watch isn't valuable, but it was a gift from my wife."

"I didn't realize you were ever married."

"I'm a widower."

Maybury nods as if things are beginning to make more sense to him now.

"For an Irishman, you're not the luckiest fellow in the world, are you, Constable O'Connor?" he says.

"I've had my share of misfortunes, sir. It's the truth."

Maybury nods again, starts to smile, then thinks better of it.

"Well, I'm guessing the money and watch are long gone by now," he says, "but I'll put on an extra patrol in that area anyway, see what we can turn up."

Back out in the corridor, O'Connor explains to Sullivan that if they ever arrest the American, he may be asked to come in to make an identification and recall the conversations they had together on the ship. But for now he should forget about all that and get on with finding a job and a place to lodge in Manchester. He gives him a sixpence for his dinner and makes him solemnly promise not to spend any of it on drink. Sullivan wants to talk some more about Maybury's suggestion that he visit the Fenian alehouse, but O'Connor tells him that Maybury was not thinking straight when he said that and someone who is not a sworn constable could never be involved in that way.

When Fazackerley sees him walk into the detective office, he winces in sympathy.

"That's nasty," he says.

"You should have seen it before. I'll be right soon enough."

"You'd be better off in bed."

O'Connor explains about Michael Sullivan and the man on the boat.

"Rogers left a note for you last night," Fazackerley tells him. "I've got it somewhere here."

O'Connor reads the note twice, turns it over, then looks at the clock.

"Do you know any Stephen Doyle?" he says.

Fazackerley thinks awhile, then shakes his head.

"Who is he?"

"I've no idea. One of my boys, Tommy Flanagan, came here at midnight asking for me and saying this man Doyle was threatening him, but the note doesn't explain who he is."

"Rogers will be back later on. You can ask him yourself."

O'Connor hangs up his hat and coat on the black bentwood hat stand, sits down, and pours himself a cup of tea.

"Flanagan wouldn't come here unless he was scared of something. It's too big a risk."

"It's money, nine times out of ten, with that kind," Fazackerley says. "He can't pay whoever he owes, and he thinks, being the nice, generous fellow you are, if he asks sweetly enough, you'll bail him out."

"It could be that," O'Connor says. "I'm meeting him at noon today, so I'll find out the truth then, I suppose."

He finishes his tea and stands up slowly. The effects of the laudanum he took with his breakfast seem to be fading already. He feels a jagged pain in his ribs and a sullen aching in his jaw.

"If Michael Sullivan comes here looking for me, you can tell him I'll see him back at George Street."

"Who's Sullivan?"

O'Connor winces and rubs his face before answering.

"The nephew," he says. "The one I told you about."

He sits in the back room of the White Lion for an hour and a half, but there is no sign of Flanagan and no message. Tommy Flanagan has never missed a rendezvous before, and O'Connor starts to wonder what could have gone wrong. He pays the waiter, then walks over to Teasdale and Sons, the dust-caked and sarcophagal tobacconists on Withy Grove where Flanagan is employed as an occasional shop man. Henry Teasdale, the proprietor, is leaning on the counter reading the *Manchester Times*. When O'Connor asks about Flanagan, he shakes his head.

"Gone," he says.

"Since when?"

"Two days ago. Last I heard, he was planning to sell his famous ratter, Victor, and travel abroad on the proceeds."

"So he's leaving Manchester. Are you certain of that?"

Teasdale closes the paper and looks up at him.

"You know Tommy Flanagan, do you?" he asks.

O'Connor nods.

"Because if you do know him, you'll know that nothing is ever certain with Tommy. I heard he's bound for the Continent, but if he ever gets much beyond Sheffield I'll be amazed."

"I owe him some money," O'Connor explains. "I hoped to find him in here."

Teasdale raises his eyebrows.

"The man who owes Tommy Flanagan money is a rare bird indeed. In my experience the obligation is usually the other way around."

"Is that why he's leaving Manchester? Is he being chased for money?"

"It wouldn't surprise me, but I can't say for sure."

"Have you ever heard of Stephen Doyle?"

Teasdale shakes his head.

"Know a man named *Arthur* Doyle," he says, "boot and shoemaker on Spear Street. Don't know any Stephen Doyle, though. Who is he?"

"If you don't know him, it doesn't matter," O'Connor says. "I'll look for Tommy elsewhere. It's not a big amount I owe him, but I like to pay my debts."

"Then you're a gentleman, and there are few enough of those around these days. Can I sell you a little pinch of something before you leave?"

O'Connor takes half a step back and glances around the shop. There are clay jars of tobacco and snuff lined up on the shelves behind Teasdale, and a glass-fronted cabinet to one side filled with a mishmash of pipe racks and cigar boxes. The yellowed walls and windows are covered over with dog-eared advertisements for Shag and Navy Cut. Everything is dark and grimy and the smell inside is brown and fierce.

"I'll take half an ounce of your best Bird's Eye," he says.

"Very good."

Teasdale weighs it out carefully on the copper scales and wraps the small brown pile in a sheet of newsprint.

"You could go to his house, of course. He lives on Thompson Street with his mother and his sister, Rose."

O'Connor nods. He knows where Flanagan lives, but he has never been there. For safety's sake, they meet in taverns and coffeehouses well away from the Irish districts, where no one is likely to recognize or remember either of them. He'll give Flanagan another day or so to reappear, he thinks, and then, if necessary, he'll talk to the sister, Rose.

He pays Teasdale for the tobacco, then walks back to the Town Hall to wait for the telegrams. It is the middle of the afternoon before they come in. The offices in London and Liverpool have no record of anyone named Byrne involved in Fenianism, but the telegram from Dublin identifies Daniel Byrne as a commonly used alias of Stephen J. Doyle, a Union veteran and a known Fenian who, according to reliable informers, was involved in the attempted uprising in March but escaped arrest. His current whereabouts are unknown.

O'Connor shows the Dublin telegram to Fazackerley. Fazackerley reads it and frowns.

"It's the same fucking fellow," he says. "Would you ever believe that?"

"We need to find Tommy," O'Connor says. "If Doyle's after him, it means he's been discovered."

"He might be dead already. When those Fenians get their hands on a spy, they don't trouble themselves with the niceties. You know that, Jimmy."

"Or he might be hiding. There are places he could go."

"It's possible."

"His sister, Rose, does slop work for the Solomons. And there's a mother too. They live on Thompson Street, behind the ropery."

Fazackerley takes a bunch of keys from his pocket, unlocks the gun safe, and takes out two revolvers. He loads them both and hands one to O'Connor.

"Should we tell Maybury what we're doing?"

O'Connor shakes his head.

"One Fenian more or less won't trouble Maybury much. If we need to, I'll tell him after."

They ascend Shude Hill past the back entrances to Smithfield market. There is a damp tang of fish guts and cheese, and the pavement underfoot is strewn with broken vegetables, malt, and sawdust. Outside the Turk's Head a barrel organ is playing "Men of Harlech" and Fazackerley pauses to listen, then gives the monkey a farthing. When they reach the corner of Thompson Street they ask a man for the Flanagan house, and he looks them up and down, then points across to number twenty-three.

Rose Flanagan is small and thin like her brother. She has dark hair tied up with a scrap of ribbon, and pale green eyes. When they tell her who they are and that they have come about Tommy, she explains that Tommy is not at home and they haven't seen him since yesterday morning. O'Connor asks if they can step inside for a moment, and she glances out into the street to see who is watching, then steps back and nods them toward the kitchen. The mother is sitting by the stove bundled up in shawls and blankets, her soft, crumpled face vacant and frog-like. She offers them a faint smile but doesn't say hello. The two men sit down, unbutton their overcoats, and put their hats on the table in front of them.

"They're police, Ma," Rose tells her. "They're here looking for our Tommy."

"*Tommy?*" the mother says. "We don't know where he's gone to at all."

"That's what I told them. He was here yesterday, but we haven't seen him since."

O'Connor reaches into his pocket for his notebook and pencil.

"Did Tommy take anything with him when he left the house yesterday?" O'Connor asks Rose.

"He took his dog," Rose says.

"Did he take a bag or a traveling case?"

"Tommy doesn't have any traveling case," the mother says.

"He just took the dog with him," Rose says. "Has he done something wrong?"

"We think he might be hiding somewhere, but we don't know where."

"Why would he be hiding?"

"Do you know a man named Stephen Doyle?"

Rose looks at him a moment before answering. Her expression is both tired and amused, as if none of this is entirely new to her. How many times in her life has she pulled Tommy out of trouble? O'Connor wonders.

"I never heard of him," she says.

"I know an Arthur Doyle, lives over on Spear Street," the mother says.

"Not Arthur, Ma, *Stephen,*" Rose says.

The mother shakes her head.

"I never heard of any Stephen Doyle," she says.

"We think Tommy might be in danger," O'Connor tells them. "Last night, near midnight, he came to the detective office in the Town Hall and said that this man Stephen Doyle was threatening him."

"So you two saw him there last night?"

"Not us," Fazackerley says. "Another officer named Rogers."

"If he was in danger, then why didn't you help him?"

"We're not sure what help he needed. He left a note for me to meet him today at noon, but when I went to the place he wasn't there."

"And you're a friend of Tommy's, are you?" Rose says. She gives him a sharp suspicious look. O'Connor wonders just how much she knows about her brother's business, and how much of what she knows she is prepared to admit in front of the mother. He looks around the kitchen. It is clean enough, but the furniture is old and badly made. There is a single candle guttering on the table in front of them and the fire in the grate is almost out.

"I'll be plain with you," he says, "since we're short of time here. Tommy has been passing me information, secrets, you could call it, in return for money, and my fear is he's been discovered."

"What secrets?" the mother says. "What secrets could Tommy know that would be of use to anyone but himself?"

"Perhaps he kept it from you," O'Connor says, "to protect you, but Tommy is close with members of the Fenian Brotherhood in Manchester."

"The Fenians?" the mother says. "Tommy knows those fellows, of course, we all do, but he's not a part of all that and never has been."

O'Connor looks at Rose. Her expression tightens.

"Our Tommy's not a spy," she says. "If he was I'd know about it."

"Do you have an idea where he could be hiding? Are there other friends? Other places he goes to? If we find him first, before they do, we can keep him safe."

Rose shakes her head.

"If you know anything about my brother, you'll know he's forever getting himself into mischief," she says, "and he generally talks his way out of it one way or another. He's gone missing before and he's always come back with some story to tell. He's an eejit all right, I'll grant you, but he's not a fool. Whatever it is he's done or not done can be made right without the police being brought in, I'm sure."

"This is more than mischief, though. If you think you can help him yourself, you can't. It's too late for that now."

"Whatever Tommy's been telling you, Mr. O'Connor, I'd take it with a large pinch of salt. He's a dreadful liar."

"That's the truth," the mother agrees. "I hate to say it about my own son, but he's awful with the lying."

Fazackerley sniffs and shakes his head.

"For christsake," he says.

O'Connor runs his thumbnail along the knife-gouged table edge. Whatever Rose knows, she is keeping to herself, and if she's scared, she is doing a fine job of covering it up. Probably, he thinks, she believes most of what she is telling them—that this is just another one of Tommy Flanagan's scrapes and that talking to the police will make things worse, not better, for all of them.

"You know what the Fenians do to their spies. You must know that."

"I know they generally kill them. But our Tommy's not a spy, I told you that already."

She flushes a little, then smiles to show she is sure of herself despite what they might think. One of her teeth at the front has a chip off the corner. Fazackerley starts to explain that if a man sells secrets for money, he is, by the popular reckoning, accounted a spy, and since Tommy Flanagan . . . but O'Connor stops him there.

"If you can't help us any, then we'll be on our way," he says. "But if you do hear anything from Tommy, you can get a message to us at the Town Hall. Sergeant Fazackerley and Head Constable O'Connor."

"You're one of those sent over from Dublin, aren't you?" Rose says to him.

"That's right."

"What happened to your face there?"

O'Connor shrugs.

"Got into some bother over in Gaythorn. Couple of hefty fellows asked me for a loan."

She steps closer in and has a look at him. She smells of bacon rind and, more faintly, lavender.

"I've got some ointment that'll take that swelling down for you," she says.

"It doesn't matter."

"No, you wait here."

She goes into the front room and comes back with a small brown-glass bottle. The label says "Dr. Abel's Best Liniment."

"It's the best thing for aches and bruises," she says. "Just try it."

"I won't, thank you," he says. "Not now."

"Here."

She puts some of the chalky white liquid on her finger ends, dabs it quickly onto his cheek and temple, then looks at him.

"Go on, rub it in," she says. "You'll feel it working straightaway."

She's playing games now, he thinks. That's all. Showing that she's not afraid of them.

"Very well, then."

He nods and rubs it in. His bruise-blackened skin feels thinned out and breakable.

"See," she says.

"We'll be on our way now," Fazackerley says.

O'Connor takes the liniment bottle off the table and looks

at it. There is a lithograph of Dr. Abel with pince-nez and a long white beard, and a description of his many accomplishments.

"You do needlework for the Solomons, don't you? That's what Tommy told me."

"I gave that up. I work in the kitchens at the Spread Eagle now. It's better paid."

"I'll look for you there, then," O'Connor says. "If I need you again."

She sniffs at the thought.

"You won't be needing me again, though. Our Tommy will be back before you even know it."

Back outside on the cobblestones, O'Connor opens his notebook and thumbs through the pages, hesitating twice and going back again, as if to check a fact or date. He first noticed something wrong when he opened it in the kitchen, but now he can see for certain that there are pages missing, five or six of them, cut out with a sharp blade. He doesn't remember exactly what was written on the missing pages, but he can make a guess from the dates before and after.

"What is it?" Fazackerley says.

"There are pages gone from my notebook," he says. "Cut out with a knife or razor."

"Fallen out, more likely. Check all your pockets."

"I already have."

"Show me, then."

O'Connor gives him the notebook and Fazackerley opens it and looks. He touches the cut-off edges with his fingertip and grimaces.

"You're sure it wasn't like this before?"

O'Connor nods.

"It's the Fenians," he says. "It must be them. That's why I was robbed in Gaythorn. They did it for the notebook, not the money or the watch. They cut out the pages, then put the notebook back in my pocket so I wouldn't notice."

"If it was a Fenian who robbed you, you would have recognized his face."

"They must have found someone else to help them, someone new, to throw me off."

"That's too clever for the Fenians. They'd never have dreamed up a scheme like that."

"It's too clever for Peter Rice, that's true, but we don't know it's too clever for Stephen Doyle."

"If he reads the pages, what does he find there?"

O'Connor shakes his head.

"Names," he says. "Three or four. I'm not sure."

"Three or four?"

"Tommy Flanagan, William Mort, Henry Maxwell . . ." He stops talking and looks off down the street. He thinks of Stephen Doyle, dark-browed, war-scarred, murderous, sitting in an attic room somewhere hunched over the papers like a priest with a breviary.

"Christ almighty." Fazackerley shakes his head. "One dead spy you might pass over as a slice of misfortune, but three all together is something else. Even Maybury will prick up his ears at a slaughter like that one."

CHAPTER 7

Tommy Flanagan is all but unrecognizable. Most of the face is shot away, and what is left is twisted, bent, and blood-blackened, like a piece of meat left too long in the oven. O'Connor can hardly bear to look at him. He feels sick at the very sight. Henry Maxwell, lying on the muddy ground adjacent, looks more or less the same. Why, if they had to kill them, they couldn't have done it in a more decent manner, he doesn't know, except, of course, he knows very well. It is a sign of their scorn, a reminder of the nature of the crime and its consequence. There will be no wakes here. No funeral parades. And if the mothers and widows want to say goodbye, this horror is all they will have to say goodbye to.

The coroner is standing off to one side, making notes, four constables in uniform are waiting around with gray canvas stretchers, Fazackerley has already been and gone. O'Connor walks over to the crumbling, weed-clogged edge of Travis Island and looks down into the black and viscid waters of the Irk. Two men dead because of his carelessness. He feels the shame burning in his stomach like something swallowed by mistake. He would like to take a drink now. He remembers the taste of whiskey on his tongue, like a long, deep cavern he could crawl into and be safe. Not a cavern, though, he reminds himself, a tomb. He closes his eyes for a moment and thinks about offering up a prayer for the dead but doesn't. Rain falls steadily from a darkened sky; it pummels the river's grimy surface and raises a fetid tang from the wet earth all around. After another minute, one of the constables comes over and tells him that the cart has arrived and they are ready to move the bodies.

There is a Belfast priest, Father Cochran, waiting for them at the infirmary. O'Connor gives him the names and addresses of the dead men and explains what has happened. He offers to give the families the news himself since he knows the circumstances, but Cochran says that it will be better coming from him. They are standing in a gloomy basement room, and the two stretchers are placed side by side on the red-tiled floor. The bodies are covered over with mud-stained blankets. The priest crosses himself twice, then bends down and lifts up an edge.

"Good God," he says. "How can you even know which one is which?"

"We went through their pockets."

"Well, the sooner they're decently buried, the better. There's no glory or goodness in any of this."

"Will you tell Rose Flanagan that when she is ready to talk to me, she knows where I can be found?"

Cochran looks at the body again, then puts the blanket back and stands up. Most of the color has drained from his face.

"Do you really think she'll be wanting to talk to the police after this?" he asks. "Do you think any of them will?"

"They won't get justice any other way."

"Justice?" he asks. "Is that what we saw last week at the prison with three men hanged?"

"This is not the same."

"Are you sure?"

There is a pause. There is no fire in the room and the only light is from a narrow window high up on one wall. O'Connor can see his own breath hanging like a veil in the dark air.

"Just as sure as I need to be," he says.

Cochran nods, licks his lips, and presses the wrinkles from his vestment with the heels of his hands.

"I believe you're from Dublin," he says. "May I ask which parish?"

O'Connor looks at him a long moment, then shakes his head.

"No," he says, "you may not."

When all the papers have been signed and the coroner is finally satisfied, O'Connor walks from the infirmary back into Ancoats. There was only one other name in his notebook, William Mort, a carpenter from Leitrim. He has been missing for two days now and his family has no idea where he could be. O'Connor wants to tell them about the bodies on Travis Island before they hear it from someone else. He goes to the house and knocks, but no one answers. He sees a curtain move in the upstairs window and tries again. As he walks away, someone shouts at him to fuck off and not come back, and a boy throws a stone, which misses. He remembers what it felt like after Catherine died. Trapped in memories. Despair like ice spreading out from the center of a pond. But there is always something left, he thinks. There must be. A gesture, a movement, a way of pulling back. Something tiny. It is a sin to just give up—not that he cares very much about sin.

When he gets to the Town Hall, Maybury is waiting for him.

"You come along with me," he says.

"There's no sign of Mort as yet," O'Connor tells him.

"If that's your version of good news, O'Connor, I must confess, I'm feeling less than elated."

"He may have escaped. It's still possible."

"If he's gone away, then he's no more use to us than if he's dead."

O'Connor doesn't answer. Maybury looks at him.

"Don't let your conscience trouble you now, O'Connor. We don't have the time for that."

"No, sir."

They walk down the corridor to Maybury's office. Michael Sullivan is already in there, sitting with his back to the fire. He is balancing a cup of tea on one knee. When he sees O'Connor, he nods and smiles. O'Connor asks him what he is doing.

"I was brought here. A fellow in uniform came to the house and asked for me."

Maybury sits down behind the desk. O'Connor remains standing.

"Michael is here because we need to find Stephen Doyle," Maybury explains, "and your nephew is the only person we know who has any connection to him."

O'Connor shakes his head. Perhaps he shouldn't be amazed by this, but he is.

"Even if we do find Doyle," he says, "without a witness there's nothing to link him to the killings. There may not even be any firm proof that he's a member of the Brother-hood."

"That's all true enough, but I'm less concerned about what he's just done, however heinous and disgraceful," Maybury says, "than about what he's planning. You've told me before that he's in Manchester to cause serious trouble."

"Yes. There's no other reason for him to come here."

"What happened with your notebook tells us he's clever, and two fresh bodies tell us he's ruthless. If we sit on our arses and wait around, who knows what carnage he might cause. Dead Fenians are bad enough, but if he starts killing Englishmen, we won't ever hear the end of it."

O'Connor glances at Sullivan, then looks quickly around the room as if hoping to find a solution to this nonsense hidden in the furniture.

"We could bring back the soldiers," he suggests. "Set them to guard all the public buildings, patrol the thoroughfares."

"That's not possible," Maybury says. "We need information. You know that."

"We've already talked about it, Jimmy," Sullivan explains. "I'll go to the alehouse and say I have some money for Daniel Byrne, a gambling debt, but I need to give it to him myself directly. When I meet him I'll tell him I've been thinking more about those things he said on the boat, about taking the fight to our enemies. I'll make him think I'm eager to join the cause."

O'Connor looks at Maybury.

"You can't think Doyle is going to start telling his plans to a young fellow he's barely met. It doesn't make any sense."

"Not straightaway, perhaps," Sullivan says, "but just as soon as I gain his trust."

"Michael's a persuasive fellow," Maybury says. "He's a decent talker."

"They'll find out he's my nephew."

"We've thought of that already. We've got him a room somewhere else, so he's not living with you. The story is that he had a letter of credit sent over from New York— enough to pay his debts and tide him over for a week or two until he finds a position here that suits him."

"Mr. Maybury says they'll pay my lodgings and give me a hundred pounds reward if it goes off all right, Jimmy," Sullivan says. "That's a good amount of money."

"And did he also tell you about the two men who just got killed for doing this kind of work?"

Sullivan looks across at Maybury and Maybury nods.

"I explained about the mistake you made with the note-book," he says, "and I promised Michael that nothing that he did for us would ever be written down anywhere, so he has nothing to fear on that score."

"I'm not afraid of the fellow," Sullivan says. "I've met his kind before. If I keep my wits about me, I'll be just fine."

"It's too dangerous," O'Connor says, "and even if it works it'll take months to win Doyle over. Now all the informers are dead, why would he delay that long? He must know we're looking for him."

"Then that's a problem we need to address," Maybury says. "We'll need to find a way of speeding things along."

"Not me," O'Connor says. "I don't want any part of this."

Maybury rests his high forehead on the tips of his blunt fingers and gives O'Connor a strained and disappointed look. He then turns to Sullivan and smiles.

"Michael," he says, "will you wait outside in the corridor a moment while I talk to your uncle alone?"

They watch him leave and wait until the door is closed. O'Connor wonders how much he truly cares about Michael Sullivan and decides he cares enough about him to not want him dead, which probably puts him a step or two ahead of Maybury.

"There must be another way," he says.

"Then tell me what it is."

"You can't force him."

"*Force* him? He's fairly champing at the bit, can't you tell?"

"I could take him down to the infirmary right now, show him what's left of Tommy Flanagan's face. That might change his mind quick enough."

Maybury picks his fountain pen off his desk, examines it for a moment, then puts it back down.

"We can do this with or without you, O'Connor. With you would be a little easier, of course, and possibly a little safer for your nephew also."

"You expect me to encourage him?"

"Not encourage, advise, guide. Make sure he doesn't do anything foolish or take too many risks. He's bright, but he's still young."

"I wouldn't say he's bright."

"Even more reason to help him, then."

"It won't work. Doyle's too clever. He'll see straight through it."

"All cleverness has its limits. Remember, he's a fanatic too. His vision is skewed. People like that are always open to flattery if you catch them right."

"I won't help you turn Michael Sullivan into a spy. I've got too much blood on my hands already."

"And you'll have plenty more if Doyle does whatever he's planning to. Have you thought of it like that? Without your informers, we'll have no way to stop him."

"I can't do it," O'Connor says again. His voice is low, constricted, restrained. He feels the sharpness of his failures jabbing like fishbones in his throat.

"You feel you have some family duty here. I understand—blood and water. Is he your brother's boy?"

"My sister-in-law's."

"I see, the late wife again. That makes it harder, I suppose."

"Perhaps."

"You can keep him safe, don't worry yourself about that. And this could be the making of him, you never know. He tells me he's interested in becoming a policeman like you are."

"He's a bank clerk. He has no idea what he's entering into. None at all. He thinks it's a great game."

O'Connor is angry but knows he mustn't show it. He's in too much trouble as it is.

Maybury nods but not in agreement. He leans back a little and pauses before speaking.

"The chief constable, Mr. Palin, is very exercised about the recent murders, as you might imagine. He thinks they reflect poorly on his stewardship of the city. In his opinion, you should be dismissed for your part in all this, sent back to Dublin for dereliction of duty. But I argued against that. I told him this was your best chance to make amends."

It is a simple threat, unsurprising and easy to make, but O'Connor feels its crude power nonetheless. If he's dismissed from his post and sent back home, that will be the end of him.

"Will you sit down at least," Maybury says to him, gesturing at a chair.

O'Connor hesitates for several seconds, then does as he is told.

"You made a mistake and this is the price. It could be much worse."

O'Connor nods.

"I'll need time to talk him through it," he says. "And we should put lookouts near the alehouse, people the Fenians won't recognize."

"I can get some fellows down from Bolton. That's easy enough."

"Is the money ready? The hundred pounds you promised?"

Maybury shrugs.

"I wouldn't call that a promise exactly," he says, "more a possibility."

"Then he'll want it put down in writing before we begin, both the amount and when it's to be paid in full."

Maybury frowns across the desk.

"So you're the lawyer now," he says. "That's a fresh development."

O'Connor doesn't answer, but he doesn't look away either. A stiff and gelid silence fills the space between them. After a long half minute, Maybury shakes his head, and stretches for his pen.

CHAPTER 8

The next day, Michael Sullivan is sitting at a corner table in Jack Riley's alehouse on Rochdale Road, with a half-full glass of porter in front of him. He has been there an hour already and is becoming fidgety. O'Connor gave him strict instructions to nurse his drink, keep his mouth shut, and wait. No skittles or dominoes or playing cards, and if someone says hello to him he is allowed to nod and smile, but that is all. Such extreme self-restraint strikes him as unnatural and perverse. If he is trying to blend in, why not just behave normally? What kind of a man goes into a tavern and sits on his own in the corner all afternoon? But Jimmy was insistent and there was something in his voice when he said it, a tinge of fearfulness or anger, that made Sullivan think he should take him seriously this time. They have given him the newspaper to read, but it is full of people and places he has never heard of. Moments like this, he wishes he was back in New York with his pals, but what's done is done, and all pleasures must be paid for somehow, he supposes, so here he is in Manchester, sitting alone in the corner of the pub, glooming over his beer like the idiot cousin at a funeral.

After a little while longer, Jack Riley appears behind the

bar, with his shirtsleeves rolled up and his waistcoat unbuttoned. He is a thin man, pale, with dark hair, oiled back,
and side-whiskers. He is missing a tooth at the top and his
nose is bent out of true from some previous fracas. Sullivan
takes another sip of the porter and looks about the room.
Just past noon and the place is half empty—there are three
men playing dominoes by the fireplace and four or five more
sitting about talking and smoking pipes. Fewer the better
is the plan, the only witness they really need is Riley. Sullivan glances at the clock again, then cranes to look out the
front window. Nothing to see. How much longer, he wonders, or is it possible they've forgotten, or the plan has
changed in some way? He picks up the newspaper again
and reads through the District News—suicide by poison in
Warrington, a stabbing in Clitheroe, in Worsley a corporal
named Cabusac has been committed to trial for shooting a
cow while drunk. He decides he will have another pint, no
one is keeping count, and, so long as he plays his part as
instructed, what does it matter? He drinks down the remains and steps toward the bar. Jack Riley looks at him.

"Porter, is it?" he says.

Sullivan nods and Riley takes the empty glass.

"Haven't I seen you before?" he says. "Aren't you that
friend of Arthur's?"

"I don't know any Arthurs," Sullivan says. "I just arrived
on the steamer from New York."

Riley leans back on the pump and nods.

"Family here in Manchester? Uncles and cousins?"

"No," he says, "no family."

"Most people that come have family. So what brings you
here?"

Sullivan shrugs.

"I had some trouble back home. I had to get away. Some
fellow promised me a job in Liverpool, but nothing came of
it, so now I'm here looking about."

The door behind Sullivan opens and a policeman in uniform, truncheon in hand, pauses a moment to take off his helmet and then steps into the parlor. Riley, watching him, frowns.

"What the fuck does he want?" he says.

Sullivan turns around to look. It's Fazackerley. Their eyes meet for a moment, then Fazackerley looks away. He walks slowly across to the bar, taking his own time about it, making his presence known. *At long fucking last,* Sullivan thinks.

Riley opens the flap of the bar and wipes his hands on a tea towel. Fazackerley, who is doing nothing quickly, pauses to take in the tableau—Michael Sullivan, an untouched glass of porter in front of him on the bar, Jack Riley with a look on his face.

"Are you the landlord?" Fazackerley asks.

"What if I am?" Riley says.

"We've had a complaint."

"Where's Rawes got to?"

"Constable Rawes is off sick today. My name's Magee."

Riley looks unconvinced.

"I deal with Rawes," he says. "Me and him have an understanding between us."

"Rawes is off sick, so you'll have to deal with me today. We've had a complaint that you're breaking the terms of your license by selling gin."

Riley snorts and shakes his head.

"Gin?" he says. "Christ."

"It's a serious matter, and if it's proven, we'll close this place down. I'm here to arrest you. You'll have to come with me to Knott Mill."

"It's a poor fucken joke. I never sold a drop of gin in my life. You can ask anyone here. They'll all vouch for me, won't you, lads?"

"We have witnesses that swear otherwise."

"Then your witnesses are liars."

"And you can tell that to the magistrate."

"Why don't you take a look down in the cellar," Sullivan suggests. "If he's selling gin, there'll be bottles down there. Evidence one way or the other."

Fazackerley turns to look at him.

"I'm not here to fossick around cellars. We have witnesses."

"And the landlord here says the witnesses are lying."

Fazackerley frowns and lays his truncheon down on top of the bar.

"Who are you?" he says.

"I'm a customer."

"Name?"

"My name's not important. What's important is you check in the cellar, so you know for certain who's lying and who isn't."

"I don't need to check the cellar to know who's lying. And if you don't tell me your name, I'll arrest you on suspicion."

Sullivan laughs.

"On suspicion of what? I've only been in Manchester for a week."

Fazackerley takes a step closer.

"You're an American, I can hear it in your voice. We've been looking for an American who's just arrived in Manchester, a man named Stephen Doyle. Is that you?"

"My name's not Doyle."

Fazackerley peers hard at Sullivan.

"But you're a Fenian, aren't you?"

Sullivan doesn't answer.

"If you're not a Fenian, then what are you doing supping in a Fenian alehouse?"

"Everyone's welcome here," Riley says. "We don't check on a man's beliefs before we give him a drink."

"I was passing by, that's all," Sullivan says.

It is Fazackerley's turn to laugh. He feels in his pocket and finds his handcuffs.

"I'll take you both back with me," he says. "We'll get to the bottom of this."

"Don't be so fucken daft," Riley says. "The lad's done nothing wrong."

"Oh, are you vouching for him now?" Fazackerley asks. "Friend of yours, is he?"

"I never seen him before today."

"So you say, but I think there's something going on here. I think there's more to this than meets the eye." He reaches for Sullivan's arm and Sullivan pulls it away.

"You can't arrest me," Sullivan says.

"Leave the lad alone," Riley says.

Fazackerley picks his truncheon off the bar and points it slowly, first at Sullivan, then at Riley.

"You two know each other," he says. "I'm not so stupid. I can tell."

Sullivan looks at Riley with what he hopes is an expression of comradely bemusement. Riley shakes his head.

"I've met some idiot fucken coppers in my time," he says to Fazackerley, "but you take the prize."

"You can both come peaceably, or I can step outside now and blow my whistle. It's up to you."

For a moment, no one moves. The domino players have stopped their game; everyone is paused, watching on in silence. Sullivan, heart drumming, hot fear gripping his insides, readies himself. Fazackerley makes a show of unlocking the handcuffs.

"Give me your wrists," he says.

"You can't arrest me," Sullivan says. "You don't have any right."

"I'll do as I please," Fazackerley says. He steps forward and grabs Sullivan by the elbow. They lock eyes for a moment; their faces are a foot apart or less. Riley is behind them, unsighted. "Go on," Fazackerley whispers to him, "now." Sullivan can smell coffee and mothballs; he can see the snotty crosshatch of nose hair. He raises his fist and punches Fazackerley as hard as he can in the side of the face. The policeman grunts and stumbles backward against the bar, dropping his truncheon and smashing the glass of porter on the way down. Sullivan steps forward again, as if to continue the attack, but Riley blocks his way.

"That's enough," he says. "That's enough now. Jesus Christ."

Fazackerley pulls himself upright. He has a red mark across his face and a drop of blood near one eye. He points at Sullivan.

"You just wait there, you little bastard," he says. "You just fucking wait there."

He runs out into the street and blows three long blasts on his police whistle. Riley looks at Sullivan and shakes his head.

"You're a fucken dark horse, you are," he says.

"He shouldn't have grabbed me," Sullivan says. He is trembling and the words are catching in his throat.

"You need to hide yourself now. They'll be coming in from all directions when they hear that whistle."

"I'll go out the back way."

"They'll be expecting that. It's safer if you stay here. There's a storeroom downstairs. I can push some old barrels up in front of the door. They won't find you down there even if they go looking."

"I don't want to trouble you any," Sullivan says.

"It's no trouble," he says. "I appreciate a fellow who can stand his ground."

Sullivan spends the rest of the day barricaded in the empty storeroom. The floor is packed clay and there are no windows. Riley gives him three candles for light, a jug of beer, and a wedge of Melton pie for sustenance. There is a wooden bucket in the corner when he needs it. He eats the pie, drinks down the beer, then falls asleep. When he wakes up shivering, and remembers where he is, he feels a mixture of excitement and fear. Jimmy's plan has worked even better than they hoped, but now he must manage the rest on his own. In his head, he goes through the preparations again— what to say and what to keep quiet about, who to believe, when to walk away. He knows he is only one step away from Doyle now. If he can convince Riley to trust him, then the rest will follow on naturally enough. He is not scared of Riley, but he wonders what questions he might still have and what suspicions he might yet harbor.

Near midnight, when the alehouse is closed and locked up for the night, Riley pushes the barrels away from the storeroom door and leads Sullivan back upstairs into the darkened parlor. He throws a handful of coal onto what's left of the fire and gestures for Sullivan to sit.

"You have another place to go to, I suppose?" he says.

"I rent a bed in one of the lodging houses on Pump Street."

Riley frowns.

"Pump Street? Is that the best you can manage?"

"I'm still looking about for work."

"That was a fine punch you landed there. Put that mouthy bastard Magee right down on his arse."

"Is he still out searching for me?"

Riley shakes his head.

"It's just the regular patrols this time of night. They don't know what you look like, and I doubt they care very much about Magee's injured pride."

"What about the gin?"

"That was nothing. There were no witnesses. They just try that kind of thing to cause me trouble. Every week nearly it's something else. I'm a freedom-loving Irishman, you see, and they don't appreciate my politics."

Sullivan nods and looks into the fire. He waits for a moment. If he is too quick or eager, then Riley might start to wonder.

"I'm not much for politics myself," he says. "I don't read the newspapers, but I heard about the three fellows they hanged. It didn't sound right to me."

"It wasn't right. It was murder, that's what it was, plain and simple. Three good men, widows, children, but they don't care about any of that. All they want is revenge."

"For that dead policeman? What was his name?"

"Charles Brett."

"Brett, that's right."

Sullivan nods, then smiles quickly. Friendly but not too friendly was Jimmy's advice. Enough but not too much.

Riley looks at him.

"What's your name anyway?" he says.

"Michael Sullivan. I was born in Dublin, on Ash Street, but we left in 'fifty-six."

"And do you remember Ireland?"

"Not so much."

"See, that's the tragedy right there. We're driven out of our own country, scattered to the four fucken winds."

"I'd go back, but I hear there's no work to be had in Dublin anymore."

"Because the British landlords suck us dry, that's why. No nation can thrive and grow if its wealth is stolen from it."

"It's a pity," Sullivan agrees. "I've thought on that myself."

Riley stands up.

"You stay there," he says.

He goes back into the kitchen and returns with a bottle

of whiskey and two tumblers. He puts the tumblers on the mantelpiece, fills them halfway, then offers one to Sullivan.

"Good health to you," he says, "and God Save Ireland."

"God Save Ireland," Sullivan repeats. The whiskey burns on his tongue and brings tears to his eyes. He takes a breath in and waits for it to fade.

"I appreciate your help," he says. "The police would have caught me for sure. I'd be locked in a jail cell by now."

Riley waves it away.

"You did nothing wrong. You stood up for yourself like a man, that's all. We could do with a few more like you around here."

They sit back down. The fire is coming to life again, the dark new coals cracking and spitting amid the mound of pale ash.

"You might be wondering what brought me in here," Sullivan says. "I know I told the policeman I was just walking by, but that isn't the whole truth of it. There's a fellow I met on the boat from New York, a fellow named Byrne, said I might find him in Riley's alehouse on Rochdale Road. I owe him a small debt and I was thinking he might help me find some work."

"Byrne?" Riley says. "I don't know anyone by the name of Byrne. What does he look like?"

"He's American like me. Thirty years old or so. Stern-looking. He has long dark hair and scars on one cheek."

Riley looks at him a moment.

"Scars, you say?"

"Here and here." He points at his own face. "Deep ones."

"And what boat were you both on?"

"The *Neptune* out of New York."

Riley shakes his head and takes a sip of the whiskey.

"I don't know anyone named Byrne," he says again, "but I can ask around."

"I thought he might help me find work," Sullivan says, "that's all."

Riley nods.

"I'll ask around."

Sullivan expects him to say something more, something that might be important, but he doesn't. Instead there is a long pause. The stuttering flames throw vague, soft-edged shadows across the floorboards and wall.

"He told me he was a draper," Sullivan adds suddenly, "but I wasn't sure that was true. He didn't look much like a draper to me. He looked more like an old soldier with the scars and the hair. I've seen a few of that type roaming about New York since the war finished. They don't know what to do with themselves now that the fighting is over. It's a sight to see."

Riley's eyes narrow. His manner hardens a touch. Sullivan wonders if he has made a mistake, then decides it's nothing.

"If a man tells you he's a draper, why would you doubt him?" Riley says. "Why would he lie about it?"

"Just the way he looked. No other reason."

Riley nods twice, looks down at his whiskey, then drinks it off.

"What kind of work are you looking for, Michael?"

"Anything," he says. "Anything at all."

"Well, I may be able to help you, then. I have plenty of friends. You should stay here with me tonight, though," Riley says. "It's safer all around. I'll make you a bed down in the cellar and we can talk some more in the morning."

Riley finds a straw mattress and some blankets, and they go back down the steps. It is chilly and damp in the cellar and there is a strong smell of mold. They clear some space on the flagstone floor and lay out the bedding.

"It's not the Queen's Hotel," he says, "but it's no worse than those fleapits on Pump Street, I'm guessing."

"It'll suit me just fine," Sullivan says. "I'm grateful."

They shake hands. Riley turns to leave, then pauses.

"You say you owe this fellow Byrne some money? Is that it?"

"We played poker on the boat to help pass the time. Just nickels and dimes, but it added up to a few dollars by the time we reached Liverpool, and I didn't have the cash to hand."

"And he gave you this address?"

"He said when I was in Manchester I could leave the money for him here."

"A trusting sort of fellow, then?"

"Looked to me like he had other things on his mind. Like a few dollars didn't matter too much in the grander scheme."

Riley nods and smiles.

"There's plenty of money in drapery, I suppose."

"I'd say there must be."

"Unless he was lying about that part."

"That was just a notion I had. I could be wrong."

Riley goes back up the steps into the parlor and stands in front of the fire. He hears the wind humming inside the chimney breast and the rain skittering against the windowpane. He is wondering what he should do next with Michael Sullivan. He stands there frowning and rubbing his chin for a while, then he remembers the happy sight of that mouthy peeler picking himself up off the floor, with his uniform half-covered in damp sawdust and a face like murder, and decides, with a smile, that a young man like that, with such an overflow of gumption, must surely be brought into the fold.

CHAPTER 9

Robert Neill, the mayor of Manchester, is square-shouldered and thick-necked; he has narrow, questioning eyes and a mouth as wide and lipless as a monkey's. He made his pile as a builder, flinging up rows of shoddy back-to-backs in Ancoats and Hulme, and there is still, despite the black frock coat and cashmere stripes, a hint of the navvy about him. You can see it in the way he moves, impatient, stooped, purposeful, and in the shape of his hands— the wide, blunt fingers, the thick knuckles, brown and gnarled as walnuts. It is as if he is ready any moment to put down his fountain pen or wineglass and pick up a trowel. A knife will not do it with a man like that one, Doyle thinks; if you get in too close, he will likely rassle you for it. It must be a pistol. That will take more time to arrange, no doubt, add to the expense and complication, but now that the informers are dead there is no reason to hurry; they can plan it out, gauge the risks, choose their moment.

Doyle is sitting in Skelly's ancient cab on Cross Street across from the Dissenters' chapel, close enough to the junction with King Street to have a view of the entrance to the Town Hall but not close enough to draw attention. It is after seven o'clock and the lights in the mayor's office are still burning brightly. Doyle is guessing Neill has another dinner to go to, or another speech to give, and is dandying himself up in preparation. They have watched him for nearly a week already with no tangible reward. They need to find him alone, in a place without witnesses, but except when he is in the carriage being driven somewhere, he always has company. They could ambush the brougham, of course, but that would take four or five men at least, and Doyle doesn't yet know four or five men in Manchester who he would trust with the task. He hears Skelly banging on the roof of the cab with the butt end of his horse whip and leans out to see what he wants.

"He's away on foot," Skelly says. "Look over there. It's him, I swear."

He points to a stocky figure crossing the road in front of the Town Hall. He is wearing a top hat and holding a black umbrella up at an angle against the gusting drizzle.

"Why would he be walking?" Doyle says. "Where's the brougham?"

Skelly shrugs.

Doyle steps down from the cab. Carts and omnibuses rattle past him; there is the hard hiss of gas lamps and a faint smell of sewage. He turns up his collar against the rain and squints.

"You stay here," he says to Skelly. "Watch out for that brougham. Follow after it if you need to."

He crosses over onto King Street. The man is thirty yards ahead of him now. Doyle quickens his pace until he is close enough to be sure it is the mayor, then slows down and steps sideways into a doorway. He feels in his jacket pocket for his clasp knife. He prizes open the short blade, thumbs its edge, thinks for a moment, then presses it shut again. He steps out of the doorway and looks to the right. The mayor is still walking steadily up the hill toward Brown Street and Spring Gardens. The wet bend of his umbrella catches the silver light of a streetlamp, then lets it go again. Something new is happening, but Doyle doesn't yet know what it is or how much it might matter. Neill pauses to check his pocket watch, then carries on walking. He passes the glaring façade of the Queen's Theatre on his left, then turns in to the narrowness and shadow of Milk Street. He walks halfway down, then stops in front of a darkened shop front and looks up. The windows above the shop are shuttered, but one of the shutters is half-open and there is a light showing behind it. Doyle steps into an alley and watches. If he had a pistol he could do it now, but all he has is the clasp knife. He looks about for a length of timber, a half-brick, but sees nothing he can make use of. Neill lowers his umbrella, steps forward, and raps on the glass of the shop door. After a minute, the door opens and he takes his hat off and steps inside. Doyle waits five minutes to be sure he is not coming out again, then leaves the alley and goes across the street to take a look. The shop window has a display of bonnets, handkerchiefs, and artfully draped swatches. The sign above says ELIZABETH STOKES, DRESS-MAKER AND MILLINER. He nods and his lips move silently as if he is reciting a short prayer, then he turns and walks back down to Cross Street. Skelly's cab is where he left it.

"He's got a woman," he tells Skelly. "She has a shop on Milk Street, number twelve, halfway down on the right-hand side."

Skelly whistles lowly, then grins. His weather-burned face is a skein of fine wrinkles, and his occasional teeth are the color of cheese rind.

"Well, the sly auld fucker," he says.

"Drive the cab up there. Watch what time he leaves the place and where he goes to afterward. Write it all down."

"I'd say we have him now," Skelly says.

"I'd say we do."

"He'll pay for his sins at last."

Doyle wonders for a moment what this means, then he remembers the hangings. Skelly is a good man, he thinks, trustworthy and useful in his fashion, but he sometimes misunderstands the task.

"It's a war we're in," he says.

Skelly nods and tips his cap.

"A war," he says, "I know that."

"You be sure to write down the time he leaves," Doyle reminds him. "The time is what matters most."

He rides with Skelly as far as Market Street, then crosses Piccadilly and walks up Oldham Street into Ancoats. The rain gilds the pavement and cobblestones and drips off the brim of his hat. After trying the Two Terriers and the Cheshire Cheese he finds Peter Rice drinking gin in the Blacksmith's Arms. He is standing up at the bar with Jack Riley; his broad face is shiny and red, and his far-apart eyes are wet with recent merriment. Doyle nods to them, then sits down at a table near the door.

Peter Rice finishes his drink and tamps his mouth on the cuff of his jacket. He says something quick to Jack Riley, then shambles over and lowers himself down onto a stool. They lean in closer and Doyle explains about the shop on Milk Street and what he saw there.

"I need two pistols quick," he says.

Rice shrugs and looks away.

"Clean pistols is hard to come by," he says.

"The sooner I do this, the sooner I'll be gone."

"There's a fellow down in Brummagem I know, but it'll be a week at least, mebbe more."

They talk for another ten minutes about the cost, and who will travel down to Birmingham to bring them back. Then Doyle stands up again and offers Rice his hand.

"There's something else before you go," Rice says. "Jack Riley has a question."

Rice beckons to Riley, and Riley comes over to join them

at the table. Doyle sits down again, and Riley tells him about Michael Sullivan and the fisticuffs with Magee the day before.

"The boy claims he knows you. Says he met you on the boat and you told him to come by the alehouse to drop off some money. Is that the truth?"

Doyle nods.

"He'll talk you to death with a drink inside, but there's no great harm in him. At least none that I saw."

"So you'll have no complaint if we give him something at the tannery?" Rice says. "Now that Jones is sick, it's been Neary and Slattery on their own in the yard for a week."

"Is there no one else?"

"It's hard, dirty work, and it doesn't pay so well as the factories or cotton mills. Most of the fellows around here will turn up their noses at the tannery, but when I mentioned it to Sullivan he was all eagerness."

Doyle shrugs.

"He's not the brightest, but if you want him, go ahead," he says. "Leave me out of it, though. If he asks after me, tell him Mr. Byrne says he can keep the money."

"I like the look of him," Riley says. "He's bold, and I like to see some boldness in a young fellow."

Doyle stands up again and buttons his coat.

"Won't you have another drink with us, Stephen?" Rice says. He smiles, but there is something snide and scornful in the way he asks.

"I need to get back to Skelly now."

"What are you doing with that old fucker?" Riley says.

"It's better if you don't know about it," Doyle says, "safer all around."

"Jack here can be trusted," Rice says. "He's no traitor."

"I'm not saying he is. Fewer is better, that's all."

There's a pause. Rice shakes his head. The tangled noises of the tavern rise up around them.

"They're following the mayor," Rice says to Riley. "They plan to shoot him when they get the chance."

"The *mayor*?" Riley says. "How can you shoot the fucken mayor?"

Doyle stares at Rice, and Rice looks back at him calmly as if nothing much has happened. Doyle reminds himself that he needs those two pistols, that the moment of reckoning might come, but this is not it, not yet.

"Whosoever knows the plan is in as deep as the man who pulls the trigger," he says finally. "Remember that. If they hang one of us, they'll hang us all."

"I can keep my counsel right enough," Rice says, "and so can Jack here. Don't worry yourself about us. We're all fighting on the same side. We're all loyal Irishmen. You do your duty and we'll do ours."

Rice holds out his hand, and Doyle looks at it.

"We'll talk about duty after I see those guns," he says.

CHAPTER 10

⎯⎯⟶▸◉◂⟵⎯⎯

It is past noon the next day when Rose Flanagan finishes her morning shift at the Spread Eagle Hotel on Hanging Ditch. She pulls on a dark wool bonnet and wraps herself in a shawl against the damp December chills. She left home well before dawn; she is tired now and her head is throbbing, but the thought of going back to Thompson Street, to her mother's pleading eyes and swollen face, to the caustic mix of shame and sorrow that fills the rooms like smoke since Tommy's death, makes her want to groan or weep. Her neighbors ignore her now. The children stop their games of tag to stare and catcall as she walks down the street. They have had a window broken, words chalked on the walls. *Is it not enough to murder and disfigure a man?* she wants to say. *Must you hound his grieving family also? Is there no decency or kindness left in the world?* They must leave Manchester, of course, there is nothing else for it, but where can they go? She has uncles and cousins scattered about, but the letters she has had back are not encouraging. Everyone knows about Tommy's crimes, it seems, the news has spread, and even those who have no great love for the Brotherhood don't wish to be linked to a traitor. If she had realized even for a moment what he was doing, she would have stopped it. She would have taken him by his collar and shaken some sense into his head just as you would with a stubborn child, because really, she knows, that was all her brother ever was—a foolish boy, too taken with himself and his own cleverness to ever believe that anyone would wish him harm.

She buys a penny bun from the bakery across the road. It is still warm from the ovens, and the smell as she holds it comforts her. She must marry someone, she supposes, that is the only escape, but who will have her now? No one in Angel Meadow or Ancoats for sure. A stranger, then, that is what she has been brought to by Tommy's greed and foolishness. As she steps out of the shop, she sees the policeman O'Connor. He looks at her, nods, and touches the brim of his bowler hat.

"James O'Connor," he says. "You remember me perhaps?"

She stares back a moment, wondering how to answer, then looks away.

"I wanted to speak to you," he says. "I thought it was better not to come to the house."

"I've nothing to say to the police. You've caused us enough trouble. You should see how my mother suffers. If all this is the death of her, I won't be a bit surprised."

"I'm sorry for that," O'Connor says. "I am."

"You could have stopped him," Rose says. "Any time, but you didn't want to, I suppose."

"He came to me first. He offered to talk."

"You could have stopped him any time," she says again.

"I told him to be careful, but I had no idea this would happen. No one did."

He is speaking in a low voice so as not to be overheard. The people walking past glance at them. A man with a white apron puts a tray of fresh loaves into the bakery window.

"What do you want from me?" Rose asks.

"I want to find out anything you know. We're still looking for the men who did it."

"My brother's been murdered," she says. "That's all I know."

"There's a place nearby here," O'Connor says. "An eating house on Thomas Street. We could talk there without being watched over. I have some questions."

Rose can still feel the faint heat of the bun in her hands. There is no good reason to talk to him except that she's curious. She wants to know all that he knows.

"How much did you pay him anyway?" she asks.

"Not very much. Five or ten shillings, once or twice it was a pound, but that was rare."

"He must have gambled it all away, then."

"I believe that's right."

She feels a moment of strange jealousy at the thought of the two of them together, her brother and this man.

"I would have come to you sooner except for the priest," O'Connor says.

"That priest was no use at all. He was scared half to death."

"I might be able to help you a little," he says. "If I knew what you needed."

She looks at him again. He is tall and thin, half-handsome in his way, but there is a slowness and sadness about him too, as if every thought and word requires careful preparation.

"You can't help me," she says. "I should be going now. My mother's waiting for me at home."

There's a pause. She waits for him to argue or insist, but he doesn't.

"I made a mistake," he says eventually. "When we called on you before, asking after Tommy, I didn't realize it."

"What mistake?"

"I can't explain it all here. It's too involved. Let me get

you a cup of tea. It's a quiet place I'm thinking of, clean, and you don't need to stay long if you don't like it."

She hesitates a moment longer, then agrees to go with him. Even if they are seen together, she thinks, what difference will it make now?

They find a table at the back, near the kitchen. When they're settled, O'Connor tells her about the notebook. She doesn't understand at first, so he explains it again.

"That was the mistake I told you about," he says.

"So without the notebook our Tommy might still be alive?"

"Most likely. Yes."

She looks down at the table, then up at the gas mantle glowing on the wall above O'Connor's head.

"They would have found him out some other way. He should have stayed clear of the police, kept his mouth shut, but he had a mind of his own. He was clever, our Tommy, but not clever enough."

The tea arrives with a plate of oatcakes and a jug of milk. O'Connor lifts the lid of the pot and stirs it.

"We can catch the men who killed him, we just need some help. Can you tell me what people are saying?"

She laughs.

"I'm about the last person to know. They won't serve me in the shops. I've been spat at twice in the street. No one gives me the time of day since they found out Tommy was a spy."

O'Connor nods. He isn't surprised. Half the point of killing an informer is to scare the life out of the ones who are left behind.

"Before he disappeared, did Tommy say anything about Stephen Doyle? Anything at all?"

She shakes her head.

"I knew Tommy was in the Brotherhood, but that was all. He never talked about it and I never asked."

"Why did he join?"

"For the fun of it, I suppose. And because it made him feel important. Why did Tommy do anything?"

"He was still young."

"Just twenty-two in June," she says. "How old are you, Constable O'Connor?"

"I'll be thirty-five next time around."

"And hardly a gray hair that I can see."

"Only one or two."

She looks more tired than she did before, he thinks, bruised and worn down by it all, but her manner hasn't changed even though her brother is dead now. She's still bright in her way, and pretty, with those green eyes and the smile.

"What kind of a place is this?" Rose says, looking around.

"Temperance."

"You're an abstainer? For how long?"

"Not so long. I'm new to it."

She takes a bite of the oatcake. She has small teeth, pale lips. There is a dark crumb at the corner of her mouth that she pushes away with her finger.

"How will you manage now that Tommy's gone? Do you make enough working at the hotel to pay the rent?"

She shakes her head.

"Not nearly enough, but we can't stay here anyway. No one will talk to me now. Even my friends are scared. I've lived here all my life and it's like I'm a stranger. My mother still doesn't understand what's going on. She sits there in the parlor every day expecting people to call to say how sorry they are for her loss. I tell her they're not coming, but she won't believe me."

"There are other places you could go to," O'Connor says. "Liverpool, Glasgow, Birmingham. Make new friends, start afresh."

She frowns.

"We've done nothing wrong, yet we're being punished. How can that be fair?"

Fair, O'Connor thinks. *Is that what she expects?*

He remembers his childhood in Armagh—the cabin by the stony conacre and the pig they fattened each winter to pay for the summer oatmeal. He was only twelve when his father killed a man in an argument about land and was found guilty of manslaughter and transported. Then, the year after, their mother died of the sweating fever and O'Connor and his sister, Norah, went to Dublin to live with their aunt Ellen in the two rooms of her dilapidated tenement off Meath Street.

Norah grieved their losses, but O'Connor was glad to be away. Despite the filth and the stench of it, he preferred the city life. He went to school for two years, where he learned grammar and history and a smattering of Latin and Greek, then became apprentice to a tailor, James O'Reilly. When he was seventeen, he had an idea to join the fusiliers. He visited their barracks at Arbor Hill to volunteer, but they wouldn't take him. They didn't say why, but making his way home afterward, he wondered if they had found out about his father's crime, if there was a thick ledger on a shelf somewhere with the name of Paul O'Connor written down and a black mark inked beside it. Just the thought made him bitter and furious. The next day in the tailor's, he argued with a customer and was given a stern warning, then, a week later, when he did it again, he was told he must leave.

After that, he found work as a drayman for O'Connell's brewery. One day, walking back to his aunt's flat in the cold dark, still wearing his hobnail boots and canvas apron, he met his old schoolmaster Felix Nugent, a Kerry man who had once told him he had a good mind and might even consider going to Maynooth to train for the priesthood. They stood together for a long time, talking. Before they said goodbye, Nugent told him he was too bright to be wasting his life as a laborer and should find something better to do. He said he had a brother-in-law who was an inspector in the Dublin police and, if O'Connor agreed, he would write him a letter. When O'Connor explained what had happened with the fusiliers, Nugent shook his head and said he doubted there could be any such book in existence, but, even if there were, his brother-in-law was a fair-minded fellow who would never seek to hold one man responsible for the errors of another.

"It isn't fair," he says to Rose. "Of course not. But if we could only find Stephen Doyle, we could end it all now."

"You won't find a man like that until he wants to be found."

"Is that what people are saying?"

"I don't know what people are saying. I told you that already."

O'Connor nods and drinks his tea.

"Even if you caught this Doyle and hanged him, that wouldn't be the end of it," Rose tells him. "There'd be someone else after that."

"That's what they want you to believe, but it's not true. We can beat them, I promise you."

"You don't need to promise me anything," she says. "I don't care either way."

"You're bitter about what's happened," he says. "I would be too."

She glares at him suddenly, then shakes her head and starts to weep. O'Connor watches her. He feels the tug of her grief, its dark, unappealable logic like a tide, and braces himself against it. He looks down at his two hands, pale pink and gray against the varnished tabletop, then looks up again. Rose gasps, shudders, wipes her eyes with the edge of her shawl, and sniffs.

"Look at me," she says. "Just look at me, will you."

It is as if she vanished for a minute, but now she's back again. He pours more tea into her cup and pushes it toward her.

"I could get you some money," he says. "Everyone knows what Tommy did for the police. When I go back to the Town Hall, I'll talk to them."

"If I had fifty pounds, we could get a shop somewhere."

"It won't be so much as that, not nearly, but let me try. See what they have to say."

He knows it's a foolish thing to promise. Maybury will likely laugh at him when he brings it up, but he wants to give her something and what else does he have?

She wipes her eyes again and drinks the tea. She looks calmer now, almost happy. Some people have that strength in them, he thinks, but he never did. It was Catherine who kept him upright and steady, and when she died it was as though the grief was doubled because he didn't have her there to help him through.

They talk more about the money, and he can see that in her head she is already making plans how to spend it.

"I can only ask them," he says. "They might say no. I'll come back to see you when I have any news. I'll wait for you where I waited today."

"Tell them it'll mean that he didn't die in vain," she says. "If we get something from it, even something small."

"I'll tell them that," he says. "I will."

There's a long pause, then Rose glances up at the clock on the wall and says she must be going now or else her mother will start to fret. O'Connor goes up to the counter to pay, and when he gets back to the table she is already standing, ready to leave. Her green eyes are pink from crying.

"Your face looks better than before," she tells him. "Almost back to normal, aren't you?"

"Nearly," he says. "Not quite."

As they say goodbye, he feels an urge to touch her, on the elbow perhaps or the angle of the shoulder, a gentle touch, small and comforting, but he doesn't do it. Instead, he nods quickly and stands aside to let her go past. As she moves by him, he breathes in the hard smells of her work—carbolic soap and white vinegar—and beneath them both, like an almost forgotten memory, the frail must of human skin.

CHAPTER 11

⸻

Peter Rice's tannery is on the east bank of the Irk, just up from the Ducie Bridge near the place they call Gibraltar. There is a tripe dresser's next to it on one side and a sizing works on the other. Michael Sullivan is employed as a yardman. When the fresh cowhides arrive into the beam room, their undersides are bloodied and membranous and the horns and tails are still attached. They must be trimmed and limed before the hair can be sleeked off with the long, dull-edged fleshing knife, and then they must be bated in pigeon manure until they are soft and receptive enough to tan. Out in the tanning yard there are twelve brick-lined pits arranged into three rows of four. The hides are moved from one row to the next until they are dark enough, then they are carried into the shed for drying and finishing. Sullivan's task is to fill and drain the tanning pits and to grind and shovel the oak bark and manure. He does this for ten hours a day, and, for his labors, he is paid fifteen shillings a week and allowed to sleep on a cot in the damp and reeking cellar.

The work is exhausting and filthy, and after two weeks of it he is no closer to finding Stephen Doyle than he was the day he walked into Jack Riley's alehouse. He has listened to the other men talking and he has struck up conversations of his own, but no one has mentioned Doyle's name even once, and there's been no sign of him anywhere. He can't get close enough to Peter Rice to learn anything that way, and if he asks Riley what he should do about the money he owes, the gambling debt, Riley shrugs and tells him to forget about it. It is as if the American has disappeared, or never even existed.

He is beginning to think that O'Connor's plan has failed, and he must give up on the hundred pounds and find some other way of filling his coffers, when, one morning, as he wheels the first cartload of ground bark out to the pits, he notices that Neary, who always starts before him, is missing. When he checks with Slattery the foreman, he is told that Rice has sent him off on an errand, and he will be back later in the day. It's the late afternoon and dusk is falling when Neary reappears. He is carrying a parcel wrapped in brown paper under one arm and smoking a cheap cigar. Sullivan calls out to ask him where he has been, and he says he has been down to Birmingham on the train to do some business for Peter Rice. When Sullivan points to the parcel and asks him what he has brought back, Neary says it's a secret.

As they are talking, Peter Rice opens the door of his office and calls him inside. Neary is in the office for fifteen minutes or so, and when he comes out again he is not carrying the parcel. Soon after, when his work is finished for the day and he has washed himself and changed his clothes, Sullivan leaves the tannery, walks across Ducie Bridge, then turns right onto Long Millgate. It is dark and the gas lamps have been lit. He counts each lamp as he passes, and when he gets to the seventh lamp on the right, opposite the butcher's, he stops and looks about. When he is sure no one is watching him, he takes a piece of chalk from his pocket, bends down as if to tie his bootlace, and marks a white cross and a number on the wall, then stands up and walks back the way he came.

Near midnight, he meets O'Connor at the edge of the pauper burial ground. It is cold and dry, and the only noise is the wind wheezing through the bare branches and the distant grind and squeal of trains from Victoria Station. Sullivan tells him about Neary and the parcel.

"How big was this parcel?"

"So big."

"Then it could be guns. Did Rice take it with him when he left the tannery?"

"I don't believe so. Least he was empty-handed when I saw him."

"So it's most likely still there in the office?"

Sullivan nods. He is cold and weary, and would prefer to be inside by a fire rather than out here in the darkness with the bones of dead people lying all around.

"Most likely," he says.

"If they're buying guns, it means whatever's going to happen will happen soon. Could you get inside the office to check?"

"Rice keeps the only key in his waistcoat pocket. I'd have to break a window."

O'Connor shakes his head.

"That won't do. You need to watch Rice carefully, see what he does with that parcel, take note of who he gives it to. If there are guns inside it, like I think there are, then my bet is that Stephen Doyle ordered them himself."

"How much longer will all this take, Jimmy?"

"I don't know that. You can quit any time, remember."

"I want that hundred pounds, though."

O'Connor rubs his jaw and sighs. The three-quarter moon casts a thick net of shadow over both of them. There is a smell of mold and leaves and autumn rottenness.

"You need to be patient, then," he says. "This isn't how we .

planned it, I know. We thought you'd find Stephen Doyle and we'd arrest him and that would be that. This way is different, but it may still work out well."

Sullivan looks suddenly solemn, struck with gloom, as if reminded of something he would rather forget.

"A fellow could topple into one of those damned tanning pits and drown in a moment," he says.

"Not if he's careful he won't," O'Connor tells him. "Not if he does exactly what's he's told and no more."

Next morning, Sullivan is shoveling mulch from one of the pits, when he hears angry shouting coming from the far end of the beam room. A minute later, Slattery the foreman appears in the yard, shaking his head and frowning. He is a tall man, big-boned and awkward in his movements. He strides past the tanning pits and knocks hard on Rice's office door. Rice comes out, they talk briefly, and then Rice follows Slattery back into the beam room. There is more shouting and cursing. Sullivan stops shoveling and listens. He hears Rice and Slattery and someone else who he thinks might be Kirkland, one of the beam men, but he can't tell what they are arguing about. He pulls himself out of the tanning pit and takes the barrow out to the frosted-over mulch pile. When he gets back to the yard, he tells Neary that the bark grinder has jammed again and needs to be looked at. He waits for Neary to leave, then wheels the empty barrow around the perimeter of the yard until he is standing beside Rice's unlocked door. He lowers the barrow and looks about. The yard is empty and he can still hear raised voices coming out from the beam room. He pauses a moment to check his courage, then opens the door and steps quickly inside.

It is warm and silent in the office, there is a dirty rag carpet in the middle of the floor and a cast-iron stove up against one wall with an empty coal scuttle next to it. The desk is empty aside from a leather-bound account book and a folded-up newspaper. Behind it are shelves filled with papers and books. There is a cupboard by the window with an almanac pinned to the door. Sullivan looks around for Neary's parcel but can't see it anywhere. He opens the cupboard door and looks inside. It is filled up with machine belts and bridles and sample strips of tanned hide in various shades of brown and black. He glances out the window to check that the yard is still empty, then starts going through the desk drawers one by one. There are bundles of receipts tied up with string, pen nibs, candle stubs, a bag of nails, a ring of rusted keys, empty tobacco tins, a nutcracker, a tape measure, a twelve-inch rule. The bottom drawer, the deepest one, is locked. Sullivan takes out his clasp knife and tries to jimmy it open, but it won't give. He takes the keys from the other drawer and begins to test them in the lock. One of them fits, but it won't turn. He takes it out, tries all the others again, then goes back to the one that fits. He eases it back and forth, feeling about for the right notch. After a minute of trying, he stands up and looks around the office again in case there is another, easier hiding place he hasn't thought of, but then shakes his head and goes back to jiggling the key. He is ready to give up, when it turns.

Inside the drawer is a metal box, secured with a small brass padlock, and, next to it, two handguns wrapped in oilcloth. Sullivan unwraps one and picks it up. It is new and smells of metal and oil. He likes the way it feels in his hand, its heaviness and tilt. He holds it out straight and squints along the shining blue-black barrel as though ready to shoot someone. *When I get my hands on that hundred pounds, I will buy myself a fine gun,* he thinks, *like this one here, but even better.* He gazes at the gun awhile longer, then puts it back. It takes him several more minutes of fiddling to relock the drawer. Then he goes over to the window and looks out again. He can see the tanning pits and the entrance to the finishing shed, but there is no sign of Neary or anyone else. He imagines what Jimmy will say, the astonished look on his face when he tells him what he just did. He opens the door and steps outside into the cold air. Fifty feet away to the left, he sees Rice and Slattery coming out of the beam room. They have a clear view of everything. He grabs the handles of his barrow, turns sharply, and starts to walk away from them, but Slattery calls out for him to stay where he is. He lowers the barrow and waits.

"Turn out all your pockets and give me your cap," Slattery tells him.

Peter Rice, thick-necked, eyes hard and staring, is silent by his side. Sullivan can tell that they are both still riled up from whatever just happened in the beam room. He does what he is told, but all he has in his pockets is a lump of chalk, two pennies, a box of matches, and a clasp knife, and there is nothing concealed in his cap. Rice asks him what he was doing in the office.

"I wanted to ask you a question, Mr. Rice," Sullivan says. "That's all. I saw the door was open so I thought you must be at your desk. I only stepped inside for a moment. When I realized you weren't there, I turned right around and left straightaway. I didn't touch anything, nothing at all, I swear."

"Why didn't you knock?"

"I didn't think to. I saw the door was left open."

"What would you need to talk to Mr. Rice about?" Slattery says. "If you have any question, you come to me."

Sullivan scratches his forehead, glances at Rice.

"It's a private matter," he says.

Slattery snorts.

"You were in there robbing, and then you saw us coming back and tried to get away. That's the truth."

"No, sir," he says. "It isn't."

"You stay there," Rice says.

He opens the office door and goes inside. Sullivan and Slattery watch him checking over the room, seeing if anything has been touched or interfered with. He takes a key from his waistcoat pocket and bends down to open the desk drawer. Sullivan feels his stomach clench.

"Anything taken?" Slattery says.

Rice stands up and shakes his head.

"We scared him off in time, then," Slattery says. "That's all."

Rice comes back outside. He leans in close and looks at Sullivan.

"Were you robbing me, Michael Sullivan?" he says. "Tell the truth now."

"No, sir, I swear. I wanted to talk to you, that's all."

"Talk to me about what?"

Sullivan hesitates for a second, looks at the ground.

"The Brotherhood," he says. "I want to take the oath."

Rice looks surprised at first, then amused. He glances at Slattery, then back at Sullivan.

"What do you suppose I know about the Brotherhood?" he says.

"Jack Riley told me you and him were both a part of it."

"Did you ask Jack Riley about taking any oath?"

"I wasn't interested then, but I've changed my mind. There's a pile of old newspapers down in the cellar where I sleep—*The United Irishman, The Nation*—I've been reading them through at night, before I go to sleep. All about the famine and the rack renters. Everything. It's opened my eyes."

Rice puffs out his cheeks and shakes his head. He turns to Slattery and tells him he can get back to work now.

"I'll manage this one, Frank," he says.

They watch Slattery walk off toward the finishing shed. The sky is a brindled slab of white and gray, and a faint mist is rising from the tanning pits. Rice bends down and prizes a rusted nail from the impacted gravel, looks at it a moment, then tosses it away again.

"You knock before you go in somewhere," he says. "Did they never teach you that in New York?"

"I wasn't thinking," Sullivan says again.

"What do you know about the Brotherhood?"

"I know that it fights for the freedom of Ireland."

"And you like the sound of a good fight, is that it?"

"I want to help my country if I can," he says. "I want to play my part."

"It's not a game, you know. People are killed in this, murdered, hanged."

"I know that."

"Jack Riley thinks you're bold."

"I wouldn't let you down. I swear."

"What if you were ordered to kill a man?"

Sullivan checks to see if he is being serious and realizes that he is.

"Then I'd kill him for sure," he says.

"You wouldn't hesitate even for a moment?"

"Not even for a moment."

Rice looks him up and down, and Sullivan tries to keep himself steady and calm, not to tremble or flinch under his silent gaze.

"I'll talk to Jack," Rice says. "I'll see what he thinks about it all. You can go back to your work."

Sullivan thanks him and picks up the wheelbarrow. He is about to walk away when Rice calls out.

"Jack tells me your people are from the Liberties. I knew a George Sullivan who lived on Park Street. He used to work at the North Wall. He married a woman named Martha McCord from the village in Clare where my father was born. Would he be any relation of yours, I wonder?"

"That's my cousin George, most likely," he says. "My auntie Sheelah's son. My da was the middle one of nine."

"Then you're less of a stranger than I thought you were."

"I haven't seen George and Martha since I was a boy. I don't know where they're living now."

"And you have no one here in Manchester?" Rice says. "No aunts or cousins? No one."

"No one," he says. "No one at all. That's right."

As he steers the barrow along the narrow walkway between the tanning pits, Sullivan's breath steadies and he feels a swell of relief. He is proud of his quick thinking—if they let him join the Brotherhood it means he will be closer to Stephen Doyle and closer to that hundred pounds as well. Slattery and Rice just gave him a dreadful fright, to be sure, but it worked out fine in the end.

It is only later, after he has met O'Connor at the burial grounds and told him about the guns and the oath taking, and he is back in the dank and dreary cellar sitting on the single rickety chair, unlacing his hobnails, that it occurs to him that he might have made a mistake by admitting that George Sullivan is his cousin. He frowns and licks his lips. Should he tell Rice that he was mistaken about George, he wonders? But no, that would only draw his attention to it and make him more suspicious. Better to leave things just as they are and trust that Rice is too busy with his own plans to worry about something so small. He turns this conclusion over in his mind a few times until he is satisfied that it makes good sense, then he pulls off his boots and lies down on the cot. He tightens the blanket around his chest and shoulders, closes his eyes, and, soothed like an infant by the shallow mumbles of the poisoned Irk, tumbles backward into a dreamless sleep.

————⟫•⟪————

CHAPTER 12

Tommy Flanagan visits O'Connor late at night. Half his face is shot away, but he has a black veil artfully arranged to cover the wound. When he speaks he has a woman's voice. *Did you forget me?* he says. *Did you forget me already, Jimmy O'Connor?* O'Connor tries to answer him, but he can't form the right words. He drools and grunts. His tongue is grown too fat for his mouth. They are sitting at a table together, and when Tommy stands up he is naked; his body is white and hairless, and he has no cock or balls. *This is what the saints look like when they ascend to heaven,* he says. *Couldn't you guess?* Looking at him standing there, O'Connor is filled with lust, but when he steps closer and lifts the black veil, he sees it is not Tommy at all but Rose. *Oh, forgive me, Rose,* O'Connor says, *forgive me. I didn't know.*

In Maybury's office next morning, a rare winter sun is slanting through the sash window and casting yellow rectangles across floor and wall. O'Connor feels the sunlight on his thigh like the heat of a hand. He explains about the discovery of the guns, and they talk about whether they should arrest Peter Rice immediately or wait. If they delay, there is a risk that any information Sullivan discovers will arrive too late, but if they act, it will give Doyle the chance to escape. O'Connor would like to move quickly, before Michael Sullivan gets himself into any more trouble, but Maybury decides they will hold back for now. If they foil a fully fledged plot and capture Doyle and the others, he reasons, it means a public victory, a visible success to balance what happened on Hyde Road. In the meantime, he will increase foot patrols around the city and put guards on all of the public buildings. He reminds O'Connor to inform him the moment he hears any more news, then picks up his pen and turns back to his papers to signal that the interview is concluded.

"There's something else," O'Connor says. "Tommy Flanagan's sister."

Maybury shrugs lightly and puts down his pen.

"Flanagan had a sister?"

"Yes, a sister named Rose and an aging mother also. Their neighbors have turned against them since the truth came out. They're being punished for Tommy's sins, and in a place like that if the people single you out, then your life's hardly worth living."

"It's not enough for them to kill the brother?"

"It seems not."

Maybury shakes his head.

"I talked to her the other day," O'Connor continues. "She wants to leave Manchester, to go somewhere new where the history isn't hanging over her, but she doesn't have the money to move. I was thinking it might be possible to make her a small allowance. Just until she and her mother find their feet. If the chief constable would agree."

Maybury frowns.

"We paid Tommy Flanagan for the information he provided, is that right? So there's no question of us owing him anything?"

"Whenever it had any value, yes, sir, we did."

"Does the sister know anything that would be useful to us?"

"I don't believe she does."

"So what would we be paying her for?"

"It would be in recompense for Tommy's death."

"Did you make any promise? Did you tell Tommy that if he was ever killed we'd give money to his sister?"

"No, sir, I didn't, but when I met her, I felt it was something we should do. I believe we're under an obligation, given the circumstances."

"Then I'm afraid your notion of obligation is different from mine. The detective office is not a charity for distressed ladies. The best way we can help Tommy Flanagan's family is to try to catch the men who killed him. That's our only obligation here."

"Even a small amount would help. Could you raise it with the chief constable?"

Maybury shakes his head.

"The chief constable is a busy man. He wouldn't thank me for wasting his time."

O'Connor tenses, then looks away. He rubs his trouser leg with one hand, and sees the glint and shimmer of dust motes rising in the brightened air.

"What difference would twenty pounds make to Palin?" he says. "Or fifty even?"

Maybury narrows his eyes and looks at him.

"Why do you care so much? Do you have some interest in the sister?" he says. "Is that it?"

O'Connor hesitates.

"That's not it," he says.

Maybury shakes his head dismissively.

"Here in England we generally pay for our own pleasures, O'Connor. I'd suggest you learn to do the same."

He knows the chance is gone now. Perhaps there never was a chance.

"That's not it," he says again.

Maybury picks up his fountain pen and points at the door.

"You can go," he says. "For a policeman, you make a dismal liar."

For the rest of the morning, O'Connor does his work as normal, but his mind is elsewhere. Just past noon, he makes his way to Hanging Ditch and waits near the back entrance of the Spread Eagle Hotel. When he sees Rose Flanagan come out, he steps forward to greet her. She has a scarf tied tight around her head and is walking with another maid. He has to call her name twice before she notices him.

"It's you again," she says.

"I need to talk to you about that money."

The other maid is small and dark, with a wide face and thick eyebrows. She could be Italian, he thinks, or Greek.

"This is Gabriella," Rose says, "the only friend I have left now."

O'Connor touches his hat.

Rose smiles as if she has just made a joke. Her face seems thinner than before, more drawn, but her eyes are still bright and lively.

"Can we go somewhere to sit down?" he says. "It's too cold to talk out here."

"Not that awful temperance place again."

"Somewhere else, then. Anywhere. You choose it."

She leads him to a small tearoom off Market Street. It's steamy and crowded inside, and there is a smell of fried onions and burned toast. They wait a minute while a waiter wipes off a table, then they sit down. O'Connor pauses before speaking. He can tell by the expression on Rose's face, eager and hopeful, that she is expecting the news to be good. He feels like a fool for making promises he cannot keep. He wishes there were some easy way to explain himself, to let her understand what has happened, but he knows there isn't.

"I talked to Superintendent Maybury today," he tells her. "I told him all about the problems, but he says he can't give you any money. He says the detective office isn't responsible for what happened with Tommy."

She looks confused at first. Then, when she realizes what it means, she looks angry.

"I'm sorry," O'Connor says. "I thought there was a chance, but it turns out I was wrong."

"Seems you've been wrong about a few things lately."

"I've made some mistakes," he answers. "That's the truth of it."

"Our Tommy was only killed because he talked to you, and we're suffering for it now. Does your superintendent not think that we deserve some help?"

"I told him all that. I explained everything, but he wouldn't listen. I'm sorry."

"Can you not talk to him again? We're not asking for much."

"If I thought I could change his mind, I'd try, but he's a hard-headed fellow. Stubborn as a brick wall. He won't budge however much I push him."

Rose frowns and purses her lips. There are spots of red now high up on her pale cheeks. O'Connor knows he has failed her. He remembers Maybury's disdain and feels a throb of anger at the position she's in and the part he's played in putting her there.

"They don't listen to me," he explains. "They never have listened. They brought me over here from Ireland to give them advice, but they take no notice of what I say. They do just as they please."

"You should go back home to Dublin if you don't like it here," she tells him curtly. "If the English won't listen to you, why do you stay?"

He rubs his right hand across his lips, then pours some milk into his empty teacup.

"My wife died last year so I've nothing to go back for now."

Rose glares at him for a moment, then sighs and shakes her head. When she speaks again the hardness is gone from her voice and they are back to where they were before. *Quick to anger,* he thinks, *quick to forget. That's how she is.*

"Your wife must have been young."

"Twenty-eight," he says. "We were married six years."

"And no children?"

"We lost a boy at nine months old from pleurisy, and after that Catherine couldn't manage it again. I don't know why. I wonder now if she was ill before we knew it, and that was the cause."

"That's a terrible thing. I'm sorry for you."

"After she died, I started drinking whiskey. It was very bad for a while. I should have lost my job because of it, but they took pity and sent me over here instead. So I can't go back there even if I want to. They wouldn't have me."

She gives him back a soft sympathetic look, as if his pain is her pain too, and he feels in response a flash of strange, absurd elation.

"We're both of us trapped here, then," she says.

"Yes," he says. "I suppose we are."

O'Connor pours out the tea and lifts the china cup to his lips. He was a constable living in the police barracks on Kevin Street when he first learned that his father was dead—killed in a barroom fight in a small town just south of Sydney. The letter, written by a local magistrate, explained that Paul O'Connor, originally from County Armagh, had been released on a ticket of leave and had traveled from Melbourne with the probable intention of purchasing land. The man who had killed him, who was in prison now and would likely be hanged, was also an Irishman by the name of Dominick Lanigan, and it was believed that the two of them had previously been close friends but had fallen out over money. The magistrate explained that some small items, which might be of sentimental value, had been discovered in his father's lodging house after his death, and he asked O'Connor to write back confirming his claim to them as his father's heir. His sister, Norah, was married by then and living on a farm near Quebec. O'Connor wrote the same day to tell her the news, and also wrote back to the magistrate, thanking him for his trouble and asking that any property belonging to his father be sold and the proceeds given to a suitable charity to save the trouble and expense of shipping them back to Ireland.

That night, in Dublin, as he made his usual rounds, O'Connor came upon two drunken men fighting each other in an alleyway. Their faces were sheened with sweat and their eyes were loose and bloodshot. When O'Connor called for them to quiet down, they ignored him, and when he tried to step between them, they cursed at him and spat in his face. He paused a moment, then raised his truncheon and hit one of them a fierce blow across the head. The man dropped to his knees, groaning, and O'Connor stepped forward and hit him again. There was no good reason for the second blow except that he was filled with rage and had no better way to show it. The man toppled sideways and lay flat on the flagstones, unconscious and bleeding from the head. O'Connor looked around, then blew his whistle three times. The other man was already gone, and no one else had seen what happened. If he was questioned, he could say that he had been attacked, and no one would know any better. He crouched down and put his fingers to the prone man's lips to check he was still breathing. After a few moments, he felt air moving in and out against his fingertips, cool then warmer. Blood was still welling up from the scalp wound and the smell of the splayed body was fierce and terrible. O'Connor thought of his father bleeding to death on a barroom floor in New South Wales. He was not angry anymore, and it was hard for him to remember just why he had hit the man in the way he had. He wondered what kind of person he must be to do such a thing.

Rain knocks against the misted windows of the Manchester tearoom. Outside, the people passing by look like blurred shadows of themselves, like souls without bodies, bewildered and drifting. Inside there is laughter and talk, the crackle of frying; waiters dance and shimmy between the tables with plates of sausages and fresh pots of tea.

"I have a little money of my own put aside, if you need something," O'Connor says to Rose. "It's not fifty pounds, it's less than ten probably, but you're welcome to it."

"I can't take your money, Mr. O'Connor. I hardly know you."

"Call me James," he says. "Please. Or Jimmy."

"Jimmy, then," she says. "And you should call me Rose."

He waits a moment, then nods.

"The money's there, if you ever need it. That's what I'm saying."

"My mother thinks I should just find myself a husband and that would solve our problems. She doesn't know what's stopping me, but I told her no Irishman in Manchester will have me. Not after Tommy. I'm too much bother."

"I doubt that's true," he says.

"Oh, it's true, all right. You should see the way they look at me now."

Her boldness always takes him by surprise. There are things he could say to her, he knows, but he doubts he has the will or courage to say them.

"My mother was married at sixteen," he tells her. "And my grandmother at fifteen. It was different times back then."

"Of course it was. I tell her, 'We're not living on a farm in Fermanagh anymore, Ma,' but she doesn't understand what on earth I'm talking about."

Once the tea is finished with, he pays the bill and they step back outside. It is colder than it was and there is rain in the air. He offers to walk back with her to Thompson Street, but she smiles at the idea and says she is in enough trouble with the neighbors already.

"Will you ever catch that man who killed our Tommy?" she says. "What was the name, again?"

"Stephen Doyle. I think we will, but I don't know when."

"You'll get him before he kills anyone else's brother or son, I hope."

"I hope so too."

She puts the scarf over her head and smiles at him quickly, and they shake hands and say goodbye. After she is gone, as he is walking back to the Town Hall, he remembers the dream he had and feels his chest tighten.

CHAPTER 13

Jack Riley has run a wet comb through his gray-black hair, and his collarless shirt is buttoned all the way up to the neck. He recites, slowly and with a somber priestliness, each line of the Fenian oath, and then has Michael Sullivan repeat it back to him. There is a dog-eared Bible on the table beside them, and Sullivan's right hand is resting on it as he speaks. When he forgets himself and makes a mistake, they start again at the beginning. They are standing in the shabby living quarters above the alehouse on Rochdale Road. Slattery, Rice, and the others are drinking downstairs, and their raucous voices can be heard occasionally coming up through cracks in the floorboards.

"So help me God, Amen," Riley says.

"So help me God, Amen."

Riley holds out his hand and smiles at him. Sullivan shakes it. *Only the things you can touch and taste are real,* he tells himself, *all the rest is just words.* They embrace. Riley is bony as all hell and smells like an ashpit.

"And now for a fucken drink or two," he says.

The oath taking is supposed to be a great secret, so when they go downstairs there is no cheering or backslapping from the others, even though everyone there knows full well what they have been up to. Riley pulls Sullivan a pint and tells him he has just done a fine thing for himself and for his country. Slattery comes across and shakes him by the hand.

"I always knew this lad was a good un," Riley tells him. "From the moment he put that copper down on his arse right over there. Christ almighty, but you should have seen it."

Sullivan drinks half the pint down in one long gulp and feels the better for it. He looks about the room at the other men. When he thinks what they would do to him if they knew the truth, it makes him nervy. He's taking an awful big chance, he knows that, but it's too late to back out now. He must find his way through it somehow. Riley is still talking. He is saying how the Brotherhood has taken some blows lately, but it can't ever be killed because the love of freedom is a sacred thing, and no matter how powerful the British are, their lies will never be a match for our truth. Slattery is nodding.

"We'll beat them fuckers in the end," he says.

"Sure we will," Riley says.

Sullivan finishes off his pint and puts the empty glass back down on the bar.

"Are all the fellows in here now a part of it too?" he says.

"Every one," Riley says, "and a better gang of men you couldn't wish for. Here, follow me."

He gives Sullivan another pint, then walks him over to the table where Peter Rice is sitting. Rice points him to a chair and tells him the names of the others. They nod at him and carry on talking. Sullivan goes through the names again in his head in case Jimmy asks him later on—Bryce, Costello, McArdle, Devine. They are talking about a prize-fight in Rochdale, and then about a horse for sale, and a man who has been arrested for selling tainted meat. Nothing about Stephen Doyle or the guns, or any scheme. When

Peter Rice stands up and goes to the bar, Sullivan turns to the man sitting next to him, Willy Devine.

"Is there a plan?" he says. "I heard some rumors."

Willy Devine cricks his neck, then gazes down morbidly at his half-drunk beer as if its piebald surface might, like tea leaves or the innards of a crow, reveal some deeper truth.

"We don't listen to no rumors," he says.

"So you haven't heard any talk about a plan?"

Devine turns to look at him. He has a dirty-looking beard and gummy eyes. He puts his tobacco-tainted forefinger up to his ale-wettened lips and winks lugubriously.

"I haven't heard nothing at all, my darling," he says, "and neither have you."

Rice comes back with a tray of fresh pints and hands one to Sullivan.

"Yank lad here asking if there's a secret plan," Devine says to him.

Sullivan takes a sip of the beer, then puts it down when he feels his hand begin to wobble.

Rice looks puzzled.

"We don't share the secret plans till later. That's how it works. You know that, Willy."

"Can't you give him a hint at least, Pete?" Devine says. "He's dreadful eager to learn. Couldn't you?"

Rice sits back down in his chair and looks around the table as if to gauge the opinions of the other men.

"I maybe could," he says. He turns to Sullivan: "Which plan do you want to hear about first?"

"Is there more than one?"

"Fuck yes," Devine says. "Do you think we'd only have one plan?"

"Then I don't mind which is first," Sullivan says. He is glad now that he took that chance with Devine. It does no good to be timid or meek, he thinks. People will sense your fear and use it against you.

"We could start with the most important, then. Which secret plan would be the most important plan, do you think, Willy?"

"They're all fucken belters," he says. "But the one that involves killing that auld bitch the Queen is my favorite."

"That's right," Rice says. "There's the plan we made to poison the Queen, with a drop of something nasty in her sherry glass." He looks at Sullivan. "What do you think of that, lad?"

"The *Queen*?" he says.

"Herself."

"Jesus Christ."

"It's a fine plan, that one," Devine says.

"And when will you do it?" Sullivan asks him.

Rice thinks a moment.

"Well, we still have to get our hands on the right poison, then we have to take it down to London, so there'll be some delay. But pretty soon, I'd say."

"How can you get in close enough? Won't she have guards?"

"It's the butler," Rice explains. "The Queen's own butler is a fellow from Kilkenny named Seamus O'Malone. He changed that, of course, now he goes by Brown."

"And he dropped the brogue," Devine says. "Talks like the fucken Duke of Clarence, now he does."

"So it's just poison you're using," Sullivan says. "No guns?"

"Just poison for this one, but there are other plans for after. Killing the Queen is just for openers."

Sullivan looks around the table. The others are nodding in agreement, but he remembers the pistols in the drawer.

"Are you telling me the truth now?" he says. "Are you being straight?"

Rice frowns and folds his arms across the bulge of his belly. He takes a long sup of ale and licks the remainder from his lips.

"These are the secret plans. It's not everyone who gets to know the secret plans."

"You've been singled out, lad," Devine says. "You should count yourself lucky."

Sullivan nods.

"I understand that."

"Well, I'm glad you do," Rice says.

"So if the first plan is the Queen, then what comes next?"

Rice looks over at Devine as if he needs some reminding.

"After the Queen, it's the Prince of Wales," Devine says. "We plan to take the Prince of Wales prisoner and hold that fancy bugger for a ransom."

"That's right," Rice says. "And after we're done with the Prince of Wales, there's the plan to steal the crown jewels, isn't there, Willy? Then the plan to burn down Dublin Castle." He frowns. "Is there another secret plan I'm forgetting about?"

"How about the plan to get a great big, red hot poker and stick it right up Mr. Gladstone's arse?" he says. "Did you forget about that one?"

Devine pauses a second, then cackles and sticks out his tongue, and suddenly they are all laughing. Red shining faces, open mouths, crooked teeth. Gibbering like apes in the zoo. He understands it now.

"The red hot poker up the arse!" Rice shouts out into the hubbub. "Christ, I knew there was something that slipped my mind!"

They are shaking their heads and banging on the tabletop as if they have never witnessed such a fine display of wit.

"You had me there, lads," Sullivan says when the noise dies down a little. "Jesus Christ, you had me there."

It doesn't matter, he tells himself. *They can have their piece of fun, and better they think me a clown than a traitor.* Rice slaps him on the back and leans in toward him. His breath smells of raw onion and his face is broad and bristly as a sow's arse.

"We always have a joke with the new ones," he says. "Don't take it to heart. You finish that beer and I'll buy you the next."

Later, someone starts up with a fiddle and Willy Devine dances a clumsy, shuffling kind of jig in the middle of the room, while the others clap and stamp and egg him on. When Devine is finished with his nonsense, another man, named Boyce, gets to his feet and sings "The Croppy Boy" in a steady, pleasing baritone. After that, Peter Rice, who is drunk but still capable of holding a tune, sings "As I Roved Out." When they ask Sullivan to give them a song, he tries to refuse, but they won't allow it, so he sings "The Rose of Tralee" with one hand gripping the edge of the bar and his eyes half-closed in concentration. His voice wavers at the start, but then in the middle verses it finds its strength and sureness, and by the end he thinks he has done well enough, or at least not shown himself up too badly. He remembers his grandmother teaching him that song when they lived in the house on Ash Street, and the memory feels like a dark weight around his heart, and he wishes for a moment he was somewhere else without the threat of awful murder hanging over him.

Jack Riley is leaning on the bar, with a bright tot of whiskey in his hand, surveying his demesne and looking ducal. When Sullivan thanks him and tells him he'll be on his way now, he straightens up and gives him a scolding look.

"Oh no, you can't be going to your bed just yet," he says. "The night's only just getting started. You sit yourself down on that stool and I'll pour ye out a drop of this good stuff here."

Sullivan sits and drinks the whiskey and when he finishes it, Riley pours him another one. He is already six or seven pints of porter to the good, and the spirits on top is

like a sudden blow to the head. Riley is talking about politics now, about the grave hypocrisies of the Irish priesthood
and the cowardice of the reformers in Westminster. Sullivan drifts away and then remembers himself. "That's right,"
he says, "I know what you mean. Good god almighty, that's
the fucking truth." They finish the bottle, but Riley has
more down in the cellar. While he goes to fetch one, Sullivan shambles out into the backyard, unbuttons his britches,
and pisses untidily against a wall. The gray steam rises all
around him, warm and fragrant like the heat of a deep
bath. He looks up at the dangling silver moon and thinks to
himself that this is the very same moon they are looking at
in New York and Paris and Dublin, and the strange thought
of this brings a tear to his eye and makes him wonder at the
beauty and vastness of the world.

When he gets back to the bar, Riley has passed a bottle
around to the others and is calling out a toast for the recently departed.

"May them three brave souls that were hanged at Salford
rest in peace, and may their sacrifice not be forgotten while
any of us here have a snatch of breath left in our puny bodies," he shouts. "And God save Ireland!"

"God save Ireland!"

They holler it back at him, then raise up their freshened
glasses and drink the whiskey down in one. Then Riley
starts up with "A Nation Once Again" and they all of them
join in the rackety chorus, putting their heads back and
bellowing the words upward into the smoke-fugged air, so
the room is rattling with raw noise and Sullivan, who is
watching on silently, feels down in his stomach something
hot and fierce that may be terror but may just as easily be
love, but he is not sure, he cannot tell.

The night stretches on, and one by one the others weaken
and drift away home, until it is just Riley and Sullivan sitting there with a near-empty whiskey bottle on the table

between them and a layer of old pipe smoke, bruise-colored and as thick as a mattress above their heads. Riley is still talking, although his voice is not as clear or steady as it was before, and sometimes he loses the drift and has to circle around or ask Sullivan to remind him what it was he was saying.

"It was something about the fellows that were hanged," Sullivan says. He is dazed and numb from the drinking. He is not asleep, but he is not awake either. His mouth is lolled open, and he has to squint to see.

"That's right," Riley says. "They were good men them three, I'll tell you, brave and proud. And they were murthered just like fucken animals, just like fucken *beasts* in a slaughterhouse. Do ye understand me, Michael Sullivan? Do ye?"

He gives Sullivan a wild, twitching glare. His mouth is fringed with whitened spittle and his bulldog eyes are pink and weepy. He is panting like he has just run a mile.

"I understand," Sullivan says. "Course I do."

Riley reaches across the cluttered table with his right hand and gives Sullivan's arm a fierce squeeze.

"You took the sacred oath tonight," he says. "You're one of us now, and when the order comes to fight, we'll be standing side by side like brothers, won't we?"

Sullivan nods, then shakes his head. He tells himself to keep on pretending. *Don't waver or weaken, not now.*

"When will the order come?" he says.

"It could come any time, any time at all," Riley says. "We can't know that. But I'll tell you something . . ." He lets go of Sullivan's arm and leans back in his chair. "There are plans moving even as we speak. Big fucken plans n'all."

"I heard that joke before."

"I'm not joking with you, though."

"So is it the Queen?" he says. "Or is it the Prince of Wales this time?"

"It's closer to home than that. Much closer."

"Like what, then?"

Riley doesn't answer straightaway. He wipes his nose on his shirtsleeve and takes a slow drink.

"By rights I shouldn't tell anyone," he says.

"I took the oath," Sullivan reminds him.

"I know you did."

Riley starts pushing his whiskey glass back and forth across the tabletop as if he is trying to trace out all the letters in a name.

"If you don't want to tell me, don't trouble yourself," Sullivan says.

Riley shakes his head and tilts forward.

"I'll tell you anyway," he says. "Fuck it. It's the mayor. They're going to kill the mayor of Manchester himself. He has a whore hidden away somewhere on Milk Street, and that's how they'll do it. They brought the guns up from Birmingham just the other day. It's vengeance for the boys they hanged."

He pauses, and for a moment Sullivan can hear the sound of his own breath coming to him hard and shallow through the sweat-stained air.

"The mayor himself," Riley says again. "So what do you think of that, then?"

"Can they really do it?"

"Certainly they can. The spies are all dead now, and without the spies the police haven't a clue, so who will stop them?"

Sullivan knows it's true by the way he tells it, by the pride and pleasure in his voice.

"The mayor is a fucking prize, though," Sullivan says.

"Yes, he is. If you kill the mayor, you spread the terror. No one knows who's next."

"So they'll shoot him, will they?"

"Through the heart."

Riley points his fingers and makes the noise.

"Bang, bang," he says with a grin. "Like that."

Sullivan winces, then leans forward against the table edge. His mouth is filling with spit, and there is a high-pitched ringing in one ear. He feels suddenly chilled.

Riley tilts his head and looks at him.

"Are you getting sick?" he says.

"I well might be."

"Then you should take some air."

Sullivan stands up and walks unsteadily toward the door. Outside, the street is dark and empty. There are green globs of horse dung scattered across the cobbles, and the usual midden stench of wet ash and urine. He leans over, hands on knees, groans loudly twice, and then spatters the pavement with the mud-colored lees of his debauch. He is dripping sweat now, and his throat is burning. The buildings around him toss and tilt like boats in a storm and, up above, the night sky drifts and pivots. Everything is loose and liquid. He leans against the alehouse wall and prays for firmness, but firmness does not appear. He waits for a gasping minute, then pukes again.

Riley comes out to take a look at him.

"By Christ," he says. "But you're in a state."

Sullivan spits and straightens himself.

"I'll be aright."

"You look like you've been buried somewhere and just dug up."

"I'll be aright," he says again.

Riley offers him a mattress to sleep on, but Sullivan says the walk will clear his head. Riley hugs him—that boniness again, that smell—then they shake hands and say their adieus.

When he gets as far as Angel Street, instead of turning right toward the Irk and the tannery, he tends left toward Shude Hill. One foot first and then the other one, anxious as a cat. He sways a tad but doesn't stumble. The rebel songs are still spinning around in his head, and when he closes his eyes he sees green fields and hills, and the marching men of '98 with cropped hair and flashing pikes. High Street, Fountain Street, Cooper. There is vomit on his boots and on the cuffs of his trousers. His throat is aching and the bright streetlamps pain his eyes. He must find Jimmy O'Connor this night or there will be hell to pay, he knows that, but which is the way to George Street from here? He looks around. Straight on, then left after the bridge? No, he thinks, far quicker to walk along the towpath. That will take him direct to Chorlton Mill.

Gingerly, he navigates the steep stone steps down to the canal side. When Jimmy hears the news he will jump out of his skin, Sullivan thinks. Kill the mayor? And they would do it too. The wild, heedless, loony, ragged-edged Fenian bastards. He wishes now he hadn't taken that oath. Not that he is much of a Catholic, but still, hand on the Bible and all, it doesn't sit well. Perhaps there is some penance he can do? Or a prayer? He will ask a priest when he finds one. The towpath is narrow and roughly cobbled. The fly boats work all hours, but he doesn't see any working now. It's deathly quiet and the water is as smooth and black as asphalt. He is so tired, he could curl up and fall asleep right here on the towpath, if it weren't so cold out and he didn't have a job to do. Jimmy will jump out of his skin, he thinks again, he won't believe what he's hearing. He yawns and blinks and scratches his arse, and wonders for a moment whether he has gone the wrong way. He turns around to check, then carries on walking. Slow and unsteady, each step an effort, if he doesn't concentrate hard he swerves.

When he comes to the next lock, he decides to go across. That way he will be on the right side of the canal when he gets to Chorlton Mill. There is a wooden railing to grip onto so it will be no trouble at all. He takes hold of the railing and pulls himself up onto the top of the gates. Water is sluicing through the square holes below the beam, and he can hear the rush and see it foaming down into the chamber below. Standing there, with the cold air blowing all around, he feels stiff and exposed. He lifts up his right foot, dangles it a moment, then sets it down again where it was. He thinks about turning around, then tells himself to sharpen up. Four or five quick strides, he thinks, that's all, then he will be at the other side, and the sooner he does it the better. The black canal water turns white as it pours over the gate. It rumbles lowly like a passing charabanc. Four or five strides, he thinks, that's all. The first stride is a solid one, and the second too, but then, at the midpoint where the two lock gates join and there is a break in the railing, he hesitates a moment, and the hesitation is what does for him. He takes another stride forward, but instead of his foot coming down where he intends, it slips off the edge of the beam. He tries to reach around and grab hold of the railing to keep himself upright but misses. As he topples off the lock gate and into the dark waters of the Rochdale Canal, he shouts out—not a word but a fleeting wail of panic, like a frightened animal might make, or a child waking up from a nightmare.

CHAPTER 14

Next evening, just past ten o'clock. Neary and Doyle are seated in Skelly's spavined hansom at the north end of Milk Street. It is bitter outside, and there is a vague brown mist hanging in the Manchester air, clammy and vegetal, like the exhalations of a bog. They have watched the mayor for long enough now, and they know his patterns well. It is always a Wednesday or a Thursday: He leaves the Town Hall around nine, always afoot, stays with the woman until midnight, then walks back to King Street with a smile on his face and takes the brougham home. They will shoot him on the way back, when he passes beneath the lamp on the corner of Marble Street, that's the plan. Neary from the front, and Doyle from the rear, one shot each should be enough, but, if they need more, they have five others in the chamber. They will be away and gone into the shadows before any alarm is sounded.

The pistols are single-trigger Tranters. Six-shooters, eighty-bore. Not new, but clean and serviceable. Doyle likes the Colt for accuracy at range, but he has heard cavalrymen argue for the Tranter or even the Beaumont-Adams as the better weapon overall, and they should know. He loaded both before they left, but now he cocks the hammers again and turns them with his thumb just to be sure. He hands one of the guns to Neary, and Neary takes it from him with a nod.

"Now we wait," Doyle says.

Neary lays the pistol down on the seat beside him and shifts forward to peer through the half-fogged window glass.

"We could have a wee pint over there in the Shakespeare," he suggests, "while the mayor's enjoying his final pleasures, I mean."

"We'll stay where we are," Doyle says again. "It wouldn't do to be seen about."

"As you will," Neary says.

Doyle leans his head back into the corner of the cab and closes his eyes to rest. He has no fears of what the night might bring. He learned in the war that the hoping and the worrying are beside the point, that there is a chaos at the heart of things—dark, unfathomable—and the best a man can do is give that chaos human form, match himself to it. In the heat of battle, he knows, the mind empties and you forget what you are. That's the reason he still fights, the truest, deepest reason, not for the cause or the glory, but for those moments out of time, which could be minutes or hours, when the world beats its savage drum, and he— unthinking and heedless—steps to its measure.

When he first arrived in America he was only thirteen years old, with his parents and three brothers already dead from the typhus. Stepping off the steamer in Philadelphia, he had two dollars in his coat pocket and a letter from his uncle Fergus with a hand-drawn map and a long list of commandments. Fergus had worked in the Pennsylvania coalfield for ten years and saved enough from his wages to buy a farm in the Lebanon Valley, twenty miles northwest of Harrisburg. The farm was not large, but the soil and the drainage were good. Sheep and cattle grazed in the lower fields, and in the upper they grew Indian corn, wheat, and rye. In lieu of a wife, he had a hired man, a Pole named Lazlo, and Anna, a thin, silent Dutch woman, who cooked and mended and slept on a cot by the stove. The house was built of logs—two rooms with a brick chimney and fireplace. There was a clapboard barn beside it, a chicken house, and a fenced-in pen for the hogs.

A portion of the land was still covered by timber, tall stands of black gum and river birch, and it was Doyle's allotted task to clear some of it for plowing. He went out each morning with an ax and a bucksaw and came back smeared with wood dust and soil and blank-eyed with weariness. In the evenings after supper, Fergus read aloud from the Harrisburg newspapers and Lazlo played the accordion and sang mournful songs in a language only he understood. Doyle was nervous and fearful at first because everything was different, but he quickly grew used to his new life and became more settled and surer of himself. Sometimes he would dream about Ireland and his family who had died, but he didn't remember the dreams afterward and the feelings of loss or sadness they provoked never lingered on for long.

When he was fifteen, he began to see Anna, the Dutch woman, in a different way. He would watch her at her work and imagine the shape of her body beneath her clothes and the smell and taste of her bared skin. Whenever he had the chance, he would sit at the kitchen table and talk to her quietly. He would ask her questions about her life. She told him she had been married once and had a child, but the husband had left her and the child had died young. He realized she was old enough to be his mother, but the thought did not discourage him. He liked the pale tautness of the flesh on her neck and forearms, and the way, as she moved

about the kitchen, the lines of sinew pushed through it like
cords in a rope. He thought about her body every night as
he lay in bed before sleeping. He imagined touching her
and being touched in return. She told him he was too clever
to stay on the farm and that he should go to Harrisburg or
Philadelphia and look for work there instead. He could
learn a trade, she said, become a cooper or a wheelwright.
She told him his uncle Fergus was a great liar who would
make promises he never kept, and that nothing he said
should ever be believed. "If I were a man," she said, "I would
build a fine house with a high wall around it and live there
alone. That is the best way to be."

One windless, stagnant night in August when it was too
hot for him to stay asleep, he rose up from his bed in the
barn and went into the kitchen looking for water. Anna was
sleeping as usual on the cot by the stove. Her nightgown
was hitched up around her thighs, and he could see the
shape and color of her breasts under the sweat-dampened
muslin. After he drank from the pail, he stood there watching her a long time. Her head was turned away from him;
her arms and legs were spread wide apart. From the woods
outside, he heard the roaring of cicadas and the sporadic
shrieks of midnight birds. After another minute, he reached
down and lifted up the hem of the gown so he could better
see the fuzz of gray-black hair between her legs, then unbuttoned his pants and started tugging at himself. Anna
mumbled, then turned onto her side and raised her knees
up toward her chest. Doyle's bare toes pressed hard into the
dusty floorboards and his breath came out in hollow, grunting rasps. He wanted her to open her eyes, to watch and
admire him, but she didn't stir again and he dared not
touch her or make any noise. When he was finished, he
wiped himself on a rag, then turned to go back to the barn.
The moon was silver-bright, and, as he crossed the yard, he

saw Fergus standing on the lip of the porch, cut in two by the slanted shadows, watching him silently.

The next morning, in the damp, half-cleared field, amid a debris of sawn logs and torn-off stumps, Fergus found him and beat him without quarter. As he served out the blows, he gasped and grunted to himself like an old man at stool. Doyle understood what was happening to him although he couldn't give it words: His errant desires were being violently reversed, hammered back inside his body like metal spikes into a rail. Later, at supper, when Anna saw the dried blood and bruises on his face and asked what had happened, he told her it was nothing at all, and when she touched him in sympathy, he pushed her roughly away. He had no wish to speak to her now, and even the sight of her, so old and ugly, repulsed him. That night, he packed his belongings into a bundle and left the farm behind. He walked five miles to the crossroads and waited there until dawn for the first wagons to roll past heading west.

He stayed in Harrisburg through the fall and winter, working in the rail yards, then drifted farther north along the Susquehanna Valley, then into New York, never settling in any place for long. For four years, he slept head-to-toe with Chinamen and Jews under damp and fetid sheets in cheap lodging houses, whoring and drinking when he had a dollar in his pocket and filching or going hungry when he hadn't. He labored beside Greeks and Poles on the coal wharves and ice ponds, and in the tunnels and the red clay railroad cuttings, digging and hauling in the cold hard dark before dawn and in the yellow liquid heat of the day. He saw men crushed by rocks and torn asunder by machines, stabbed or beaten senseless in taverns and alleyways, but such sights didn't scare or trouble him. He owned nothing but his boots and the clothes on his back and had no friends to speak of. When he talked, his gray eyes flickered from side to side and his voice was low and hesitant, as though stretching out for words that were just beyond his reach.

The recruiting sergeant in Albany offered every man a cold glass of beer and twenty-five dollars if they would sign for a three-year term. He explained that if the traitorous Southerners won this fight, the whole nation would revert to savagery and ignorance, and all their hard-won greatness would be lost. Then he smiled and pointed his finger straight at Doyle and said that right there was a bold-looking young fellow who he knew would do well in the fight and would he be the first to come up here and sign his name? Doyle had no interest in politics or affairs of state, no knowledge or understanding of the arts of warfare, and no great love for the darkie either, but he liked the look of this sergeant, who had waxed mustaches and a brass-buttoned coat, and twenty-five dollars at once was more money than he had ever held in his life.

They gave them all new boots and uniforms and put them on a train headed south. In the camp, they drilled each morning for three hours straight: A hundred men conglomerated, moving together in time, the whole company moving together, like a well-trained animal or a fine machine, turning on command, wheeling, marching, halting. Doyle didn't see the purpose, but he did as he was told. He was content for the moment to be warm and well fed. He thought he would stay in the army so long as it suited him and then he would leave. When the other men told their battle stories, he listened but gave them no credence. They were all boasters, he thought. He had seen fighting and bloodshed before, so why should this time be any different?

It was Fredericksburg that changed him. After that, he understood that war was true and real in a way that nothing else was, or ever could be. As he charged toward Marye's Heights into a hail of rebel bullets with the men dropping

dead on either side—some falling silently like stunned cattle, others howling out with terror and pain—he lost all
sense of himself as a singular or particular being. He was
everywhere and nowhere at once: in his body, but also outside it; in the corpses of the dead, and in the screams and
curses of the living; in the sound of the shells exploding
above, and in the trampled, bloodstained earth below. It
was a kind of vision, except *vision* was not the right word
because there was no right word, and when it dissolved,
when he was safe again and the fight was finished, he felt
not relief so much as grief and sadness at the loss.

They made him a sergeant after that, then a captain. He
followed their rules like a monk follows the rules of his chosen order—because such discipline was a way of conjuring
truth, of allowing the mystery to become real. He survived
Chancellorsville and Gettysburg and the bloody angle at
Spotsylvania, and by the time they reached the siege works
outside Petersburg he was the longest-serving man left
alive in his regiment. His blue uniform was ripped and
faded, the soles of his boots were held on with baling wire,
and the aimless years of his orphan youth were like a
weightless dream.

He is woken by the sound of a church bell counting the
hours. He rubs his eyes and straightens himself. Neary
nods and smiles as if welcoming him back from a journey.

"The fog's worse now," Neary says. "You can hardly see
ten feet ahead."

Doyle looks out into the muddy darkness, shrugs, then
checks his pocket watch.

"Tell Skelly to drive around awhile," he says. "Then he
can let us down at Piccadilly and we'll walk back."

Neary opens the door and calls up the instructions. Skelly
gees the horse and there is a creak and a rattle of harness

as they move away. After a few minutes, they turn right onto Mosley Street past the banks and shops and cotton warehouses. The fog holds them tight in its gray-brown fist—carriages emerge then disappear, dark figures shimmer briefly into life like shadows on a cavern wall.

Neary has a long, drawn-out face; a square jaw; sunken, cadaverous eyes. He is not quick-witted, but he's steady and sure, and Doyle trusts him. The others, Rice and Riley and the rest, still think like children. They drink down their whiskey, bawl out their tearful ballads, and dream of a peasant army marching over the Wicklow Mountains with pikes and scythes in hand. Nine months before, Doyle was up on Tallaght Hill at midnight when a hundred or more of the bold lads dropped their Enfields and ran like rabbits at the sight of half a dozen policemen, so he knows what that dream amounts to and it isn't much. The British won't be beaten on the open field, anyone with an ounce of sense will tell you that, but they can be made to suffer and bleed if you do it right. When that bleeding becomes too much and they cannot rest from the awful, nagging pain of it, then they will break and this war will finally be over, and when it is, it will have been won not by the apostles or speech makers, but by the ones like Patrick Neary who waited in the shadows and did whatever dark deeds were required of them without comment or complaint.

They go around once again to kill the time, then Skelly stops the cab by the steps of the infirmary and the two of them get out. They walk back toward Milk Street, heads lowered, collars upturned. This fog is a blessing, Doyle thinks. It will muffle the noise of the shots and bewilder any onlookers. By the time the peelers understand that a fresh outrage has been committed, the perpetrators will be far away and safe.

———

O'Connor is sitting in his usual place in the Commercial
Coffeehouse on Oldham Street. The evening newspaper is
open on the table in front of him, but his mind is on other
things. He has been thinking about Rose Flanagan, on and
off, for most of the day. He is wishing now he had not offered to give away his money. That was reckless of him. If
she asks, he will have to do as he promised, but if he gives
it to her, what will it mean? Will it mean nothing, except he
is sorry for her and she needs his help, or will it mean they
are attached in some new way? And what kind of attach-
ment does a gift like that imply? He rubs his face and takes
a sip from the glass of sarsaparilla. He will be more careful
in the future, he thinks; he will hold his tongue until he has
thought these things through.

A moment later, the bell sounds and Frank Malone steps
inside and looks about. He notices O'Connor in the corner,
nods at him, and makes his way across. Malone is a cheerful fellow, talkative and fond of his own opinions. You could
call him arrogant, O'Connor thinks, but he's not the worst
of them for that.

"It always gives me a raging thirst coming into a place
like this," Malone says. "It never fails."

He feels in his jacket pocket and hands O'Connor a note.

"For you," he says. "Came in from Knott Mill Station
this afternoon. The sergeant thought you might want to
see."

The envelope is gummed shut. O'Connor checks the
handwriting on the front, tears it open, and unfolds the
paper inside. He reads it through once, then reads it through
again to be sure.

Malone asks him if it's bad news.

"They've got one of my informers locked in the cells over
there," he says. "They pulled him drunk out of the Rochdale
Canal last night, and now that he's sobered up enough to
talk, he's telling the sergeant that the Fenians have hatched

a plan to kill the mayor. He says it'll happen on Milk Street, but he doesn't know when."

Malone looks doubtful.

"Where did he hear all this?"

"It doesn't say where."

"There's nothing on Milk Street but a few old houses and a milliner's shop. There's no reason on earth the mayor would ever go there. The story makes no sense at all."

"Perhaps he got the name wrong."

"If he was drunk enough to fall in the canal, he most likely dreamed the whole thing up."

"I need to talk to him anyway. Find out if there's any truth to it."

O'Connor tucks the note into his pocket and gets up from the table. He folds the newspaper and puts it back on the wooden rack. Every time they meet in the graveyard he warns Sullivan to tread carefully, to keep quiet and not draw attention to himself, but the boy is foolhardy and reckless. They pull bodies out of that canal every month. He might easily have drowned. Not that death is real to them at that age. It's just an idea, or less than an idea, he thinks, just a word, a sound. You can warn them all you like and it makes no difference. It occurs to him, as he settles his bill at the counter and takes his coat and hat from the stand, that if his son, David, who had died, had lived instead, this is what fatherhood might have felt like: this constant irritating fear, this sense that a vital part of your life is being lived elsewhere, in secret, by someone you may love but can't possibly trust. Not that he loves Michael Sullivan, of course, not that he even likes him much. The boy is a flagrant fool and a wastrel, but they are knotted together now, it seems, whether they want to be or not, until all of this is over with.

"It'll be nothing," Malone says again. "When they're in drink the Fenians like to blow their trumpets, but nine times out of ten it's all a lie. We both know that."

"How far to Milk Street from here?" O'Connor asks.

"Five minutes," he says. "Less probably."

"Then we can stop off on the way."

Outside, the fog is the color of weak gruel, and the air tastes bitter and gamey. When they reach Milk Street they walk halfway down, then pause beside a lamppost. It's just as Malone described it—a few modest houses, shuttered and dark, and a milliner's shop. There's no movement or sound and no sign of anything unusual. O'Connor is about to turn to go back, when he hears a sudden whistle, like birdsong but louder. He looks at Malone.

"Could be burglars about," Malone says. "Good weather for it."

"Do you see anything?"

Malone shakes his head.

O'Connor looks about. The blank fog surrounds them, head high, like the walls of a vague and ghostly stockade. Probably nothing to be concerned about, he thinks. The mayor is safe asleep in his villa in Higher Broughton, and they are standing on an empty street hearing the usual squeals and rattles of a city at night.

"Could be the rats," he says, "or a cat coming into heat."

Malone doesn't answer. He is peering past O'Connor now, over his shoulder into the thick darkness behind.

"There's a fellow standing in that doorway over yonder," he says in a whisper. "I just seen him move."

"One man only?" O'Connor asks.

"So far as I can tell."

O'Connor turns and looks.

"Police," he shouts out. "Who's over there?"

There's no answer, no sign of movement at all that he can see. He wonders if Malone was mistaken.

"We know you're in there," Malone shouts again. "Show yourself now."

They gaze at the doorway and wait. Most likely just a beggar taking shelter, O'Connor thinks, or a drunk. He checks in his pocket for the handcuffs.

Malone walks forward, but before he gets to the doorway, the man steps out. He is wearing a ragged tweed overcoat and a bowler hat. His hands are pushed deep into his pockets and his thick shoulders are hunched against the chill.

"What's your name?" Malone asks him. "Who are you?"

Beneath the curled brim of his bowler, the man's eyes are dark and full of eagerness. His lips are slightly ajar. Before answering, he glances off to the left and right, then looks back at Malone as if deciding how much or little he is required to say.

"My name's Harrison," he says. "I'm a visitor to the city."

"And what were you doing hiding in that doorway?"

"Not hiding," he says, "just waiting."

"For what?"

The man pauses again.

"For who," he says. "A woman. Her name is Annie something. You can find her in the Swan most nights."

Malone turns to O'Connor and shrugs.

"Annie Smith," he says. "I know the one."

O'Connor recognizes the man: It's the one he saw talking to Tommy Flanagan at the funeral parade, the one with the scars on his face. He feels a strand of coldness trembling and twisting in his gut.

"I've seen you before," he says. "And your name's not Harrison."

The man shakes his head.

"You're wrong, sir. My name's Harrison. I'm a draper over from New York."

"Raise your hands above your head," O'Connor tells him. "Let us check your pockets."

The man doesn't move. He frowns and then gives Malone

a puzzled, quizzical look, as if he believes that Malone, out of the two of them, is the one most likely to listen to reason.

"Has it become a crime just to stand in a doorway now?" he asks.

"You're lying to us," O'Connor says. "Let us check through your pockets."

"There's nothing in my pockets," he says.

"Then show us."

He still doesn't move.

Malone turns to look at O'Connor. Half his face is sunk in shadow and the other half is made visible by the choked glow of the streetlamp behind. The thickened darkness streams around them like black water around a rock.

"You say you know him?" Malone says in a low voice.

"It's Doyle."

"You're sure of it?"

O'Connor nods. He is watching Doyle's hands, which are still pushed deep into the pockets of his ragged overcoat.

"There are more of us waiting at the end of the street," he says. "You can't get away."

"I'm a draper and my name is Harrison," Doyle says again, but the way he says it this time, lifeless, flat, mocking, like a bored child tripping out his bedtime prayers, makes it clear to them all that he is growing tired of the pretense.

"Enough of this shite," Malone says.

He pulls his brass handcuffs out from his pocket and moves to grab Doyle's arm. Doyle pivots away from him; his right hand jerks upward. When O'Connor sees the pistol, the curved steel cylinder and barrel catching and angling the yellow gaslight, he knows it is already too late, that the decision, which will not have been a decision at all, but an act born of instinct or fury or need, has already occurred. There is a muzzle-flash and a roar. Malone grunts and

gasps like the air has just been kicked out of him, and then
bends and twists back into himself, clutching and fumbling
at his seeping belly, as if trying to keep hold of something
that doesn't wish to be held.

As Malone drops down to the cobblestones, bleeding and
moaning, Doyle puts the pistol up to O'Connor's forehead.
Shadows swirl and knit around them. Fog swags like
stained laundry in the windless air. Here is death, O'Connor
thinks. Not the instrument or the image of it only, not the
echo or borrowing this time, but the thing itself. Foul and
reeking. He feels it pressing, red, against his face and chest
like the heat of a wildfire. Just one inch closer, he knows,
and he will catch and melt in its roar.

Doyle's eyes are like two black holes skived into the darkness.

"Which cunt told you about our plan?" he demands. "Who
was it?"

"No one told us. We came here by chance."

"I can kill you here and now," he says. "Don't think I
can't."

"I know that."

"So tell me the truth."

Malone is curled up on the mucky pavement, gasping
and mewling like a newborn. O'Connor hears a sash window squeal open somewhere behind, then a door.

"You should run while you can," he says. "You don't have
any time for this."

"Give me the name," he says, "or I'll kill you."

"You won't get away," O'Connor says. "It's too late."

"I'll ask you just one more time and then I'll shoot you
dead, I swear."

O'Connor can feel the hot mouth of the muzzle pressed
hard against his forehead. All we ever get to know is this
one moment, he thinks, this single now. The darkness re-

leases us, and then the darkness takes us back, and if it's not pure and abject fear that keeps us living, then what else can it be?

"Who is the traitor?" Doyle says again.

"It's Rice," he says. "Peter Rice is the traitor."

Doyle's lips tighten and his face twitches sideways, but he doesn't speak or lower his arm. *I had that one chance to save myself,* O'Connor thinks, *but now the chance has passed.*

"Peter Rice."

It is not a question but an echo, as if he wants to hear the name again from his own mouth, taste it, just to be sure.

O'Connor nods.

"Yes," he says. "He told me all about the plan to kill the mayor. He told me everything."

There is the long blast of a police whistle from the direction of Market Street and then another. Doyle looks away quickly, then turns back again.

"See those handcuffs there on the ground," he says, pointing downward. "You put one link around your wrist and one around your friend's. You do it now."

Malone's left hand is black and wet with blood. He's only half-conscious and his eyes are rolling up into his skull. When the cuffs are locked in place, Doyle gestures for the key and O'Connor gives it to him.

"I'll see you hanged for this, I swear," O'Connor says.

Doyle shakes his head.

"No, you won't," he says. "They only hang the stupid ones, and I'm not that."

He drops the Tranter back into his overcoat pocket; then, moving without haste or guile, as if this place and time are no different from any other, neither better nor worse, turns and walks away. The wet fog, rough-grained and maculate as old timber, breaks open to receive him, then shuts behind like a door.

CHAPTER 15

When the banging starts, Dixon is asleep in bed with Victor the ratter splayed out beside him. He shouts that he is coming, then pulls on his boots and goes up to see who is there. He remembers Neary's face from before but not his name.

"It's Doyle's chap," he says. "And what time of night do you call this?"

Over Neary's right shoulder, on the far side of the narrow street, he can see Skelly's ragged-looking hansom stopped beneath the gas lamp and Stephen Doyle standing in front of it, holding a pistol against his thigh and looking palely furious. Neary tells him they need to use the railway arch tonight and they will give him a sovereign if he will take them there. Dixon asks him what the gun is for, and Neary sniffs, then tells him there are some things it is better if he doesn't know about. Dixon thinks a moment longer, then asks to see the sovereign, and Neary shows it to him. "I'll get the keys," he says. He goes back down to the cellar, dresses himself quickly, and takes a ring of keys from the brass-headed nail on the wall. Victor sighs in his sleep and fidgets, and Dixon lays a hand on his ribs and whispers an endearment into his felty ear.

They get into the cab together and drive past the end of Stanley Street and across the broken and waterlogged ground to where the viaduct crosses the Bolton Canal. The fog is wrapped so thick about them that Skelly has to slow the horse more than once and peer about to be sure they are still on the road. When they reach the place, they all get out. Neary lights a match and Dixon undoes the padlock and opens the door. The archway is cold and black inside like a cavern set deep in the earth. Near the entrance, there is a workbench scattered with rusted tools, a cast-iron stove, a cabinet, a table, and some archaic armchairs with horsehair poking through the rent fabric. Farther back, in the shadows, there's a head-high pile of dust and bones, and another, similar-sized, of planks and broken furniture. The floor is cement, and rainwater drips, now and then, from cracks in the brickwork overhead. Dixon finds a paraffin lamp, wipes away the dust, then trims and lights it.

"You'll need to hide the hansom in the next archway over," he says. "If you leave it outside, they'll see it from the coal wharves yonder as soon as it gets light. There's no fodder for the horse in there, but I can walk to the livery stables to get you some."

"You stay here with us," Doyle says. "Skelly will tend to the nag."

Dixon nods.

"It's quiet here," he says. "No one'll find you, if you don't want to be found."

Doyle is still holding the pistol in his right hand. He examines it for a while, turning it over and back as if wondering what it might be worth at market, then puts it into his jacket pocket.

"There's been some trouble tonight," he says. "A man's been shot."

"One of yours, is it?" Dixon says. "A brother?"

Doyle shakes his head.

"A policeman. It's not likely he'll live."

Dixon stares at him a moment, wide-eyed.

"No," he says. "You can't stay here if you just killed a copper. They'll hang us all."

Doyle's face doesn't change. In the light from the paraffin lamp, the whites of his eyes gleam like polished ivory. His swollen shadow jitters against the high curve of the wall.

"Two days only," he says. "I'll pay you well for this place and the more help you give us, the quicker we'll be away again."

Dixon rubs his neck and scowls.

"It's not my fight," he says. "I'm not one of you."

"If you keep calm and do all I ask, we'll be gone before you know it. You can forget this ever happened."

"I'm not a killer."

"And I'm not asking you to become one. That's not what I have in mind."

Dixon looks across at Neary, but Neary's expression doesn't alter.

"You're fucking mad, the lot of you," Dixon says.

Doyle waits a moment, then takes a step forward and puts his hand on Dixon's shoulder.

"Listen to me now," he says. "I have a job for you. There's a man called Peter Rice. He owns a tannery near the Scotland Bridge. Tomorrow morning, I need you to go out and find him for me. I'll tell you where to look and who to talk to. As soon as you find him, you come back here and tell us, and we'll do the rest ourselves."

"That's all of it?"

Doyle nods.

"There's one more thing I should tell you, though, just in case you're thinking that instead of going out looking for Peter Rice you could run to the police."

"I wasn't thinking that at all."

"Just in case you were. The man we robbed before was a

detective, name of James O'Connor. The moment O'Connor sees your face, you'll be charged with conspiracy to murder. You may not believe you're one of us, but that's not how the judges will see it."

Dixon looks at Doyle's right hand still pressing down on his shoulder.

"We robbed a peeler?" he says.

"I would have told you before, but it wasn't to the purpose."

Neary goes outside to help Skelly with moving the horse and cab, and Doyle finds kindling and lights a fire in the stove. When they come back inside, Skelly is carrying blankets and a bottle of whiskey. They sit down on the broken armchairs and pass the bottle back and forth until it's finished. Skelly sings them a song. Sometime after midnight, Dixon falls asleep. When he wakes up again it is still dark, the paraffin lamp is alight, Neary is snoring, and Doyle is standing at the workbench, sorting through a box of old rusted nails, dividing the ones that can still be used from the ones that can't.

"You're a strange bastard, you are," Dixon tells him. "The police must be tearing down the city looking for you. Any normal man would be long gone by now if they had the chance, but here you are."

Doyle turns around to look at him.

"I'm a soldier. If I have a job to do, I like to keep on until it's finished."

"I'd never be a soldier. Marching about like that, following other men's orders. You couldn't ever pay me enough."

"You think the thieving makes you free?"

Dixon sighs and scratches himself.

"I don't think on such things," he says. "I just do what I want."

A train passes overhead. There is a distant muffled roar,

and the darkness shakes around them. Skelly grumbles out
a curse and shifts about in his broken chair.

"So you follow your own pleasures, is that it?" Doyle says.
"Go wherever they point you and don't worry too much
about the consequences?"

"Something like that."

Doyle nods.

"I remember how that feels. I used to think like that myself, but then I changed. I went off to the war and learned a
thing or two."

"What did you learn?"

"That a man's life on its own is nothing much to talk
about. That it disappears just like that, in the blink of an
eye."

He turns back to the workbench and picks up a bent nail
from the wooden box. Dixon watches him silently as he hits
it twice with the hammer, then checks it again and puts it
in the good pile.

"Really, you should leave now," Dixon tells him again. "If
you stay, they'll find you and hang you for sure."

Doyle doesn't trouble to turn around this time. He picks
up another nail from the box and examines it in the dim
light of the paraffin lamp. His white breath forms ghoulish
shapes in the black and frigid air.

"If they hang me, there'll be someone else coming after,"
he says. "Someone who remembers my name, and who I
was, and why I was here. That's what this all means. There's
always another."

CHAPTER 16

By morning, there are thirty Fenians in the Swan Street lockup, and another fifteen down at Livesey Street. O'Connor checks the list of names. Neary is missing, he notices, and so is Skelly. His hand trembles as he turns the pages of the ledger. Someone offers him brandy to steady his nerves, but he asks for tea instead. The broken handcuff is still in his pocket and there are patches of blood on his shirt front and up one arm of his overcoat. He wishes now he had stayed in the infirmary with Malone. The thought of him suffering alone, unwatched and uncomforted, is like an ache in O'Connor's chest. He looks at the clock on the wall and promises himself he'll be back there within the hour.

Fazackerley explains that they have made a start on questioning the suspects, but they've uncovered nothing useful so far.

"Peter Rice is the one who will know," O'Connor says. "If anyone knows."

"That's what we figured too."

"Where's Michael Sullivan?"

"Cell three. He was effing and blinding when they brought him in, but I gave him the look and he quieted some."

"We should leave him in there for a while. See what he can pick up from the others."

Fazackerley nods.

O'Connor takes a swallow of the tea and glances about. The charge office is crowded with policemen. They stare at him, then look away again. He senses their anger and their fear, the questions they want to ask him but won't.

He turns to Fazackerley.

"Do they think it's my fault?" he asks. "Is that it?"

"Don't be foolish," Fazackerley says. "Why would they think that?"

"Is Maybury waiting somewhere?"

"He's upstairs in the surgeon's room. I'll take you to him."

The room is small and bare: three chairs, a narrow desk, a sink in one corner with a mirror above it, and a cupboard for the medical supplies. When O'Connor and Fazackerley walk in, Maybury is behind the desk writing. He glances up, then nods for them to sit.

"We'll bring Peter Rice in here presently," he says. "We'll stand him over there, and you'll tell him what you told Doyle. If he's going to talk to us, we need to put the fear of God into him. Do you think you can manage that?"

O'Connor nods.

"I'll do what I can," he says. "I'm guessing Rice and Doyle don't like or trust each other much, but whether that means Rice believes Doyle would actually kill him is another thing. Even if he does, Rice may not know where Doyle is hiding, or Doyle may have fled already. He could be halfway to France by now."

"You told me that he'll stay here in Manchester until he's found the man who betrayed him. That's what you said to me before."

"I think it's likely, but I don't know that for sure. I may be wrong. Since they killed Tommy Flanagan and the others, I've had nothing solid to go on."

Maybury's eyes widen. He shakes his head impatiently, then turns to Fazackerley.

"Likely," he says. "Good god, we're chasing our own fucking tails here, Sergeant, I swear."

O'Connor looks out the window. The morning sky is the color of dust and ashes.

Frank Malone is dying, he thinks, *and Tommy Flanagan is already dead; I have enough guilt on my back to last me a long lifetime, so what does it matter what else Maybury cares to throw on the pile?*

"If you don't need me here, I have better things to do," he says.

Maybury's face darkens.

"You'll sit there until I tell you to go," he says.

"Everyone is distressed about the shooting," Fazackerley explains. "It's only natural. O'Connor's not thinking right, is all."

"I'm thinking fine," O'Connor says.

There are several seconds of clenched silence between them, then a knock on the door and Peter Rice is brought in wearing handcuffs. Maybury tells the constable that he can leave. He asks Rice for his name, address, and occupation and writes the information down slowly, as if it is new and important. He then asks him where he was last night, and whether he has any knowledge of an American named Stephen Doyle. Rice says he was at home asleep with his lady-wife and, no, he has never heard of any Stephen Doyle, but he knows a Willy Doyle from Donegal, if that is any help to them. Maybury pauses awhile for effect, then tells him that they know very well who he is and they know very well he is lying about Doyle, and if he has any sense at all he will listen carefully to what they are going to tell him next, because his life may very well depend on it.

Rice looks calm and easy, unconcerned. He rubs his head with both hands and yawns loudly. His curled-up tongue has

the color and sheen of a kidney, and his blunt fingers are
stained brown from the tanning liquor. He points at O'Connor
and asks whose blood that is on him, and when O'Connor
explains, he nods and smiles as if he knew it already but just
wanted to be sure. "It's a great shame, that," he says. "A terrible piece of bad luck for the young fellow." O'Connor says it
is not bad luck but plain murder and Rice's problem is that
he will likely be the next one killed. Rice frowns at this information and looks suitably bewildered. O'Connor then tells
him what happened on Milk Street, explains that Stephen
Doyle put a gun to his head and demanded to know the name
of the man who had betrayed him.

"And do you know whose name I gave him, Peter?"
O'Connor says, standing up so their eyes are on the same
level, and he can smell Rice's tobacco-stained breath and
the musk of his unwashed flesh. "I gave him yours."

There is a moment of silence, and then Rice snorts as if
he's been told a great joke.

"I don't know any Stephen Doyle," he says. "And he don't
know me. I'm an honest tanner, that's all I am, so why you
should be giving some murderous Fenian fellow my name I
can't for the life of me imagine."

"Well, that's a great mystery, then," O'Connor says. "Because when I gave him it, he seemed awful pleased, awful
satisfied, as if I'd cleared up something that had been trou-
bling him for a good long while. He could have shot me dead
then and there, but he didn't because he believed I was telling him the honest truth. Just think on that awhile."

O'Connor watches Rice carefully. Beneath the boldness
and bravado he thinks he sees the beginnings of something
new.

"Why would he ever believe a copper anyway?" Rice says.

"You know why, Peter. Because I'm the one the traitors
like to talk to, I'm the one who knows."

Rice shakes his head.

"All that means nothing to me," he says. "Nothing at all."

"Tell us where Doyle's hiding," Maybury says. "That's the only way to save yourself now. If we don't catch him first, then he'll be coming for you. You know he will."

Rice shifts his jaw sideways, then back again. His face tightens.

"I'm not a squealer," he says. "Never have been."

"He looked angry when I gave him your name," O'Connor says. "That was his big plan, wasn't it, killing the mayor, and now it's all in shreds and tatters and he wants someone else to blame. Maybe you can talk your way out of it, but I'd be surprised. He's not a man to show much mercy when it comes to spies. Just tell us where he's hiding, though, and your difficulty goes away."

Rice frowns and rubs his bristled jaw. He gazes up at the ceiling for a while, sniffs, sighs, then looks back at O'Connor.

"I bet you made the same fine promises to Tommy Flanagan, didn't you?" he says. "Said you'd keep him safe and warm if he told you what you wanted to know? And look how well that turned out for poor Tommy. Beaten half to death, I heard, then finished off with a shotgun, wasn't it?"

O'Connor doesn't answer. Maybury grinds his teeth and looks down at the tabletop in front of him. Rice's mouth broadens into something close to a grin.

"You may be clever enough in your own fashion, Jimmy," he says, "and you know how to keep your lords and masters happy, I can see that, but you'd better believe you'd be the last man in Manchester I'd ever trust my secrets to, the very last one."

O'Connor looks down at the floor between his feet a moment to steady himself, then starts to speak again, but Maybury stops him.

"We'll talk to you again, Peter Rice," he says. "Don't imagine this is the last of it."

"I'll be back at the tannery, if you ever need me," he says.

"It's in Gibraltar, just by the boneworks. You can ask any-one thereabouts. They all know who I am."

Fazackerley calls the constable in and tells him to take the prisoner back down to the cells and bring up Michael Sullivan in his stead. They wait in silence until the two men's footsteps die away, then Maybury unspools a string of violent curses.

Sullivan is pale and disheveled. One side of his face is badly bruised, and the left arm of his jacket is ripped and gaping. He still smells faintly of the Rochdale Canal. May-bury offers him a chair, and he sits down on it slowly, then yawns and rubs his eyes like a child waking up from a nap. They ask him how he is feeling and if he needs to see a doc-tor and he shrugs and says he will manage. Maybury sends the constable down for a pot of tea, then picks up his foun-tain pen.

"Will you tell us all that happened, Michael?" he says. "How did you learn about the plan to kill the mayor?"

Sullivan describes his conversation with Jack Riley at the alehouse. He explains that he was on his way to George Street to look for O'Connor when he slipped and fell into the canal.

"Knocked myself out cold on the lock gate," he says, point-ing to his damaged face. "If there hadn't been a copper nearby to hear the commotion, I'd probably be drowned."

Maybury asks him why he didn't tell the officers at Knott Mill Station about the planned attack as soon as he arrived there, and Sullivan says he was too confused and in no con-dition to talk or even think right.

"When I woke up the next day, I remembered all about it, though," he says. "That's when I asked them to send the note to Jimmy. They wouldn't do it at first. They thought I was talking nonsense, but I told them they'd all be in trou-ble if the mayor was killed just because they wouldn't send a note to the Town Hall and that changed their minds."

"If that note had reached me when it was sent, we could have set a trap," O'Connor says. "We would have been waiting for them when they arrived."

"It wasn't marked as urgent," Fazackerley says. "That was the mistake they made. Easily done."

Maybury grimaces. He asks Sullivan how many others knew about the Milk Street plan apart from Jack Riley.

"I don't know for sure. He acted like it was a great secret, so maybe just the fellows at the top: Peter Rice, Willy Devine, Costello, McArdle."

"Charlie McArdle was there too?"

Sullivan nods.

"They all were, except for Doyle, of course, and Neary and Skelly. Them three were nowhere to be seen."

"If Jack Riley told you about Doyle's plan, that shows he trusts you," Maybury says. "After you leave here, you must talk to him again as soon as you can. You must find out if he knows who else was involved and where they're hiding. We don't have much time."

Sullivan shakes his head.

"Oh no," he says. "No. I'm finished with the spying now, Mr. Maybury. I've done all that you asked of me. I told you about the Fenian plan, and if you didn't catch Stephen Doyle red-handed like you should have, it wasn't my fault."

Maybury looks at him a moment.

"You've done well for us so far, Michael," he says. "But this job's not finished yet."

"It is for me. It's too dangerous to go on longer. Those men are all killers. I sat with them in the alehouse that night and you could see it in their eyes."

"What about the hundred pounds? Did you forget about that already? The money's yours, but I can't give it to you until we find Stephen Doyle."

"I didn't forget, but I can't spend the money if I'm lying dead."

Maybury turns to O'Connor.

"You talk to him," he says. "Make him see sense. There's Frank Malone dying in the hospital. This is not the right time to be backing out."

O'Connor looks at Sullivan sitting there, arms crossed tight over his chest, and his face and body tensed and belligerent. He remembers him on Ash Street, clinging onto his brother's back as they played, laughing and screaming like two devils.

"Michael's right, sir," O'Connor says. "The work's too dangerous and he's too young for it. He's survived by luck so far, as much as anything, but his luck can't last forever. If he wants to stop now, then I believe we should let him."

"Is there another informer inside the Manchester circle that I'm not aware of?" Maybury asks. "Someone else who'll be able to tell us what they're planning to do next?"

O'Connor shakes his head.

"No, sir."

"No one at all?"

"No one."

"Then how can we possibly allow him to stop? There are murderers on the loose, the town is in an uproar, and Sullivan here is the only one who might be able to tell us what the enemy is thinking. This is when we need him the most."

"You can't make me keep on with it," Sullivan says. "I've had enough."

"We have no power over him, sir," O'Connor says. "He's free to do as he wishes."

Maybury waits a moment, rubs his jaw, then opens up a cardboard file on the table in front of him and removes a slip of paper. He looks at it for a moment, to be sure it is the right one, then holds it out.

"He's not so free as you think, O'Connor. That's a telegram from the New York Police Department dated last week. It confirms that your nephew Michael Sullivan is wanted for embezzling the sum of one thousand dollars from Elling Brothers Bank, where he worked as an assistant teller. They thought he might have fled to Dublin, but it hadn't occurred to them that he was over here instead. They were pleased to get my message."

O'Connor takes the telegram and reads it through. He feels shame more than anger, as if it's him, not Michael Sullivan, who has been exposed, whose stupid lies have just been revealed for what they are. When he has finished reading, he hands the paper to Fazackerley.

Sullivan stares down at his feet, then looks up at the ceiling.

"What did you do with that thousand dollars?" O'Connor asks him. "How did you spend it?"

"On the horses mainly. Some on cards. I had a run of bad fortune like you wouldn't believe."

Fazackerley puts the telegram back on the desk, and Maybury thanks him and returns it to the cardboard file.

"The fellows in New York want me to send you back over there to stand trial," Maybury says. "That's what they're asking for. When this telegram reached me, I replied straightaway explaining that you were involved in important work for us here and couldn't be spared, but if you won't continue with that work, if you're determined to give it up, as you say you are, then there is no longer any good reason to refuse their request."

"You've got me trapped," Sullivan says sullenly. "Over a barrel. I can see it."

"We need to know where Stephen Doyle is hiding. You need to find that out for us. If you do it and we arrest him, I'll not only give you the hundred pounds, I'll also write to the fellows over in New York to see if the embezzlement charges might be dropped. If you give us what we need, it's possible you could go back there and live as you did before.

Although I can't make any promises, of course. What do you say, Michael?"

Sullivan looks over to O'Connor. His expression is help-less, bewildered. He's nothing but a child, O'Connor thinks, a vain and greedy boy who imagines the world is created for his pleasure and convenience alone and is amazed to dis-cover, too late, that it isn't.

"What should I do now, Jimmy?" he asks. "Should I carry on with it?"

"I warned you before. I told you it was too dangerous."

"I know you did."

"I can't help you anymore, Michael," he says. "You must choose for yourself."

Later, as he walks back down Tib Street toward the infir-mary, past barrows piled with turnips, onions, and salted fish, O'Connor's head aches and he feels a slow, rebarbative burning in his throat and stomach. When he first joined the Dublin police, he thought it was a chance to escape the darkness and disorder of the past, to wash away the mem-ory of his father's crime and all its consequences and start afresh, but he wonders now if the darkness and disorder are inside him, if what he was trying to escape from is who he really is. He tells himself this isn't true, it can't be, but even the possibility of it fills him with a dreadful gloom.

When he gets back to the ward, Malone is already dead. The narrow cot is empty, and the nurse tells him that the body has been taken down to the mortuary in the basement. He waits in the corridor for a while, stiff and raw with re-grets, wondering what to do next. Then a thickset man ap-pears, wearing laboring clothes, and says his name is Alfred Patterson and he is Malone's brother-in-law just come across from Ashton on the train. They shake hands and O'Connor explains what has happened. Patterson, who looks surprised more than saddened at the news, says he will need to see Frank's body for himself, with his own two eyes, or his wife will likely not believe him when he gets back home. They ask a porter for directions, then make their way downstairs to the mortuary. The large, white room is cold and windowless; there are deep wooden shelves attached to every wall where the bodies are stacked four and five deep. It takes them several minutes to locate Malone. He is lying on a bottom shelf, below a thin, gray-haired woman with yellow-tinged flesh and bruises on her face. Patterson crouches down just to be sure, then rubs his chin and stands up again.

"Him and me were never pals," he says. "I didn't like him overmuch, too big for his britches I always thought, but the wife will take it hard."

"The shooting was a mistake. He should never have been where he was."

Patterson shrugs.

"Such things happen as they will," he says. "A man can't choose his end no more than he can choose his beginning, I say."

Patterson is a carpenter by trade. He spends his days sawing and hammering, laying floorboards and hanging windows and doors. While they wait in a side room for the death certificate to be written out and signed, he talks about spindles and hinges, sashes and casements, the differing properties of oak and pine. O'Connor hears the words but doesn't listen. The coldness of the mortuary has sunk deep into his bones, and the sight of Malone's abandoned body, stiff and lifeless as a waxwork, has left him feeling queasy and adrift. The hours and days ahead of him now seem unending and impossible, like a task he can't abandon but will never complete.

Once the papers are all in order, they walk back to London Road Station, up the hill, past the long line of hansom cabs.

Dark clouds shuttle across the sky and the raw wind pokes
and pushes them. The departure board shows half an hour
before the next train to Ashton, so they find a corner table in
the Albion Refreshment Rooms and sit down together. It is
crowded and noisy inside and the air smells of wet overcoats.
O'Connor orders a bottle of stout and a ham sandwich for
Patterson and a ginger beer for himself. The sandwich, when
it arrives, looks meager and ancient, but Patterson declares
it delicious nevertheless. Despite the somberness of his mis-
sion, he appears to O'Connor to be in a holiday mood now,
glad of the excuse to lay down his tools for the day, and
pleased to have someone new to tell his stories to.

"I know some Irish fellows over in Ashton," Patterson
says. "Bricklayers mainly. Now what are the names?" He
frowns awhile in thought. "Patrick Devlin? Joseph O'Toole?"

O'Connor shakes his head.

"John McDonell?"

"No," he says.

Patterson looks surprised.

"They all talk like you do," he says. "Just the same."

O'Connor checks the clock and asks Patterson if he'll
take another drink before he leaves.

"I'll get these ones myself," he says, standing up. "It's my
treat."

He walks over to the bar and comes back holding two
glasses of cheap brandy. He sits back down, puts one of the
glasses on the table in front of O'Connor, and lifts up the
other for a toast.

"To poor Frank Malone," he says. "May he rest in peace
and may the good Lord forgive his many sins."

"Thank you," O'Connor says. "But I don't."

Patterson shrugs and smiles.

"Come on," he says. "It's for Frank, and it's only small."

O'Connor looks down at the glass in front of him: the
brown disc of brandy against the darker blankness of the

tabletop. He pauses, then lifts it up and smells. The scent is like a wide door swinging open in front of him. *How long has it been?* he thinks. *How long, and for what?*

"To Frank," he says.

He takes a first quick sip, then drinks the rest straight down without thinking. His mouth burns, and the world becomes louder and brighter around him.

CHAPTER 17

The room is cold and filthy, and there is a smell of cured meat and offal rising up through the floorboards from O'Shaughnessy's butcher shop below. Riley is there already, seated by the ash-filled fireplace puffing on his pipe like nothing much has happened lately. There's a copy of that morning's *Manchester Times* lying on the table unread. Rice takes off his hat, steps to the window, and shifts the muslin curtain an inch to one side. He forgets for a moment who he is looking for; then he remembers.

"Where have the others got to?" he says.

"There are a dozen or so still locked up in the cells at Swan Street. The rest are back home or out looking for Doyle."

"Any sign of Neary or the hansom?"

"Nothing."

Rice shakes his head.

"So if they're still in Manchester, they're hiding from us."

"More likely they're long gone, if you ask me," Riley says.

Rice lets go of the curtain and steps back into the center of the room. His face is set hard in a frown.

"I don't believe he'd come for you anyways," Riley says. "He can't be so cracked as to give credence to what that

Jimmy O'Connor tells him without even an ounce of fucken proof."

Rice looks at the empty chair but doesn't sit down.

"Doyle thinks Manchester is riddled with spies," he says. "That's the very first thing he asked me about on the day he arrived here from New York: *Where are the spies? Why haven't you killed them all yet?* You remember?"

"Those Yanks think they know our business better than we know it ourselves," Riley says. "Why else would they send a fellow like Stephen Doyle over here to show us what to do?"

"He set out his stall all right with Tommy Flanagan and the others, I'll give him that, but now he's overreached hisself with the mayor and he's raging with fury and wants to find an easy place to put the blame. I know just how that works."

"You can't go killing the fucken mayor and get away with it. It can't be done. I could have told him that for nothing. Not that he ever thought to ask."

"You remember how he was when we met him in the Blacksmith's? Just last week it was. Looking down on us like we were more or less nothing. He thought he knew better, but he didn't, and now another copper's lying dead in the infirmary, and we're the ones that'll take the blame for it. There'll be a noose around some poor bastard's neck afore this is over, I swear, and so long as he's Irish they won't care too much who it is."

"You should go up to Glasgow," Riley suggests. "Talk to Murphy about it. Let him sort it out. He's the Head Center now, that's his job."

"Maybe I will."

The two men fall silent for a moment. A dog barks twice in the street outside, and there are muffled voices from the shop below. Rice picks up the *Times* from the table and looks at the front page. According to the report of the murder, which extends across the first two columns, Detective Francis Malone of E Division encountered Stephen Doyle by chance on Milk Street near midnight, recognized him as the notorious and wanted Fenian, and was fatally shot in the stomach while courageously attempting to make an arrest. There is no mention of O'Connor or the mayor or the mayor's whore. The incident is described as the latest in a series of horrifying outrages committed by the Irish traitors in the pursuit of their foolish and unrealizable goals.

"Wherever he may be, if we find him before the coppers do, we might talk some small sense into him," Riley says.

"He won't be found if he don't want to be. A man like that."

"He's clever enough, it's true. And violent too when he needs to be."

"I'll sleep in my own bed tonight," Rice says after a pause, "in my own house. I'm not hiding away from anyone."

"Nor should you. God knows you're better than any of us, and you've got no reason to stand accused of any crime."

Rice nods at this, and sits himself down at last. He takes out his pipe and taps the bowl on the table.

"Is there no chance of a decent blaze in here," he says, looking about, "or a cup of tea?"

"I'll go talk to O'Shaughnessy now," Riley says, standing up. "He's usually quicker than this."

He goes downstairs and comes back up five minutes later with a coal scuttle and a handful of kindling.

"There'll be a pot coming in a little while," he says. "The boy's just stepped out for some milk."

Rice watches on as Riley lays the fire and lights it. There are curlicues of gray-blue smoke peeping from the gaps between the coals, then small, flickering tongues of orange flame that give off no heat. He rubs his thighs and leans backward in the chair. It creaks beneath him, and the kindling cracks and hisses in the grate.

"Someone talked," he says. "How else would O'Connor have known to be there at just the right time? If we knew who it was that blabbed, we could set Doyle straight. Sort it out that way."

Riley is still leaning over, with his hands on his knees, examining the fire. He turns his head to one side, then nods and straightens up.

"That would fix it," he agrees.

"Who would have heard about their plan besides Doyle and Neary and the two of us? Did you ever speak about it at the alehouse? Did you overhear anything?"

"There's allus some loose talk as the night goes on," he says. "You know how that is, Peter. You couldn't stop it if you tried. But they're all good fellows at the alehouse. You know they are. I'd swear by every one of them."

Rice scratches his neck and nods.

"Tell me some more," he says.

Riley doesn't answer straightaway. He winces and looks briefly pained, as if he is being asked to reveal a secret that he'd rather keep hidden.

"That lad Sullivan from the tannery," he says. "That night he took the oath, I may have said something to him about Doyle's plan, just a little something to make him feel a part of it all like. But it can't have been him."

"Why not?"

"He's only a lad. And he only just got here. Why would he be off telling tales?"

"Was anyone else listening, or was it just you and him?"

"Just the two of us. There's allus some loose talk, it's only natural."

Rice frowns and looks away.

"You shouldn't be talking to a private like that, Jack," he says. "You know the fucken rules."

"Aye, but he's a good lad, Sullivan. And he has no fondness for the coppers either. You should have seen him flatten that one before."

"What else do we know about him? Remind me."

Riley shakes his head.

"He had that trouble over in New York. Some fellows were after him. That's why he's here now. He has a brother in Brooklyn still, and other family in Dublin somewhere. The Coombe, isn't it?"

"The Coombe," Rice says. "That's right. He has a cousin, George Sullivan, married a girl from my father's village in Clare. He told me that."

"Well, there you are, then."

"Who else do we know from around there?"

Riley thinks.

"Tom MacRae comes from Cork Street," he says. "That's not so far away."

"You should talk to Tom MacRae, then. Find out if he knows anything about the Sullivans."

"There'll be nothing to tell. He's an honest lad, Michael. If I'd had any doubts at all, I'd have sent him on his way. Whoever talked to O'Connor, I can promise you, it wasn't him."

The boy comes upstairs with a pot of tea, two cups, and a jug of milk on a wooden tray. Riley takes the tray from him and puts it on the table.

"You know," Rice says, "today at the lockup, after Maybury and O'Connor tried their nonsense on me, the next one called from the cells was Michael Sullivan. Directly after me. Why would they care so much about little Michael Sullivan, I wonder?"

Riley shrugs.

"That's just coincidence. Nothing more," he says. "Here you are."

He holds out the cup and Rice stands up to take it. He

blows, takes two sips, then puts it down on the empty mantelpiece. He rubs his hands together and holds them out to the fire.

"You go talk to Tom MacRae anyhow," he says. "Find out what he knows. It can't do us any harm."

CHAPTER 18

O'Connor watches Alfred Patterson amble off down platform two, waits a minute more to be sure he is truly
gone, then turns and goes back inside the Albion. The
barman—oiled black hair, rolled-up shirtsleeves, a starched
apron—gives him a sideways glance, and O'Connor licks
his lips and points across to the brandy bottles. *Every law,
however needful, must have its limits,* he thinks, *and a
drink will do me no harm right now after the fearsome night
I've passed. Something to mend the shredded nerves, that's
all. It would be a cruel kind of man who would begrudge me
that.*

His hand shakes as he lifts the glass. He can still smell
the rank air of the mortuary, still see, if he closes his eyes,
Malone's pale, scarecrow body, sagged and lifeless on the
wooden rack. It is the solitude of death that frightens him
most. Not the pain but the loneliness. To see all the familiar
details slip away, the places, the people, to know they are
gone forever, that is the true horror, he thinks, not the
pitchfork or the fires of hell. Blasphemy, of course, to think
like that, to imagine you can understand the mysteries, but
that is how it strikes him always. The cruelty of it, even if
it makes no sense to think that way, that is how he feels.

He has one more brandy, then pays and leaves. The news of Malone's death will be general by now, he is sure. The evening newspapers will all carry their reports, there will be conversations in corridors and drawing rooms and bars, urgent letters will soon be written to the editor, and forceful speeches made in parliament. And how long will it all last: a week? a month? a year? Then there will be something else, another outrage more awful, yet somehow just the same. *We are all marching on the same treadmill,* he thinks, *strapped to a great slow-turning wheel. We think we are moving forward, but we are only going around and around again.*

He stops at the Feathers, then at the Brunswick, then at the Shakespeare on Fountain Street. By the time he arrives back at the Town Hall, it is the late afternoon. Darkness is falling quickly, and the full moon is showing like a bruised fruit in the mold-black sky. His mood is changed from before. The tiredness and gloom are gone, and he feels a new kind of energy swelling inside him, febrile and vaguely belligerent. He remembers all the slights and insults he has suffered since his arrival in Manchester and tells himself he is a man maligned, a victim of ignorance and English prejudice. *If the world was arranged as it should be,* he thinks, *according to reason and good sense, then I would be recognized and rewarded for who I am. Instead, I am mocked and belittled.*

He finds the detective office alive with rumors. There are reports of Doyle being seen as far away as Burnley and Southport, and a man fitting his description has just been arrested in Crewe. Some believe he must still be hiding out in Manchester, others that he has escaped abroad already, disguised as a priest or manservant, or hidden inside a beer barrel. When he asks Fazackerley's opinion, Fazackerley tells him they have had men kicking down doors in Ancoats since midnight and it is clear as day that no one has a fucking clue where Doyle is, not even the Fenians themselves.

"Where have you been hiding yourself anyway?" he says. "We've been looking out for you."

O'Connor shakes his head, as if the question is pointless.

"I've been occupied," he says.

Fazackerley looks at him more closely, then leans in and sniffs.

"Ah, Christ, no," he says, stepping back again. "Not that, Jimmy. Not now."

"Just a brandy or two for the nerves," O'Connor says. "That's all it is. Would you begrudge me that?"

"I don't begrudge you a thing," Fazackerley says. "Christ knows I'd likely be the same after the night you've had. But you can't be here in that state. You know the regulations. Go home now. Go to bed and come back in the morning. If we find Doyle, then I'll send a man to George Street to fetch you back. But I'm betting we won't find him, not tonight at least."

O'Connor doesn't answer. He has a blank, distracted look and when he speaks it is as if he is speaking to himself.

"After he shot Malone, I swear I thought he'd shoot me too," he says. "When he pointed that gun right at my forehead, I thought it was the end. God love me, I thought I was dead. I've been frightened before, but that wasn't fear I felt, it was something else altogether. I don't know the right word for it. Perhaps there isn't one."

"It's a bad business all around," Fazackerley says. "I know that. I feel it myself. We all do. But it won't do to soften now, when there's still work to be done."

O'Connor straightens himself and blinks. He doesn't want to go home yet. The thought of lying alone in bed with his racing thoughts appalls him.

"Where's Rice?" he says. "Did you follow him like we said?"

"He's with Jack Riley above the butcher's on Tib Street. We've got Barton in one of the shops opposite keeping an eye open in case Doyle ever shows himself. Though I don't believe he ever will."

"I could go over there now. Keep Barton company awhile. What do you think?"

"He doesn't need any company, Jimmy. You should go on home, like I told you. We can talk about it all tomorrow."

O'Connor shakes his head and looks away. Through the window he sees Franklin the lamplighter with his bent back and his ladder and pole working his way up King Street. *I'm tired of being pushed aside,* he thinks, *passed over as if I'm nothing.* He glares at Fazackerley, as if Fazackerley has become the distillation and the cause of all his miseries.

"Frank Malone might still be alive now, if you'd sent me Michael Sullivan's message when you first got it. Christ almighty, the lad risks his life, and when he gives you what you asked for, you let it sit there as if it's nothing."

He's talking louder now, shouting almost, and waving his hands around. Sanders, who is sitting close by, writing a report, puts his pen down and looks up. Fazackerley looks back at him and shakes his head.

"Jimmy's upset, that's all," he says. "It doesn't matter."

"He should show some more respect," Sanders says.

Fazackerley pats O'Connor on the shoulder and smiles.

"Come on now, Jimmy," he says.

O'Connor shrugs it off. *I've stayed quiet too long,* he thinks, *I've let other men drown me out.* He feels more words, scathing and necessary, gathering on his tongue.

"Sanders?" he says, turning. "What the hell do you know?"

"I know Frank Malone's lying dead with a Fenian bullet inside him, and you're standing here without nary a scratch on you. I know you Irish bastards like to stick together."

O'Connor shakes his head and breathes out slowly. His

lips and tongue are dark with spittle, and he is sweating although the room is not even warm. He tucks his chin into his chest and looks up, like a schoolmaster addressing a dunce.

"By Christ, I've met some dull and dim-witted fuckers in my time," he says, "I truly have. But you must take the crown."

Sanders' eyes open wide in outrage. He jumps up from behind the desk and grabs O'Connor by the throat with both hands. They struggle awkwardly for a moment, grunting and gasping, their boot heels scraping and banging against the bare floorboards, before the others step across to break it up. They push Sanders down into a chair and hold him there, and Fazackerley tugs O'Connor out into the empty corridor.

"That Sanders is a great prick," he says, "but you've become a fucking mischief maker. You go home now, like I told you to, and don't show your face back here until you're in a fit state."

O'Connor is unrepentant. He is happy to have things in the open now, happy to shake off the falsehoods and evasions at last.

"Doyle's still close by, you know," he says. "I'm sure of it. He won't give up."

"You leave Doyle to us."

"I've seen him in the flesh. Heard him talk, remember. He was standing just as close to me as you are now."

"And you think you understand him because of it? Is that right?"

"He's a man, that's all, not so very different from you or me."

"Christsake," Fazackerley says. "You best not let the others hear you talk like that."

"I don't much care what they think. I'm finished here. You know I am."

Fazackerley lets go of his arm and looks at him.

"You take it all too hard, Jimmy," he says. "You always have done. A man can't live that way."

"You're saying I bring it on myself?"

"That's not what I'm saying."

O'Connor turns aside. Rain is beating against the windowpane, and there is a low hiss, like a half-heard whisper, from the gas mantle on the wall above their heads.

"By the time you know anything, it'll already be too late," he says. "Doyle will be away and gone. I promise you."

"We'll see about that."

They go outside together, and Fazackerley puts him into a hackney and tells the driver to drive to George Street. After half a mile, O'Connor leans out and calls for him to stop. He pays what he owes and sends the cab away. The evening is cold and the steady rain lends a dull polish to the muddy cobbles and to the smoke-blackened walls. He stops in the Unicorn, then makes his way toward Tib Street. The drink has cleared his mind, given him new strength and power. *I'll follow my own lead from now on,* he tells himself, *I've had enough of other men's advisements. I'll take the saddle off my back and the bit from my mouth and do, for once, as I see fit.* When he gets to the corner of Whittle Street he looks about for Barton. He finds him eventually, seated in the window of the chemist's shop across the road from O'Shaughnessy's. His face is half-concealed behind the bottles of hair oil and dusty cartons of Epsom salts and toilet soap.

"Changing of the guard," O'Connor tells him lightly. "You can go on home now."

Barton doesn't question it. He is young, newly married, and eager, O'Connor imagines, to get back for his supper.

"Anything new to report?"

Barton shakes his head.

"Riley left a few hours ago, but Peter Rice is still up there."

"On his own, then?"

"Far as I can tell."

"I'll take the gun too," O'Connor says, guessing there must be one.

Barton gives it to him and O'Connor checks it is loaded properly before dropping it into his jacket pocket.

"They don't need you at King Street until the morning," O'Connor tells him. "Fazackerley knows all about it."

"So they haven't found him yet?" Barton says.

"Not yet but it won't be long. It's all in hand."

After Barton leaves, he takes off his jacket and settles himself down into the chair. He keeps careful watch for nearly an hour but sees nothing. There is a light glowing in the window above the butcher's shop, but no other sign of life or movement from inside. The chemist, short, middle-aged, with straggly gray hair and a dubious, world-weary look, is standing behind the counter pressing pills and sorting them into bottles. O'Connor turns and asks him if he has ever seen a man shot, and the chemist frowns and says he hasn't ever seen such a thing and he doesn't hope to either.

"Doyle may surrender without a fight," O'Connor says. "That's possible too."

"Or else he won't appear at all. That other one, Barton, told me he's most probably miles away by now. Said this here is just a sideshow and the real business is going on elsewhere."

O'Connor shakes his head.

"He'll come by here. I know he will."

"Made you a promise, did he?"

"It's a feeling I have."

The chemist snorts.

"Feelings is for girls," he says.

"He'll be here," O'Connor repeats. "And when he comes, you'll be my witness to what happens next."

"I should charge you rent for that there chair," the chemist says, pointing to it. "Sixpence an hour. What do you say?"

"I say you can talk to the chief constable about it," O'Connor answers. "Mr. Palin. You'll find him to be a most pleasant and genial kind of fellow. Generous with his money too."

"Will I now?"

O'Connor laughs. The chemist shakes his head and goes back to pressing pills. After a minute, the door chimes and a young woman comes in, a factory hand in a grubby blue gown with a scarf over her head seeking something for her pounding headaches. The chemist asks her some questions, then mixes up a bottle and charges her a shilling. When she is gone, O'Connor gets up from the chair and puts his jacket and hat back on. He is feeling restless and the heat and smell of the place are making him queasy.

"I'm going outside for a spell," he says. "Walk about, get some air."

CHAPTER 19

When Riley returns, unobserved by James O'Connor, to the room above O'Shaughnessy's, it is just past nine o'clock. Peter Rice is snoozing openmouthed by the fireplace amid a scattered wreckage of dinner plates, newspapers, and teacups. Riley shakes him awake and explains what he has learned on his travels. Rice listens, then sits up straighter in his chair and asks him to repeat it over again, but more gradually.

"And you're sure of all this?" he says when Riley has finished.

Riley nods.

"About as sure as I can be."

"If it's true, then we've both been made to look like fools," Rice says.

Riley nods again and grimaces.

"I can't hardly believe it myself," he says. "I truly can't."

"And where has he got to now?"

"We don't know that, but there are some boys out looking. When they find him, they'll bring him direct to the tannery. That's what I told them to do."

Peter Rice shifts about, scowls, and reaches for his pipe.

"Of all the fucken nonsense," he says. "Of all the fucken, fucken nonsense."

"I know, Peter. It's a great surprise to me, I can tell you."

"You should never have believed him in the first place. Lad walks in from nowhere, why would you give him any credence at all? Why would you offer him the time of fucken day?"

"There was that thing with the peeler. That was what warmed me to him."

"Jesus Christ."

"It could be a coincidence still. You never know."

"O'Connor's nephew? It's not a fucken coincidence. It can't be. Not after what happened with Doyle last night."

"So what will we do?"

Rice stands up and paces about the room, blowing out gouts of blue pipe smoke and scratching at his bristled head as if he has a dose of the scrofula.

"Is anyone watching Jimmy O'Connor? If the lad suspects something, that's where he'll run to first."

"He can't suspect anything," Riley says. "Not so soon."

"What about Doyle and the others? Any sign yet of them?"

"Nothing yet. They're all away and gone if you want my opinion."

Rice turns and gives Riley a furious stare.

"I don't," he says. "After this, you'll forgive me, Jack, if I leave your opinion where it fucken stands."

Riley shrugs and makes a contrite face.

"He fooled us all," he says. "He's a smart little bastard and that's the truth."

Rice sits back down in his chair. He rubs ash from his trouser leg and shakes his head.

"They must think we're awful stupid, sending in a boy."

"They got lucky, that's all. It was a pure accident he found out about the plan."

"I hate a fucken traitor," Rice says. "There's nothing I

hate more. The enemy is the enemy, you know where you stand, but a traitor is something else. Like a creeping disease. Like something rotting away inside that you don't even know about until it's too late."

"Two-faced bastards," Riley says.

"We need to find out what else he knows, and what else he's told them, then we need to show them that there's a price to be fucken paid."

"The boys will find him soon enough," Riley says. "I'm sure of it. He'll be out drinking somewhere."

Rice nods and gnaws his bottom lip in ponderment.

"Then we'll get over to the tannery now and wait," he says. "I want to be standing right there when they bring the bastard in."

They leave through the back entrance. Into the yard, past the outhouse, and then through the gate and out to the cindered alleyway. The alleyway is dark and Rice stumbles once and curses. Riley, a few feet ahead, waits for him to catch up.

"We can find a cab at New Cross," he says. "Save time."

"We'll walk it," Rice says. "I've been sitting up there on my arse all day long."

They're walking down Angel Street with St. Michael's churchyard on the right when they hear someone calling Rice's name from the other side of the waist-high wall. They glance at each other quickly, then turn to look.

"Who's there?" Rice shouts back. "Who wants me?"

There's no answer. Wind rattles the branches of the birch trees. The church's square tower looms gray against the cloud-streaked blackness of the sky. They can see to the first crooked line of gravestones but no farther.

"I can't see a fucken thing," Riley says.

"Who's there?" Rice calls again.

After a moment, Patrick Neary steps out from the shadows and nods at them both.

"Just me, Peter," he says.

"Where's Doyle? Is he with you? Is he back there now?"

Neary shakes his head.

"He's not here, but I'll take you to him. He wants to talk."

Neary steps closer so they can see he is alone, and holds out his hands so they can see they are empty.

"What does he want to talk to me about?" Rice says.

"He needs your help to get away. There are peelers everywhere now. The town's gone mad after what happened last night."

"I heard he thinks I'm the one who told on him."

"He's not worrying much about who told on him. He just wants to get away safe. He doesn't want to end up hanged like the others were."

"Well, you can tell him it wasn't me who did it, but we know who it was. We just found out."

Neary nods but doesn't answer.

"Why didn't you run when you had the chance?" Riley asks him. "After you shot the fellow? You could all be on a boat to Dublin by now."

"Things didn't go like we planned," Neary says.

Riley snorts.

"Trying to shoot the fucken mayor and you end up killing a peeler instead? I'd say they didn't."

"If Stephen Doyle needs my help, he can come to me direct," Rice says. "I'll be at the tannery. We're going there now."

Neary frowns and shakes his head.

"Too dangerous. There'll be people out on every corner keeping watch. I'm taking a big risk myself just being here with you."

"Then tell us where Doyle's hiding, and we'll go there ourselves."

Neary shakes his head again.

"I can't do that, Peter," he says.

Rice looks back at him and nods.

"So that's how it is, then."

"He just wants to talk awhile."

"You tell him to come to the tannery. I'll be waiting for him there."

Rice gives Neary another look, then turns and starts to walk away. Riley falls in beside him.

"You did the clever thing there," he whispers. "That's a fucken trap if ever I smelt one. I never trusted that Neary much, never liked the look of him."

"Is he following after us?" Rice says.

Riley looks around to check.

"The shadows are too thick. I can't exactly see what he's doing."

"How did they know we'd be passing this way?" Rice says. "Did you think of that?"

Riley frowns.

"How did they?"

"Because they've been watching us all day, that's how."

Riley stops walking for a moment and opens his mouth to make a comment, but Rice grabs his arm and tugs him onward. A few seconds later, a hansom pulls up to the curb just ahead of them, and a thin man in dark clothes gets out and looks about. Neither Rice nor Riley recognizes him. He turns away from them and reaches into his pocket, and when he turns back they see he is holding a pistol. He raises the pistol and tells them to stop where they are.

"And who the fuck are you?" Riley asks.

Before the man can answer, Neary comes in from behind and hits Riley across the back of the head with a bludgeon. Riley drops onto his knees, groaning, and Neary leans over and hits him again. The man with the pistol tells Rice to put his hands in the air and Neary handcuffs him, then they put a flour sack over his head and push him inside the cab. It is all over in a moment, and there are no witnesses except for Riley, who is lying facedown, unconscious and bleeding on the pavement. As the cab drives away, a cat shrieks in the bushes nearby, and the churchyard clock, like a slow-witted child, slowly counts its way up to ten.

CHAPTER 20

———⟫•⟪———

The Old Fleece is just around the corner from the chemist's shop. O'Connor steps inside and asks the barman for a tuppenny ale and a tot of rum. *I won't stay here long,* he thinks, *but the watching is tedious work and a drink inside me will help the time pass quicker.* He finishes the rum in two swallows, then takes the ale and sits down at a table. He gazes at the fire for several minutes—orange flames stuttering and curling between the pitch-black coals—then takes a long sup of the ale, licks his lips, and sighs. If he closes his eyes, the world disappears completely, but when he opens them again it surges back into him, all the colors and the noises, like water bursting through a dike. The men at the next table are arguing about the price of bacon. He takes another long drink, and then another one. The pint glass is empty now and, realizing this, he feels suddenly lost and alone.

He notices a woman standing up at the bar talking to the barman. Her round cheeks are shiny in the gaslight and her brown eyes are bright and full of pleasure. The two of them are laughing. O'Connor puts his empty glass down on the bar and the barman asks him if he'll take another one.

"No, thank you," he says. "I should be getting back now."

The woman turns to look at him and smiles as if they already know each other.

"One more won't hurt," she says. "Least it never hurt me none."

"And you're a fine example to follow, aren't you?" the barman says.

The woman makes a face at him and waves him off.

"You have yourself another one anyhow," she says, giving O'Connor a friendly look and touching him lightly on the forearm. "I'm sure you must deserve it."

"I'll have a rum," he says.

The barman turns and reaches for the bottle. O'Connor leans forward to check what the woman is drinking.

"And another gin."

She smiles and thanks him. She has a broad face, almost square, and lively, wide-set eyes. She is about as tall as Catherine was, O'Connor thinks, but thicker in the shoulders and the waist. Her sleeves are rolled up to the elbow and her forearms are smattered with freckles and have a faint fledge of yellow hair. She says her name is Mary.

The barman pours the two drinks and moves away.

"I haven't seen you before, have I?" she says.

O'Connor shakes his head.

"This is my first time in here."

"Makes a change to see a handsome face."

Her hair is brown and wavy and held back with a wooden comb. She has a scrim of dirt under one thumbnail and silver hoops in both her ears. There is a small U-shaped scar on her chin. He knows what she is but doesn't mind. She is pretty, he thinks, blurred and worn away at the edges, but not so dulled or desperate-looking as some.

"Do you work in the mills? Most of the fellows who drink in here work in the mills, either the mills or the Smithfield market."

"I don't work in the mills or the market. I'm a detective."

Her eyes briefly widen.

"Are you out looking for someone now? Is that what you're doing?"

"I was," he says, "but I'm not looking anymore. I'm resting from my labors for a while."

"Then you're just like everyone else in here."

O'Connor smiles at the idea.

"Perhaps you're right."

"You look sad, but I know a way to cheer you up."

"I'm not sad," he says, "just tired."

"You work too hard."

She's right, he thinks. *I work too hard and all for what? However hard I work, the crimes will never end. If Doyle is caught and killed, there will be someone else and someone else again. There is no true and lasting order, no law beneath it all, just urge and counter-urge forever. Why not step away, then, surrender, accept that I'm just a man, stupid and simple like everyone else, thrashing around in the darkness looking for pleasure wherever it can be found? There's no shame in that,* he thinks, *no shame in being human.*

There is a pause, then he nods and raises his glass, and she raises hers. She smiles again and looks him in the eye, direct and unashamed, as if there is some strange secret absence hidden deep inside, which she is pledged to fill.

Later on, after they've drunk some more, they go back to her narrow room on Diggle's Court. Mary lights a candle stub and puts more coal on the fire, then undresses herself quickly and gets under the blankets. Her movements are cheerful and careless. Her flesh, in the frail yellow light, looks sheer and unsullied, like something more imagined than real. When O'Connor lies down on the thin mattress and pushes himself into her, it is as if he is slipping out of time altogether, as if the barriers between past, present, and future are dissolving, and all that is left is a shapeless, wordless moment. Afterward, when he returns to himself, to the raw, dull surfaces of his own body and to the dark, depressing angles of the everyday, he feels sick and ashamed, as if he has betrayed a solemn trust. Mary strokes his arm and tells him to be calm. She kisses his cheek and smiles as if nothing has happened and nothing is wrong.

"Whatever it is you're thinking of," she says, "you should just forget it."

"I can't do that," he says.

"You're here now. With me."

"Of course I am," he says. "I know that."

She has soft, rounded shoulders, small, dark-tipped breasts. It would take years to explain everything to her, he thinks, a lifetime or more.

"You can stay if you'd like to," she says. "I won't be going out again tonight."

"Do you have a bottle of something?"

"No, but there's a shop on the corner. If you give me the money, I'll go down."

"I'll go myself," he says.

They talk for a while longer, then he stands up and gets dressed. Outside, the rain repeats itself, low and constant, like the hum of a machine or the words of a prayer. He hears the creak of an ungreased axle, the low, grunting bark of a chained-up dog. The man behind the counter is drowsy and disheveled. He shuffles about the shop, scratching his bald head and mumbling to himself as he goes. O'Connor buys a bottle of gin, a penny loaf of bread, butter, cheese, and a quarter ounce of tobacco. The man asks if he wants the gin wrapped up with the rest or left separate, and O'Connor says left separate will be fine. He puts the bottle in his pocket, pays what he owes, and walks back to the room with the brown paper parcel under his arm. Mary is lying as he left her. When he comes in, she turns to look at him and smiles.

"Will you come back to bed now?" she asks.

"I will in just a minute."

The candle is on the mantelpiece and the fire is still glowing, but the rest of the room is sunk in thick shadow. He puts the parcel on top of the dresser, unwraps it, and cuts two slices of bread from the loaf with his clasp knife. He spreads butter on the bread and gives one slice to Mary, then cuts the piece of cheese in two and gives her half of it.

"That's good," she says. "I've hardly et all day."

Smiling, she folds the slice, bites into the fold, then chews and swallows. O'Connor twists the cork from the bottle and drinks. The hot taste takes him by surprise and makes him cough. He passes the bottle across and Mary drinks from it, then gives it back to him. She wipes butter and crumbs from her mouth with the back of her hand and pushes a loose strand of hair behind one ear. He notices a kidney-shaped bruise, rough-edged and almost black, high up on her arm, as if someone has grabbed or punched her there.

"Does that hurt you?" he asks.

She shrugs.

"It's nothing," she says. "Just some fellow who got out of hand."

He cuts two more slices of bread and spreads them thickly with the butter.

"Jesus. We're the king and queen tonight, aren't we?" she says.

"I'd say we are."

He undresses again and gets back into the bed beside her. She smells warm and musty, and when they kiss he can taste the gin in her mouth. He has forgotten about Tib Street already, and about Stephen Doyle. This room is become a world itself, complete and entire, and whatever lies outside—the buildings and people, the dark, extended earth and weeping sky—has no more substance than a dream.

"Are you feeling better now?" she asks him. "You looked low before. As if you had something else on your mind."

"I'm well," he says. "That was nothing that a good drink won't cure."

"A good drink will cure most things," she agrees. "That's the truth."

He reaches down between her legs. She pushes against him, then stretches and sighs and rolls on top. The second time, it is the same as the first, except easier and more familiar, as if they are old friends now and everything important between them is understood and accepted. When it's over, they drink down the remains of the gin and fall asleep, their four pale limbs warped and wefted together like threads on a loom.

CHAPTER 21

O'Connor is woken by the clangor of factory bells. He gulps down water from the metal jug, then dresses himself slowly and gets ready to leave. When Mary stirs, he touches her hand and tells her to go back to sleep. Outside, the rain has stopped, but there is a cold, damp wind blowing in from the west. He feels weakened and queasy from the gin, and his mind is muddled. Instead of going home or back to the Town Hall, he walks to the public washhouse on Miller Street and pays sixpence for a bath and a shave. As he lies in the long copper tub, the water hot and hard against his skin, his body feels newly minted. It is as if he has remembered something about himself that had slipped his mind or been covered over by time. *This is my flesh,* he thinks, *these are my bones. Will you look at me now, lying here?*

Afterward, he buys a half-pint of rum at the Turk's Head, then walks to the Spread Eagle Hotel on Hanging Ditch. In the vestibule, he writes a note and asks for it to be given to Rose Flanagan, then orders a pot of coffee and sits down in an armchair to wait. He pours rum into the coffee and drinks it; then, after a while, he falls asleep. He dreams that he has committed a great crime and is about to be punished for it, but he can't remember what the crime was, or what the punishment will be. When he wakes up, Rose is standing in front of him with her hand on his shoulder. Her face is pale and angular and her green eyes are shining. She complains that he should not trouble her at work like this, and that she will get a bad reputation if Mr. Bryant, the hotel manager, ever hears that a policeman has been asking to speak to her. She asks him what is so important, anyway, and he tells her he can't explain it all right now, but there is no reason for her to be concerned. They arrange to meet in the same place they went to before.

As he waits alone in the tearoom, O'Connor remembers Mary again, her smell and her softness, and wonders what Rose Flanagan would think of him if she knew. In Dublin, before he was married to Catherine, he had friends, other policemen, who would go to Mrs. Gleeson's place on Duke Street on Saturday nights after drinking in the Crown, but he never went with them, even though they asked him to more than once. He would go back to the barracks on his own instead and read a book or spit-and-polish his boots. They would laugh about it afterward and ask him if he was practicing to join the priesthood. Perhaps he thought he was better than they were, or perhaps he was just afraid. Back then he was still so young, his mind was full of thoughts and feelings he didn't understand. Now he is older and everything is clear and visible. There are no mysteries left to fathom, no hidden truths. He must take whatever kindness he can find and be grateful for it.

When she arrives, Rose looks at him impatiently and asks again what it is he needs to talk about that couldn't wait until her work is over for the day.

"I'm giving up the police," he says. "Resigning my post. It's not right for me anymore, and I'm not right for it. I wanted to tell you first."

"I hope it's not because of what happened with our Tommy. I told you before, it wasn't your fault and you shouldn't blame yourself."

"It's not that, no."

She looks at him more carefully. She sees there is something different about him now, in his eyes and the way he moves his hands, something softer and less certain.

"You're just tired of it all, then. Is that it? Had enough."

"Did you hear that another policeman was killed the night before last, a man named Frank Malone? He was shot on Milk Street."

"Of course. It's all over the newspapers."

"I was there when it happened, standing not ten feet away." He points to the bloodstains on the arm of his coat and Rose stares and looks amazed.

"If you were there, you could have been shot yourself then," she says. "Isn't that right?"

"I believed I would be. The man held his gun up to my head, but he didn't pull the trigger. I'm here by blind luck, more than anything."

When he stirs his tea, she sees his hand is shaking. She can smell the drink coming off him and guesses what it must mean. She is touched to see him like this—reduced and made vulnerable—when before he has always tried so hard to be stern and sure.

"You're wondering why I took you away from your work to tell you all this, I suppose," he says. "Asking yourself what difference it makes."

"You've seen a terrible thing," she says. "A man killed right in front of your eyes."

"When we talked before, I had the feeling you were someone I could trust. You've lost your brother, and I've lost my wife. It's not the same thing, I know that, of course. Not the same thing at all, but perhaps not so very different either."

She shrugs and offers him a guarded smile.

"It can't be changed. None of it can be changed. It must be suffered, that's all. That's what my mother tells me every day, and she's right."

"But better not to suffer it alone. If possible. Wouldn't you agree?"

"Of course," she says. "A trouble shared."

They look at each other for a moment across the table, then O'Connor looks away. It's raining outside, and the light coming through the window is murky and spare.

"What will you do now?" she asks him. "If you've given up your post with the police. Where will you go to?"

He shakes his head as if she has asked him the wrong question.

"I wish I could have helped you with that money," he says. "That fifty pounds you needed. I wish I could've done more."

"That doesn't matter now," she says. "We'll manage somehow, I'm sure."

He nods, then sighs and rubs his face.

"I can still help you, Rose," he says. "If you'll let me. There are other ways. Better ways. We can help each other if we want to. Don't you see?"

He reaches for her hand across the table, grips it for a moment, then lets it go again.

Rose looks down at the bland surface of her half-drunk cup of tea. Twin dots of crimson appear on her cheekbones. She shakes her head, then looks back at him but doesn't answer.

He wonders if he has made a mistake already, misunderstood something vital. He has never been clever when it comes to women, except for Catherine. And even with Catherine, he made blunders, was forgetful, took things the wrong way as often as not.

"It's marriage that I mean," he says.

"I know what you mean."

There is a pause as O'Connor looks at Rose, and Rose looks across the room. She wonders why she is so surprised by his offer, why she didn't see it coming and prepare herself better.

"What do you think of me?" he asks.

She takes a moment to gather herself before answering.

"That's no kind of question," she says.

"Tell me."

"I think you're a kind man and clever and quite handsome, but sad as well. And I think you're very upset about that terrible murder you saw, and you've been up all night, and you've taken a drink, and now you don't even understand what you're saying to me."

"I do understand what I'm saying."

"How would we live if we were married? Where would we go?"

"Wherever you wanted to go."

"I can smell the drink coming off you, Jimmy."

"That's nothing," he says. "Really. Just something to steady my nerves."

She shakes her head.

"I have to get back to my work now, or they'll get angry and dock me the time."

As they stand up together, the teacups rattle in their saucers, and the chair legs scrape against the floor. O'Connor looks confused, upset, and Rose feels sorry for him despite his clumsiness.

"Will you think on it, at least?" he asks.

"Come to see me next Sunday after mass," she says. "Come to the house. My mother sleeps in the afternoon, so we can talk then without being disturbed."

"If you don't want it, I understand. I won't blame you."

"Come on Sunday, please," she says. "That'll give me time to think."

———

In the afternoon, he goes back to the detective office and returns Barton's pistol to the gun safe. A little later, while he is sitting at a table in the recreation room writing out his letter of resignation, Fazackerley sees him there and walks briskly across. He waits for O'Connor to look up before he begins to speak.

"What time did Peter Rice leave the room above O'Shaughnessy's shop?" he says. "And where did he go to afterward? Wherever it was, I'm assuming you must have followed him there."

"I don't know where he went or when he left. I wasn't watching."

"You took over from Barton. He just told me all about it. He says you told him I'd sent you. You also took his gun away from him."

"I only stayed in the chemist's until nine o'clock, then I went to the Old Fleece for a drink. I was intending to go back to the chemist's, but I never did."

"So there was no one watching all the rest of the night? Stephen Doyle could have appeared and done a jig in the street outside and we'd be none the wiser?"

"You might ask the chemist fellow what he saw."

"Where were you, Jimmy?"

"It doesn't matter where I was. I'm resigning from my post now, so that'll be the end of it."

He shows him the letter and Fazackerley reads it and swears and gives it back. His face is red with rage.

"If that bastard Doyle gets away from us, it's on your conscience now," he says.

"There's a good deal on there already. I'm not sure you'll find much extra room."

He can hear Fazackerley breathing hard beside him, but

he doesn't look up. He finishes the letter and signs and folds it.

"Will you give this to Maybury for me?" he says. "I'll write another one to Dublin Castle later."

Fazackerley turns the letter over in his hands.

"You don't need to do this, Jimmy," he says. "You made a bad mistake all right, but we can find some way around it. If you write a report to say you were there watching all night, I'll sign it, and we'll forget about the rest."

O'Connor shakes his head.

"I asked Rose Flanagan to marry me this morning. She said she'd think on it and give me an answer next week. If she says yes, we'll go back to Dublin together. I'll find another job there."

Fazackerley stares at him, then closes his eyes and draws his hands slowly down his cheeks as if applying an unguent.

"Rose Flanagan?" he says quietly. "Tommy Flanagan's sister?"

"It'll be two years come April since Catherine died," O'Connor explains. "Two years is long enough. I have to start again now."

CHAPTER 22

Glasgow. The Clyde.

As the ship moves away from the quayside, the crowded underdecks are filled with the cries of tightly swaddled infants and the smells of saltfish, sweat, and sauerkraut. Stephen Doyle stands alone among the ragged swell of wide-eyed transients—Swedes, Norwegians, Germans, Poles—and remembers himself, a boy of barely thirteen, leaving Ireland for the first time with the houses and the harbor wall of Kingstown shrinking behind him and the empty gray sea ahead getting bigger and bigger every moment. His parents and three brothers were all dead from the typhus and he was filled up to the brim with grief and fear, yet he knew enough not to let it show. If you keep your weaknesses hidden, give them neither light nor air, then soon enough that childish part of you dies and all you are left with is strength. That was the lesson he learned in his youth—that you must murder the softness in yourself, smother it in its cradle, because if you don't, then you will pay the price later on.

He should have killed James O'Connor on Milk Street when he had the chance. He knows that now. So what stopped him? Was it a misjudgment, or something else? That was a clever lie O'Connor told about Peter Rice, and it took some nerve to tell it with a gun pressed against his forehead. He could have killed him afterward, he *should* have. There was no reason not to, but, when the moment came, he held back. Something in the man's eyes, he thinks now, or in his face perhaps, some shade or sadness that gave him pause. Hard to believe. Strange to think of it. How many men has he killed before in his life, pleading sometimes, praying, weeping, begging him on their knees for mercy, without even a second's hesitation? Next time he will know better, though. If their two paths ever cross again, if the opportunity repeats, he won't make the same mistake.

CHAPTER 23

Next morning close to noon, as O'Connor dozes on his bed on George Street, with a volume from the lending library lying open on his chest, there is a hard knocking on the front door and Mrs. Walker, grumbling, shuffles along the hallway to see who it could be. When O'Connor hears the familiar voice, he puts his jacket on and goes downstairs. Fazackerley, standing in the doorway, nods at him but doesn't smile. Whatever friendship they had is in abeyance now.

"They need you over at the Town Hall," he says. "Maybury was dismissed from his post yesterday and Palin's resigned this morning. There's a new fellow just come up from London and he wants to pick your brains."

A cab is waiting for them at the corner. The driver is bundled against the cold and steam is rising from the horse's back and flanks. On the drive to the Town Hall, Fazackerley explains that the men come up from London are arrogant and secretive, and no one knows what they want or what they're thinking.

"What did you tell them about me?" O'Connor asks.

"I told them you'd handed in your resignation yesterday afternoon, and you were no longer a serving detective so

there was no cause to bring you in, but they insisted anyway."

"That's all?"

"They know about the fight with Sanders. And they
talked to Walter Barton already, I believe."

"You think they're looking around for a scapegoat?"

"They might be. If they can't find Stephen Doyle, they'll
need something else for sure. If I were you, I'd stick to the
bare facts. Keep your famous opinions to yourself."

O'Connor nods, then takes a flask from his pocket and
drains it.

They sit in silence after that. Through the fogged windows the world outside comes and goes like slides in a magic
lantern show. They are nearly at King Street when O'Connor
speaks again.

"Do the new fellows from London know about Michael
Sullivan?"

"I told them about Michael, but what'll happen to him
now that Maybury's gone, I couldn't say."

"They should honor Maybury's bargain, that's only
right."

"That's what they should do, but whether they will or
not, who knows?"

O'Connor shakes his head. He remembers Michael sleeping those two nights on the bedroom floor. The grainy, fer-
mented smell of him and the steady rasp of his breathing.
Of all the sins on his head, colluding with Maybury to turn
that boy into a spy might yet be the worst of them.

"You'll need to be the one who talks to him now, instead
of me. Do you remember the sign we use for a meeting?"

"A chalk mark by the lamppost on Long Millgate. I remember it."

"You tell him to be careful when you see him. Not to take
any more chances."

"I might say the very same to you."

———

The man from London is short and heavyset with sloping shoulders and a thick, bullish neck. His dark hair is oiled sideways, and his newly razored jowls are pink and damp as sausage meat. His name, he says, is Inspector Robert Thompson and he reports direct to Colonel Percy Feilding, head of the Special Investigative Unit.

"You'll know Colonel Feilding's reputation as a Fenian hunter from your time in Dublin, I suppose."

O'Connor nods. He remembers the name.

"The colonel will remain down in London, but I'm here in his place. I'll be in charge of the Detective Division until they find a more permanent replacement for Superintendent Maybury."

They are seated in Maybury's old office. The room is warm and smells of cigar smoke and old sweat. There are boxes and papers piled up on every available surface.

"I resigned my post yesterday," O'Connor says. "I believe Sergeant Fazackerley explained."

"And if you hadn't resigned so promptly, you would almost certainly have been dismissed," Thompson says. "That's what he told me."

He picks up a sheet of paper from the pile in front of him and reads from it.

"Drunk on duty, assaulting a fellow officer, disobeying a direct order, taking a firearm without permission."

He puts the paper down and looks at O'Connor.

"That makes it sound like something bigger than it was," O'Connor says.

"Is that so?"

O'Connor nods. It is best to say as little as possible, he thinks. The more he says, the longer they will keep him here.

"Tell me what happened when Frank Malone was killed."

"You can read it all in my report. It's somewhere among those papers, I'm sure."

"What did Stephen Doyle say to you exactly?"

"He asked me who the traitor was and I told him it was Peter Rice."

"You think he believed you?"

"I'm not sure."

"But he didn't shoot you."

"No. If he'd have shot me, I expect I'd be dead."

"So he must have believed you?"

"Perhaps."

"He could have shot you anyway, of course. Even if he did believe you. That would have been safer all around. No witnesses."

"He's not that kind of man."

"Not that kind of man?" Thompson looks surprised. He puts his pen down and leans forward a little. "Then what kind of a man is he? In your opinion, I mean?"

O'Connor hesitates.

"I couldn't really say."

"You spoke to him face-to-face. What was that like?"

"I thought I was going to be killed. I was sure of it."

Thompson nods and makes a careful note, as if the answer interests him.

"He held that gun up to your head, but he didn't kill you, so whatever you said to him, it must have been the right thing to say."

"I already told you what I said."

"The man's a murderer, a pitiless assassin. Yet when he has you at his mercy, he lets you go."

"He was there to kill the mayor, not me."

"Is it because you're both Irish? Is that it? Did he hear the brogue and change his mind?"

O'Connor smiles at the idea.

Thompson's face darkens. He looks suddenly enraged.

"A man's dead and you sit there smiling," he says.

"I know what happened. That's not why I'm smiling."

Thompson gazes back at him without answering, as if challenging him to speak again, but O'Connor stays quiet.

"A policeman is dead," Thompson continues eventually, "and the man who murdered him appears to have escaped scot free. I'm new to the city, so perhaps there's something I've missed. But I'm wondering how that could have happened exactly. I'm wondering who helped him get away."

"It would be easy enough to escape from Manchester if they had any kind of plan in place. We can't check every road and railway station. It's impossible."

Thompson nods and writes another note. His anger has disappeared as quickly as it came and O'Connor wonders if it was ever real or just a feint.

"Tell me about the notebook," he says.

"Someone cut the pages. They attacked me near the Gaythorn Bridge. Knocked me senseless."

"And why didn't you report the missing pages immediately?"

"I didn't realize they were gone."

"Until the next day?"

"That's right."

"And when you realized they were gone, it was too late. The informers were already dead."

O'Connor nods.

"What did you think of Tommy Flanagan? Did you like him?"

"You don't have to like them."

"So you weren't the least bit troubled when he was killed?"

"I felt responsible for his murder."

Thompson looks surprised by this suggestion.

"You were attacked without warning, you told me, knocked unconscious. What else could you have done?"

"I might have realized sooner that the notebook had been

tampered with, but I was distracted. The morning after the attack, my nephew arrived unexpectedly from America."

Thompson turns over a sheet of paper and puts his finger on the name.

"Michael Sullivan?" he says.

"That's right."

"Who was the man who attacked you?"

"I never saw him before. I know most of the Manchester Fenians by sight, but I didn't recognize that one."

"And there were no other witnesses to this attack?"

Thompson hesitates before the word *attack* as if its meaning might yet be in question, as if the attack might not have been an actual attack at all. O'Connor understands he is being goaded now, that Thompson would like him to lose his temper, say more than he wants to. He doesn't believe they will do him any real harm, despite what Fazackerley said, but he is already tired of the game.

"Shouldn't you be out looking for Stephen Doyle instead of wasting your time with me?"

"You just told me Stephen Doyle had escaped already."

"I told you he could have escaped."

"Do you know where he is?"

"No more than you do."

Thompson gives back an agnostic half-smile.

"I don't know too much. That's why I'm asking these questions. Manchester's all new to me, I just came up from London yesterday on the train, but you've been here nearly a year now. Time to make all kinds of friendships, I'd say."

They look at each other again.

"Did anyone else see what happened on Gaythorn Bridge?"

"It was late at night. Dark. There was no one else around, but plenty of people saw the bruises afterward. You can ask Fazackerley about that, and Maybury too."

"A man can get himself injured in different kinds of ways,

I suppose. You drink a little too much whiskey one night, for instance, say the wrong thing to the wrong fellow, and the next thing you know . . ."

"I wasn't drinking then," O'Connor tells him.

"But you're drinking now, aren't you? I can smell it on you."

He tilts his head back and sniffs the air to emphasize the point.

"I'm not on duty," O'Connor says. "I'm not even a policeman any longer."

Thompson nods his head in agreement. The coal shifts and rustles in the grate.

"I've known enough drunkards in my time to form a clear opinion about that way of life. Do you want to know what my opinion is?"

Thompson waits, as if he expects O'Connor to answer yes or no, but O'Connor says nothing.

"My opinion is that the man who drinks to excess is too feeble to face life as it is. He lacks courage and character. He's also, typically, a liar. So, you see, when you sit there smelling of liquor at noon and telling me you don't know where the murderer Stephen Doyle is hiding or how he escaped, I don't assume, based on my previous encounters with men of your type, that what you're saying should necessarily be believed."

"I was attacked near the Gaythorn Bridge. They cut pages from my notebook and used the information they found to kill two men. Why would I lie about that?"

"Without any witnesses, I have only your word for what happened, or didn't happen, by the bridge. We know that the informers were betrayed, and we know that you were injured somehow, but that's all. The story about the attack and the notebook hardly rings true. I think it's more likely that you were threatened or persuaded by the Fenians and you gave up the names of the spies. You knew you would lose your position if the truth ever came out, so you made up a story to cover yourself. Then after that first lie, of course, the Fenians effectively had you in their power."

"That makes no sense," O'Connor says. "If I was working with the Fenians, why would I prevent them from killing the mayor?"

"It makes perfect sense. You didn't want Maybury to use your nephew as a spy, but Maybury insisted. That put you in a difficult place. If you tell the Fenians about it, what will they do? Possibly they'll kill Michael Sullivan, since they're fond of killing spies, but even if they choose not to kill him, you can't expect them to just play along and pretend they don't know who he is and what he's there for. So you decide to keep it a secret from them. After all, any information Sullivan gets will go through you and so you will be able to make sure nothing comes of it. Unfortunately for you, when Sullivan hears about the assassination plot he doesn't just tell you, he writes it down. I'm guessing Frank Malone read the note before he delivered it. You claim now that it was your idea to go to Milk Street, but more likely it was his alone. You tried to stop him, I expect, but he wouldn't listen. Then Malone is killed by Doyle, and you walk away entirely unharmed. I don't know everything you said to him, but part of it was a promise to help him escape from Manchester, I'm certain of that."

He is testing me out, O'Connor thinks, *seeing if I weaken any. The story is just wild guesswork, but he thinks if he scares me enough I might tell him something else he can use against me.*

"I know what you're about. You've lost Stephen Doyle and you can't put a fine gentleman like Palin in the dock, so you need someone else to blame. I'm not perfect, I have sins on my head as much as any man, but I did my duty and there are plenty around here can testify to that."

"I wouldn't be so sure," Thompson says. "The fellows I've

spoke to don't hold you in high regard. They don't like your manners or the things you say. They're not certain you can be trusted."

"Speak to Fazackerley, then. He's the one who knows me best."

"Sergeant Fazackerley says you've lost your way. He doesn't know what's got into you of late."

"He knows I'm not a traitor."

Thompson lets that question hang for a moment before speaking again.

"You're a smart enough fellow, O'Connor," he says. "But you're not nearly as smart as you think you are. Did you really believe you could just resign your post and walk away from all this?"

O'Connor's head is beginning to throb. Is this what he expected when he came into the room? This persistence? He can't rightly remember. The cab ride from George Street already feels like something that happened months before. He wishes he could lie down somewhere and rest his eyes, but Thompson shows no sign of letting up. He is pleased with himself, O'Connor can tell, proud to have been chosen to clean the mess that other, lesser men have made. Beneath the calm surface, there is something brutal and relentless about him. He will do what is needed to satisfy whoever sent him here. He will find a truth, and if no truth exists, he will fashion one to suit.

"Why did you go to Tib Street on the night after the murder when, by all accounts, you were blind drunk? Why did you tell Walter Barton, falsely, that you had been sent as his replacement?"

"I wanted to get my revenge on Stephen Doyle, and I thought it possible he would come there looking for Peter Rice. I was angry about what had happened to Frank Malone."

"Yet, after only an hour, you abandoned your post, and

you were not seen again until the next day when you came in here to tender your resignation."

"I got tired of waiting. I went into the Old Fleece for a drink, then I spent the night with a woman. Her name is Mary Chandler and she lives on Diggle's Court. If you go there, you'll find her easily enough. She'll tell you where I was."

"This Mary Chandler is a whore, I assume?"

O'Connor nods.

"And how often do you see her?"

"That was the first time."

Thompson gives him a disbelieving look, then starts to write it down. His hand moves slowly across the page; he sniffs occasionally and pauses between sentences to be sure he's got it right.

"Is she Irish?" he asks.

"She's English. She has nothing to do with Doyle or the Fenians. Nothing at all."

"So she wasn't important. That's what you're saying. Just something to do after the real business of the evening was finished with? After you'd got rid of Walter Barton, and left Peter Rice free to carry out the plan?"

"What plan are you talking about?"

Thompson puts down his pen, leans forward, and blows across the page to dry it.

"The escape plan. I don't know just what agreement you came to with Stephen Doyle," he says, "but I know you went out of your way to make sure that no one was watching that butcher's shop on Tib Street."

"They were only watching it in the first place because of me, because I told Doyle that Rice was the one who betrayed him."

Thompson nods.

"The plan must have changed," he says, "or something unexpected happened. Peter Rice was supposed to distract us, that's clear to see, but then at the last minute he was needed, I'm guessing, so you had to find some way to get rid of whoever was watching him. The Fenians must have contacted you that afternoon, told you what to do, threatened you too most probably. Is that what started you drinking again?"

O'Connor rubs his face and stares down at the floor. Has the decision already been made, he wonders, has he been singled out as the one to take the blame? He tells himself that can't be true. The Londoners have not had enough time. But even the possibility scares him. As he sits there silently, he feels his strength and willpower seeping out through the pores of his skin like sweat.

"I was shaken by Malone's death. I was in distress. I needed something to calm my nerves. That's why I took a drink. The only reason."

"You felt guilty, I expect, because you knew Malone would likely be shot, but you chose not to warn him?"

"What happened that night was an accident. I didn't know he would be shot."

"You went in there unarmed. What did you imagine you would find?"

"It was a mistake," he says quietly. "I made a mistake, that's all."

Thompson looks at his pocket watch, then stands up and walks over to the door.

"We'll keep you here while we make more inquiries," he says. "There's a room upstairs that's empty. You can wait in there. I'll put a constable outside."

"I have other business to see to today. I can't stay here."

"I could arrest you now and put you down in the cells. But the cells are still full of Fenians, so I'd prefer to avoid that course."

"You have no witnesses," O'Connor says, "no evidence at

all to back you up. No magistrate would take your story seriously as it is."

"That's why you'll stay here until more inquiries are carried out. If we find nothing else against you, then you'll be free to go."

He turns the brass handle and pulls the door ajar. There is a man in uniform, whom O'Connor doesn't recognize, waiting in the corridor outside. O'Connor gets up to leave. He is angry but also afraid. If the truth is all he has for protection, he knows it may not be enough.

"You're wrong about me," he says. He is standing close enough that he can smell the oily sweetness of Thompson's pomade. "I'm no more a traitor than you are."

"If you're not a traitor, then you're a great fool," Thompson answers calmly. "We'll find out which it is soon enough, I promise you that."

CHAPTER 24

O'Connor is left alone for the rest of the afternoon. The room is empty aside from two bentwood chairs, a lop-sided table, and several tea chests filled with broken boots and old uniforms. The narrow window looks out onto the gabled roof of the York Hotel. O'Connor sits on one of the chairs and smokes his pipe to pass the time. Occasionally, he stands up and walks around the perimeter of the room, then sits down again and groans, or keeps his eyes closed for minutes at a time as if trying to fall asleep. There is no fire in the grate and he is cold, but he doesn't ask the constable standing outside for coal. He tells himself that this will be over soon enough. The other detectives may not like or trust him much, but he doesn't believe they will go so far as to lie, and Fazackerley will speak up for him, he is sure. When Thompson finds there is nothing solid to support his notions, he will start to look elsewhere. He thinks of Rose Flanagan again and feels a sadness and a yearning out of proportion to the depth and duration of their acquaintance. When he thinks of her, he knows he is also thinking of Catherine and he wonders if he should be embarrassed or ashamed of this fact, and whether he is betraying his dead wife's memory in some way,

by allowing it to merge with these feelings for another woman
who is young and still alive.

The sky outside is turning dark when Fazackerley pays
his visit. He is carrying a metal tray with soup and bread
and a mug of tea. When he sees the condition of the room,
he goes back out into the corridor and orders the constable
to fetch a bucket of coal and an oil lamp from downstairs,
then he puts the tray on the table, wipes the loose dirt off
the empty chair with his forearm, and sits down. O'Connor
blows on the soup, picks up the dented spoon, and starts to
eat. He gazes at the mug of tea and fervently wishes it were
something else.

"Are the fellows up from London all like him?" he says.

"I'd say Thompson's the worst, but not by much."

"You've heard what he accused me of?"

"He's been in the parade room asking his questions, so
everyone knows by now. I've told him it's all a nonsense."

The soup is hot and salty. As O'Connor eats, pale lumps
of turnip and pieces of gristly meat bob to its surface like
jetsam on a brown and greasy tide. He dips the bread in the
lees and gobbles it down, then puts the bowl up to his lips
and drains the final drops. He didn't know he was so hungry; since the interview with Thompson, he has been in a
daze.

"What about the others?" he asks. "What did they tell
him?"

"They've told him all they saw and heard, but that doesn't
amount to much. There are a few of them would be happy
enough to see you in jail, but they're not stupid enough to
perjure themselves to get you there. I'd say Thompson will
come to his senses soon enough and realize he's wasting his
time. If you stay patient and hold your tongue, you'll likely
be out of here tonight."

O'Connor thanks him and the two men shake hands.

Fazackerley stands up and looks around the dim room as if committing its modest dimensions to memory.

"Those cockney fellows don't worry me," he says. "I've seen their kind before. They'll be gone soon enough. Then things will get back to the way they always were."

"Except without me," O'Connor says.

Fazackerley shrugs and looks off at an angle.

"You were always a visitor here, Jimmy," he says. "We both know that."

The constable comes back in with the bucket of coal and the oil lamp, and they watch as he lays a fire in the grate and lights it. O'Connor wishes, for a moment, that he had told Fazackerley more about himself, more about Catherine and the child they lost and the different ways they suffered afterward, but he realizes it is too late for that now. When Fazackerley remembers him in the future, he thinks, he will remember him only as the man who was there on the night Frank Malone was killed, the one who lost his head afterward and had to resign before he was dismissed. The rest of it will quickly be forgotten.

The fire has taken hold and the soft warmth of it makes him drowsy. He smokes another pipe, then falls asleep in the chair. He is woken, hours later, by voices coming from the corridor and the rattle and creak of the knob being turned and the door being pushed open. He is expecting Thompson, or one of his men, come to tell him he is free to leave, but it is Sanders standing there instead, poised and rigid. He is bare-headed and collarless, and his shirtsleeves are rolled up to his elbow. His pinched face is a sour medley of amusement and disdain.

"You're to come with me, O'Connor," he says. "I'm to take you down to the cells."

O'Connor hears more sounds of movement from the corridor and wonders who else is waiting outside, and what they are doing. He wonders if Thompson knows that Sanders is here, or whether this is a joke they have thought up by themselves.

"Who sent you?" O'Connor asks him.

"Inspector Thompson. I'm following his orders. He wants you in the cells."

"I won't go to the cells. I haven't been arrested, so there's no cause to lock me up."

"You'll be arrested when the time is right."

O'Connor shakes his head.

"Where's Fazackerley?"

"Fazackerley's gone home."

"I'll talk to Thompson direct, then. We can go down to his office now."

"My orders are to take you to the cells."

"I won't go down there. I already told you that."

He senses Sanders' agitation, his fretful eagerness to do whatever is planned and his fear that he will lose the opportunity, through some complication or trickery, that the moment will be stolen from him.

"We all know what you are," Sanders says. "You had Maybury fooled, but Maybury's gone now, and the new fellows are a sight cleverer than he was. They can see through your lies well enough."

"The stories aren't true. I'm no more a traitor than you are."

Sanders' face suddenly reddens.

"Frank Malone was a friend of mine," he says. "And my good friend was murdered by you filthy Irish bastards. Shot dead, in cold blood. An innocent, unarmed man. So don't you dare accuse me of being a traitor."

The door is pushed open again, and the two men who were waiting outside step into the room. O'Connor recognizes one of them but not the other. The one he recognizes, Payne, another detective, asks Sanders if he needs any help.

"He says he won't go to the cells. Says he wants to see Thompson first."

"We'll put the snaps on him, then," Payne says easily. "Ankles and wrists. Carry him down arse first, if need be. Is that really what you want, though?"

He turns to O'Connor and shows him the handcuffs. Payne is tall and thin, with a crooked nose and narrow eyes. He has a reputation, O'Connor recalls, for laziness and for losing at cards.

"You don't need to use the cuffs," he says. "I'll come willingly."

He puts his pipe in his pocket and stands up from the chair. *Thompson must be running out of ideas,* he thinks. *He's trying to scare me, that's all. It's a joke, a game, which it's wiser to play along with than resist.*

The four men leave the room and walk together along the narrow corridor, then turn right through an open doorway onto a metal staircase painted gray. O'Connor doesn't recognize where they are but guesses they must be in the rear part of the building. They descend into the basement and go through a succession of dim-lit corridors before they reach the cells, then they wait while Sanders goes looking for someone to the unlock the door. There is shouting coming from another room and a strong smell of piss and carbolic. The red brick floor is damp and there are specks of dried-up blood on the green paint below the wainscot.

"Here's the place where a man like you belongs," Payne says, "locked up with all his Fenian friends."

The other man, the one O'Connor doesn't recognize, nods and smiles at Payne's remark, then tells O'Connor that if there is any truth or justice in this world, they will hang him for what he's done.

"Who are you?" O'Connor asks him. "What do you know about me?"

"My name's Grayling. I know what I've heard," he says. "And that's all I need to know."

Sanders comes back with a key, and they unlock the door of the empty cell and point him inside. There is a slatted wooden bed to the left and a galvanized pail in the far corner. The gray stucco walls are smeared with filth and gouged with the gnostic mottoes of the recently interred. O'Connor wonders for a moment how it has come to this, then reminds himself that his imprisonment can't last, that Thompson holds no evidence against him, and Fazackerley will be back by morning. Before they close the door, the three men pause to curse at him again and tell him that he is a bastard traitor who will get what he deserves. After they have gone, he curls up on the wooden bed and tries to sleep, but the cold makes him shudder and every now and then a shriek or bellow from the cells nearby jolts him back awake.

The next day, he is given bread and tea at dawn and a bowl of barley soup at noon. The soup is watery and has a urinous tang to it that he tries to ignore but can't. When he complains about the cold, they bring him a brown blanket that is damp. He waits patiently all that afternoon for Fazackerley and when Fazackerley doesn't come, he begins to feel afraid again. He wonders if they are really searching for new evidence against him, as Thompson claimed they would, or if he is being held here out of spite and malice only, as a revenge for his imagined crimes. Who else, besides Sanders, Payne, and Grayling, even knows where he is? And who will look for him if he doesn't reappear? He urges himself to stay calm, to remember that reason and the law still exist somewhere even if he cannot see or sense them. But, compared to the crude truth of his present conditions, such promises feel airy and false, like the vague and threadbare categories of a superseded faith.

There is no candle or lamp in the cell, and the only light creeps in through a narrow pane of glass above the iron door. In the late afternoon of the first day, as he sits on the bed in the three-quarter darkness, holding his knees up to his chest and trying to ignore the stench of the slop pail and the growing aches in his hips, neck, and spine, the door opens and Sanders comes in.

"This is too much," O'Connor tells him. "The joke has gone too far now. You know very well there is no evidence against me, and no good reason to keep me here any longer. I've not even been arrested. You must release me now, immediately."

"Release you?" Sanders laughs as if he has just been told an amusing story. O'Connor notices he is carrying a truncheon in his right hand. There are cake crumbs in his beard and he smells of ale and onions.

"Thompson has all the evidence he needs against you," Sanders tells him cheerfully. "More than enough to see you hanged. They'll be moving you to Belle Vue Prison soon enough."

"You're lying," O'Connor says. "I know you are. I doubt Thompson even knows I'm down here."

"How could he not know? He's the one who ordered it."

"Where's Fazackerley got to? Why has he not come to see me yet?"

"Fazackerley? Fazackerley is under suspicion himself now. He's a good friend of yours, so it's probable he knew what you were doing. There may be others involved also. Maybury? Palin even? We don't know how deep it goes."

O'Connor shakes his head. Such wild inventions are far beyond the nous of a man like Sanders, he knows that, but does that mean Sanders is actually telling the truth or only that someone much cleverer has taught him how to lie?

"I need to talk to Thompson now," he says. "We need to stop this before it goes any further."

"Are you ready to make a confession of your crimes? If you are, I'll take you up there now."

"I have nothing to confess to," O'Connor says. "I'm an innocent man."

Sanders steps forward quickly and, holding the truncheon horizontally with both hands, thrusts it hard up into O'Connor's windpipe. The back of O'Connor's head thuds onto the cell wall, and his eyes begin to bulge. Sanders presses long enough for the first signs of panic to appear on O'Connor's face. Then he steps away again.

"I could break your innocent neck for you," Sanders tells him. "Easy as that. Don't you forget it."

It takes a minute for O'Connor's breathing to settle again. He rubs the feeling back into his throat and jaw and glares at Sanders.

"Why have you come down here?" he says. "What do you want with me?"

Sanders nods once, as if glad of the reminder.

"I need your wallet, your braces, and your boots," he says. "You're a prisoner now, so that's the rule."

O'Connor knows very well that there is no such rule and there never was one but thinks he will not help himself much by arguing the point. There are guards outside, and if he refuses, Sanders will likely take the items from him by force.

"When will I be moved to Belle Vue?" O'Connor asks.

"Whenever it suits us."

If they want to move him, they will have to put him before the magistrate first, he knows, and if they do that, then they will have to let him see a lawyer. He will be out of this limbo, back in the real world.

"Tomorrow?" he suggests.

"Whenever it suits us," Sanders repeats.

He picks up O'Connor's boots, sneers at them for a moment, then holds his hand out for the wallet and braces.

After Sanders leaves, O'Connor lies back down on the slatted bed and closes his eyes. When he wakes again, his ears and throat are burning, and he feels a soreness and swelling deep in his gut. He stands up, unbuttons his britches, and squats over the pail in the corner of the cell. With both knees bent, and his back pressed against the wall for support, he strains, then empties himself. There is a moment of relief, of almost-joy, then another wave comes, louder and more abundant than the first, and then a third. When it's over, he climbs back onto the bed and covers himself with the brown blanket. Although the air is cold, he is sweating now. The pain in his gut is gone, but he feels weakened and queasy, and his legs and back are stiff and aching. After a few more minutes, he rolls over and vomits onto the stone floor. He wipes his mouth with his sleeve, spits out the remnants, and calls for water, but no one answers. He guesses it is after midnight. There are no sounds coming from the corridor, just the yellow glow of the gas lamps through the crude fanlight. He closes his eyes again, brings his knees up to his chest, and hugs himself for warmth.

The sickness lasts two days. He is dizzied by fever, sweating and shuddering, dropping in and out of a fractured and restless sleep. At times, in his confusion, he believes he is back in Armagh or in the rooms on Kennedy's Lane. When he hears voices from the corridor, he thinks it is Catherine singing to the baby, or his parents arguing. He tries to call out to them, to ask for help, but it is as if he has forgotten how to speak. Instead of words, he makes hoarse guttural noises only, shrieks and yelps like the crude agitations of an imbecile or a frightened ape. Although he knows what he wants to say, he cannot say it however hard he tries. His throat closes and his tongue becomes thick and useless. Listening outside, the guards shake their heads and laugh at his clownish gobbledygook. "It's that Fenian cunt O'Connor chanting his Latin again," they say.

When the fever recedes and his mind begins to clear, he asks for soap and water and a cloth to clean himself. He washes his face first, then his arms, then his chest and belly. His body feels like a house he has returned to after a long time away, like a friend whose name he has forgotten. He wrings out the cloth, then pulls down his trousers and continues cleaning. He has soiled himself while sleeping and his arse is caked and raw. Slowly, feeling the way with his fingertips, he picks away the dried-on excrement, then wipes and rinses. Next, he cleans his thighs and genitals, then his feet. The gray water is cold against his skin, and the effort of standing and bending makes him breathless. When he is finished, he wraps himself in the brown blanket and lies back down on the wooden bed. His dirty clothes lie scattered across the floor, but he is too weary to reach for them.

An hour later, when Thompson opens the cell door, he sniffs once, then steps back into the corridor and calls for the guards. While he waits outside, they remove the slop pail and scrub and mop the floor. Pale and naked under the verminous blanket, unshaven and hollow-eyed, O'Connor watches on in silence. When Thompson comes back in, he is smoking a small cigar against the smell.

"I heard you'd taken ill," he says. "Are you recovered now?"

O'Connor hesitates a moment. He remembers the dreams, the mangled words clogging his throat. Thompson tilts forward an inch and looks at him more closely.

"Do you hear me, O'Connor?"

"I'm well enough," he answers. "Weak, that's all."

"When you eat you'll feel better, I'm sure. Soup and bread. Your strength will soon return."

"I've been here for four days already and I've not been arrested or charged with any crime. You have no right to keep me against my will. No right at all."

Thompson nods.

"Four days is longer than I'd hoped for, but a peculiar case like yours takes time to fathom out. The complications are unusual. I know you're most likely a traitor, but I don't have enough evidence to prove it yet, and if I let you go free you'll disappear forever. So what am I to do? Yesterday, I wrote to Colonel Feilding about my dilemma, and I received his reply just this morning. He's a clever fellow, the colonel, and he gave me some good advice. He told me to think about the gun. He said the gun was the answer to my problem. It took me a moment realize what he meant, but once I realized, I could see the way forward as clear as day."

"Which gun?" O'Connor asks.

"Barton's gun. The one you stole from him. It wasn't yours and you had no right to take it, but you took it anyway. You lied to get it. That's stealing and a loaded gun is no small thing to steal."

"I returned it the next day. I put it back in the safe."

Thompson nods.

"The records show it was put back in the gun safe at half past twelve in the afternoon. Barton estimates you took it from him around eight the previous evening, so you had it for sixteen hours or more. A man can do a lot of mischief with a loaded gun in sixteen hours."

"I was drunk. It was in my pocket all night, but I forgot it was there."

"You think your drunkenness lessens the crime? I'd say it only makes it worse."

Thompson's manner is the same as before: self-satisfied, insidious, unstoppable. He swallows a mouthful of smoke, then lets it seep back out through his broad nostrils.

"You'll go to the police court in the morning to be charged with the theft of a firearm," he says. "We have witnesses, of course—Barton himself, the fellow who owns the chemist shop, Fazackerley—it won't be a difficult case to decide."

"I intended to kill Stephen Doyle if I could. That's why I took Barton's gun. I was in a wild rage."

"Barton says you were calm and seemed sober, at least so far as he could tell. He says he argued with you about the gun, but you forced him to give it up."

"He didn't argue. He gave it willingly."

"Barton's a respectable lad, clean and honest-looking. When he stands up in the court I expect he'll be believed."

"What's the purpose of all this?"

"To keep you where we want you. You're a dangerous man, an enemy of the crown, and a risk to the public. If we can't try you now, at least we can keep you safely locked up."

O'Connor shudders and pulls the blanket tighter around his shoulders. He feels a wave of nausea breaking over him. *A dangerous man?* He wonders if Thompson can mean what he is saying, or if it is all part of the same preposterous stratagem.

"I'm not a danger to anyone," he says. "I'm an ordinary man, loyal and decent."

"We know now that you disgraced yourself in Dublin, and they sent you over here to give you a second chance. That was their mistake, of course. Once a man has lost his way like you did, he can't get back again. It's impossible. Once the weakness has revealed itself, there's only one direction he can go. Maybury should have seen it much earlier. He should never have trusted you. That was *his* mistake. But now everything is revealed. Now we know what you are."

"Nothing is *revealed*," O'Connor insists. His breath is short and the words come out in bursts. "Nothing is revealed at all. You accuse me of betrayal, but I'm the one who is being betrayed. This is the true betrayal: this false accusation, these ridiculous lies."

"You're a common drunkard. Let's agree on that at least."

"I suffered a loss," O'Connor says. "My wife."

Thompson nods complacently.

"Catherine," he says. "We know about her, but if you're looking around for pity, you'll have to look elsewhere. I'll save my tears for the men who were murdered by your Fenian friends."

O'Connor shakes his head and turns away. The fever has left him confused and weakened. He doesn't trust himself enough to make an answer. Thompson waits a minute longer, then crushes the cigar butt underfoot and pushes open the cell door. There is a quick spill of yellow light and the bright sound of a man whistling in the corridor, then the door bangs shut again and the world goes back to darkness and silence.

CHAPTER 25

She wants to be happy and safe, to have children and a home, but what does he want? Comfort, she supposes, and love of some kind, a way out of all the trouble and the sadness he has known. She needs his help and he needs hers, so they will help each other. It won't be pure or perfect like in the songs, but everything in this life is a risk, and when the thinking and talking are over, all you can do is offer up a prayer and hope for the best. So that's what she will do. When he comes to her, whenever he comes to her, she will tell him she accepts his offer. She will smile and say yes, and it will be, for that one moment at least, as if the past has disappeared completely, as if the world has begun again from nothing.

It is past nine o'clock on Sunday and Rose Flanagan has just settled her mother down for the night when she hears the knocking. *At long last,* she thinks. *He has taken his time about it, but finally.* When she opens the door she expects to see James O'Connor standing on the step looking nervous or expectant, or some mixed-up combination of the two, but it is someone else entirely: an old fellow dressed all in black, with a shabby gray mustache and cloudy, oysterish eyes. He says his name is Harold Newly and he is an attorney-at-law. He offers her his card and she takes it. She tells him that she has no need for any attorney-at-law, and he smiles back and explains he is currently in the employ of Mr. James O'Connor, and Mr. James O'Connor has asked him to convey a message to Miss Rose Flanagan.

"Would you be Miss Flanagan?" he asks.

She nods.

"Then may I come inside for a moment?"

Rose doesn't answer straightaway. She looks at the card again and wonders what it all could mean.

"Why would a policeman have any need of an attorney?" she says. "That don't make any sense."

Newly smiles again and says that the situation is certainly unusual, but he can explain it easily enough if she will allow him. He has a slow, defusing manner as if he is used to being disliked or mistrusted. She steps aside and lets him into the hall. There is no fire left in the front room, so they walk back into the kitchen. He puts his hat on the table and tilts his umbrella against the wall. Rose offers him a chair by the stove and he thanks her and sits down. "Tea?" she says, but he declines it with a small shrug.

"Where has Jimmy gone? Why could he not come here himself?"

Newly nods as if to concede that her question is a reasonable one to ask. His face is creviced and dusty, and his thin lips are pale on the outside but darker within. He reminds Rose of a church organist or a schoolmaster gone to seed.

"This will no doubt come as a surprise to you, Miss Flanagan," he says, "but Mr. O'Connor is currently confined in the New Bailey Prison over in Salford. He's been charged with the theft of a police firearm, and the magistrates have remanded him for trial at the spring sessions. I am hopeful he will be freed when the case comes up, since the accusa-

tions against him are weak, but, until then, the prison regulations require that he be treated as a felon. His freedoms
are severely limited: He cannot receive visitors, except for
his legal representative, and he cannot send or receive any
letters at all."

Rose stares at him, then shakes her head. What he is
telling her sounds so strange and unlikely that she is
tempted to laugh.

"How can they put a policeman in jail?" she asks. "Isn't
that against the law?"

"Mr. O'Connor is not, strictly speaking, a policeman any
longer; he resigned from his post, but even if he were one,
that doesn't give him immunity. A crime is a crime just the
same, whoever commits it. That's what the law says."

She still can't believe what she is being told. It seems
impossible to her that O'Connor's fortunes could have
changed so rapidly, but then she remembers what he told
her in the tearoom about Maybury and the others—how
they ignored all his good advice and treated him like dirt.

"Someone's took against him then, because of where he's
come from. He told me how it was at the Town Hall. He has
no friends there at all. The English don't see him as an
equal. Something has happened, I'll bet, some other fellow
has broken the rules, and he's being made to take the blame
for it."

"There's some truth in that," Newly agrees. "Usually a
man would be dismissed from his post or merely repri-
manded for what Mr. O'Connor did, not threatened with
jail, but feelings have altered since the recent Fenian murders. Forgiveness and understanding are in short supply
these days. They say he stole a pistol, when all he did, in
truth, was borrow it for a while without asking the proper
permissions. He had taken a drink at the time, which
doesn't help our cause, but no harm was done and no one
was injured. It was a foolish mistake, no more than that,

but in the present climate, if you're searching for a scapegoat, it's the kind of thing that can be made to sound a lot
more sinister than it was."

"When did all this happen?"

"Sunday last. In the evening, while they were out searching for the men who murdered Constable Malone."

"I saw him the day after. He came to the place I work, the
Spread Eagle Hotel. He talked about leaving the police, resigning his post, but he didn't say he was in any kind of
trouble."

"He didn't know it then. He went back to the Town Hall
the next day not suspecting anything was wrong. They
started asking him some questions, and when he got up to
leave they put him in the cells. It's a man named Thompson, an inspector just come up from London, who's the cause
of it all. He has a belief that Mr. O'Connor is a traitor, that
he was colluding with the Fenians somehow, but he has no
evidence to prove it, so the accusation of robbery is the best
he can manage. This Thompson looks the part, they say,
and he convinced the magistrate easily enough, but when it
comes to the sessions it's another story. A good barrister
will better him, I'm sure of it."

Rose frowns and shakes her head. She remembers the
bloodstain on the sleeve of O'Connor's coat. *He risked his
own life for them*, she thinks. *He might have been killed,
and now they're calling him a traitor. That's the kind of
thanks you get.*

"How is he coping in the jail?" she asks.

"He's been ill with a fever and his spirits are much reduced. A prison is a fearful place, Miss Flanagan, it is designed to be fearful—that is its express intention. Mr.
O'Connor is suffering there, as any honest person would,
but he asked me to tell you that you have been on his mind
a good deal and the thought of you has often brought him
comfort."

"Is that his message for me?"

"That's a part of it. The rest is more particular."

Rose presses her lips together. She thinks of the New Bailey Prison, rising up from the banks of the Irwell, somber and massive, like the black weight of all the city's griefs made visible. Even if they let him go, as Newly says they will, he will be tainted by what has happened, she thinks, invisibly weakened. Whatever troubles he had before will be magnified and made much worse.

"When I heard you knocking on the door just now, I thought it was him," she says.

Newly nods and narrows his eyes in sympathy.

"Then I'm sorry to disappoint," he says. "I must make a very poor kind of substitute."

"How much did he tell you about me?"

"He told me that he made you an offer of marriage, and you were thinking on it. He wants you to know that, given the changed circumstances, you should not feel under any obligation to make an answer now. As soon as he has secured his release, he will seek you out again to renew his offer. That will be the very first thing he does. He hopes you will give him an answer then, and the answer will be a happy one, but until that time you should consider yourself entirely free. That's what he wanted you to know."

"Free to do what?" she says.

"Your brother is dead, as I understand it, and your mother is infirm. If other possible sources of help appear, then you should consider them, at least. I believe that's what Mr. O'Connor is meaning."

Rose straightens in her chair. She is taken aback by the coldness of the offer.

"Does he give me up so easily as that?"

"It is intended as a kindness, nothing more. He doesn't wish your fortunes to be damaged by his stroke of ill luck."

Rose looks down at her hands—the broken nails, the red

fingers roughened by work. Whichever way she turns there is only more heartache. She feels the wrongness of it all like an aching in her bones. She sighs slowly, then smooths her skirt and looks up again.

"How long until the sessions meet?" she says.

"Three months from now, in April."

"And what if he's found guilty?"

"It's not likely he will be. This Thompson is playing games with him, I think."

"But what if he is?"

Newly pauses and wipes his bony hand across the wooden tabletop.

"If he is, the sentence will be a year at least, possibly longer."

After Newly leaves her, Rose goes back into the kitchen and sits there looking at the fire. She reminds herself that she is still young and that nothing has been decided yet. She can do as she wishes. She thinks about this for a long time, then stands, lights a candle, and goes upstairs. Tommy's room is dark and empty still. It has not been touched since the murder. There is no lodger who will take it and she can't bear to sleep in there herself. In the other bedroom, her mother is already snoring. Rose undresses quickly, pulls on her nightdress, and slides down into the cold bed beside her.

CHAPTER 26

They walk in circles: thieves and blackmailers, sodomites and ponces, embezzlers, garroters, pickpockets and cracksmen, everyone different yet everyone the same. O'Connor stares at the hunched shoulders of the man in front and hears the cough-and-spit of the man behind. Their prison clogs clatter on the wet asphalt. Beside the path, where the guards stand, the winter grass is worn away to mud. All talk is forbidden; even a glance or a smile will be punished. After exercise, they go to the chapel, then on to the felons' workshop—winding bobbins, picking oakum, the smell of creosote and the cold brown air full of dirt and dust.

He meets Newly every other Wednesday in a timber-walled consulting room between the gatehouse and the governor's office. They talk about the witnesses who will be called, the evidence, the likely barristers, what the judges might or might not think and say. Newly's manner never varies, he is careful and calm to the point of dreariness, he speaks slowly and never strays from the matter at hand; but afterward, when their allotted time is up and they shake hands, O'Connor feels, always and despite himself, a moment of raw, unbridled sadness, as if he has just been separated from a lover or a dear friend.

At night, he hears screams from the other cells, sobbing, the sound of quick footsteps and iron doors being slammed shut. The narrow cell is as cold as a tomb, and the thick darkness presses down on him like a fist. If he dreams, he dreams of Catherine, but mostly he lies awake gripped by fear, thoughts and memories threshing like steel blades inside his skull.

Some days, he is filled with indignation and anger, he feels misused and on the edge of violence; it is all he can do to contain his rage. But on other days, he drops into a nerveless, helpless lassitude. He thinks of everything he has done and not done, his mistakes and failures, his painful history, and he wonders if this punishment is what life demands. Is this the fate that has been waiting to embrace him? Is this his purest patrimony come at last? He has been in the New Bailey Prison for two months already, and sometimes he fears he is losing his mind.

Fazackerley arrives unannounced just after breakfast one morning. O'Connor is cleaning his cell—sweeping the slate floor and rolling up the blankets and mattress—when the door opens. Fazackerley looks tired and gloomy. His blue eyes are framed with gray. He steps into the cell, removes his dented bowler, and pushes the limp hair back off his wide forehead.

"I would have come before," he says, "but they wouldn't let me. It's a shame what they've done to you, Jimmy, a shame. I told that to Thompson. I said it to his face."

"And how did he answer?"

Fazackerley shakes his head.

"He's the new broom, ent he? The worse he makes us look, the better it is for him. He's got his eye on Maybury's job for sure."

"Chief of detectives?"

"He might even get it. I think he will. They're in such a fucking panic now."

O'Connor offers Fazackerley the stool from the corner, then finishes rolling the mattress and sits down on the edge of the bed. The cell door is still wide open, and he can see the kitchen trusties stacking empty food trays on the landing opposite. There is the usual breakfast smell of oatmeal skilly and night soil.

"I brought you some bacca," Fazackerley says. "Here."

He gives the twist to O'Connor and O'Connor sniffs it and nods.

"I would have stopped all this if I could, Jimmy. I hope you know that, but there was nothing I could do."

"You warned me about Thompson. I do remember that."

"I should have told you to get out while you still could."

"Newly tells me that you'll be a witness at the trial."

"I will. Of course. If it comes to that. I'll do whatever I can."

Fazackerley looks around the cell and rubs the point of his chin against the back of his hand.

"Belle Vue is a better place than here," he says. "It's cleaner, and they let you keep your own clothes when you're on remand. You should ask for a transfer. You'd feel more like yourself in your own clothes, I'd bet."

"It's not the clothes that's the problem."

Fazackerley smiles for a moment, then stops himself. He puts the bowler down on the floor by his feet and rubs his hands on his thighs as if trying to keep them warm. His overcoat is still wet from the rain, and he smells of tobacco smoke and the winter air.

"We'll get you out of here one way or the other," he says.

O'Connor wonders why he has come. He must have bribed a guard or been given permission from the magistrate, so there must be something particular he needs to say, something that he couldn't say through Newly.

"Have they found Stephen Doyle?" he asks. "Do they need me to talk to him?"

Fazackerley tilts back on the low stool and looks surprised, as if the conversation has taken a confusing turn. He shakes his head and tugs down on one ear.

"They're still looking, but he could be anywhere by now."

"I'm the only one who knows him. The only one who's seen his actual face. You remember that?"

"I do."

Fazackerley sniffs and looks down at his feet. If it's not Doyle he's come about, O'Connor thinks, then what could it be?

"Have you heard from Michael?" he asks. "Did you meet with him yet?"

When Fazackerley looks up, his face is different: darker, more strained.

"It's Michael Sullivan that I've come to talk about," he says.

"Is he in trouble? Does he need our help?"

Fazackerley doesn't answer straightaway. O'Connor watches him for clues. A guard walks past, pauses to look inside the cell, then continues walking. The long innocent moment holds them in its gentle hand, then lets them go.

"Yesterday morning a fellow found a body on the waste ground near Stanley Street," Fazackerley says. "Someone had tried to bury it, but they hadn't tried too hard. The state it was in, looked like some dogs had got to it. I'm sorry, Jimmy."

"Michael's body?"

Fazackerley nods.

"By the coal wharves?"

"That's right. Near the Bolton Canal, not so very far from here."

O'Connor knows the feeling from before: numbness first,

then pain. Sorrow like a crevice cracking open inside him. Like a blind, furious animal released from its cage.

"How was he killed?"

"Shot once in the head, but they beat him pretty bad before that."

"He should have taken his chances in New York."

"We couldn't know."

O'Connor reaches his arms across his chest and hugs himself tight. He leans forward and waits for the feelings of sickness and dizziness to lessen. Fazackerley sniffs, then takes a grubby handkerchief from his jacket pocket, wipes his nose with it, and puts it back.

"It was Doyle who killed him, but Peter Rice and Jack Riley were there too. We found blood in one of the railway arches near where Michael's body was found. The fellow who rents the arch is named Dixon. At first, he claimed someone had broken in, but when we told him he'd hang for the murder, he changed his mind quickly enough. This Dixon's nothing, just a filcher from Salford. Doyle found him one night in the vaults on Sidney Street and paid him to rob you. Then later, when they needed a place to hide, he called on him again. He's not a Fenian, he's not even Irish, but he was there and he saw everything that happened. According to Dixon, Doyle believed what you told him at first. He thought Rice was the traitor, but then Rice convinced him it was Michael. Somehow, they'd found out that he was your nephew. I don't know how. Michael tried to deny it, Dixon says, but they got it out of him in the end."

"When did they do it?"

"The first night after Frank Malone was shot."

O'Connor clenches his face as if in sudden pain. He looks up at the whitewashed ceiling and groans. The bell rings for morning exercise and the guards on the landing start shouting out the numbers.

"They arrested Jack Riley at the alehouse last night. Peter Rice has disappeared for now, but he won't get far. They'll both go on trial for conspiracy to murder, and with Dixon as witness it's likely they'll hang for what they did. Doyle's long gone, but that doesn't worry Thompson much. Two dead Fenians will do the trick for him; it doesn't matter who they are or exactly what they did. He sees it as a stroke of good fortune."

"If I'd kept watching the butcher's shop that night, I might have stopped it."

"They would have killed him anyway, Jimmy."

"I could have followed them to the railway arch."

"If you had, they would have shot the both of you together. We'd have two bodies lying side by side in the morgue instead of one."

A guard comes to the door and tells Fazackerley that he will have to leave soon, and Fazackerley thanks him and then waits for him to go.

"I talked to Thompson before I left the Town Hall this morning. He won't admit he was wrong about you, even now, but he agrees that whatever happened with the gun doesn't matter anymore. We've got our eyes on bigger things now. He's going to write to the magistrate to ask for you to be allowed out of here on bail, and when the case comes to the sessions, they won't be offering any evidence. It may take a day or two, or a week at most, but you'll be freed quite soon."

O'Connor shakes his head. He closes his eyes tight, then opens them again.

"It's not right," he says.

"It's never right, Jimmy. It's better, or it's worse sometimes, but it's never right. You must know that by now."

———

One side of the exercise yard is in shadow, and the other is lit by the weak winter sun. O'Connor walks in slow circles with the other prisoners, into the brightness then out again. Warm and then cold, the same each time. When the guards are not looking, the man behind him whispers urgent questions: *My name is Ezra,* he says. *What is your name, my good friend? I am a coiner. What are you?* O'Connor hears him well but doesn't answer. The man in front has a withered right leg; his body tilts and sways as he walks. The circle turns again: shadow and then light, walls and then sky, brown smoke leeching from the chimneys and clogs rattling on the wet asphalt. A dog barks somewhere. Crows hunch like sentries on the ridge tiles. Everything different, he thinks, but everything the same. Time becomes memory, and memory becomes the ditch in which we drown.

CHAPTER 27

Five days later, O'Connor is released from the New Bailey
Prison with two shillings and sixpence in a buff envelope
in the pocket of his waistcoat. His jacket and trousers are
still stiff and odorous from the fumigator. He buys a meat
pie from a barrow on Worsley Street and eats it slowly, sa-
voring every bite. When he finishes, he buys another one
and the pieman remarks on his appetite. Free, with no
walls around him and the gray clouds like a mantle above
his head, he feels dizzy and disarranged, as if he has just
woken up from a strange dream or stepped back onto the
land after a long time alone at sea. When he has finished
the second pie, instead of crossing the Albert Bridge and
walking back into Manchester, he descends the worn stone
steps to the boat landing, then turns right onto the narrow
muddy path that runs along the north bank of the Irwell.
He remembers the night of the Fenian hangings: the watch
fires and the barricades, the eager crowds of people gath-
ered by the prison wall. Tommy Flanagan was still alive
that night and so were Henry Maxwell and Frank Malone.
Doyle has had his revenge, he thinks, even if it didn't happen the way he planned it. Three dead men to balance the
three who were hanged, blood for blood, and that could

have been the end of it, except it never is the end. There's always another wrong to be made right, another lesson to be taught or learned.

The path begins to broaden and change direction and soon, to his right, instead of the high backs of mills and factories, he can see only a dank floodplain of dead grass and shriveled weeds, cut across here and there by brick-lined drainage ditches. He continues on until he reaches the river lock where the Bolton Canal meets the Irwell, then turns away from the river and follows the towpath toward the coal wharves. The railway arches are a hundred yards ahead of him now, a looped curve of red brick, water-stained and smoke-blackened. Most appear empty and un-used, but some are boarded up, and a few have tall slatted gates or narrow doors with signs nailed above them.

In front of one of the arches there is a fire burning and two men are loading empty barrels onto a dray. One of the men is whistling. O'Connor tells them his name and what he is looking for and why. The man who was whistling stops, then rubs his head and points off. "Over yonder," he says, "keep walking straight and you'll see the spot." O'Connor walks, then turns around, and the man, who is still watch-ing, waves him farther onward. The wet ground is covered over by a sapless tangle of shrub and vine, bent and disor-derly. Dead thistles catch at his trouser legs. He stumbles twice but doesn't fall. He can't see what he is looking for yet and he wonders if the man was confused or lying. Then he notices it, away to the right: a patch of broken ground, the fresh-turned soil glowing dark as a wound against the brown-gray clamor of brambles and thorn. Coming closer, he sees the open grave, crudely dug, thin and shallow with footprints pressed in all around and the grass on both sides trodden flat. He circles it once, then crouches down and picks up a burned match and a button. Careless, he thinks, clumsy, to bury him here, so close, but Doyle didn't care by then. They already had evidence enough to hang him, so one more body made no difference.

He stands up and looks about. The men with the dray are gone, but their fire is still burning brightly. A train whistle sounds, and brown smoke drifts sideways from the factory chimneys. He is hungry again, but the hunger feels trifling and shameful. The dead are in command, he thinks, now and always. Every step away is a step toward, every turning is part of the same circle, and what we call love or hope is just an interlude, a way of forgetting what we are. He bends down and picks up a handful of wet soil from the soft edge of the grave, stares at it for a moment, then rubs it away. There are certain cruelties that he will not let himself imagine. *Better to be stupid or ignorant,* he thinks, *better to just pretend.*

A letter from Rose Flanagan is waiting for him at Newly's law office. The letter explains that she has moved to Glasgow and is living in a women's lodging house in Oatlands and working as a kitchen maid in one of the big hotels by the railway station. She is happy, the letter says: The lodging house is clean and well looked after, and she has made new friends already. Near the bottom of the letter, like an afterthought, she explains that, despite his kindness, she cannot accept his offer of marriage. It would not be right. She knows his face will always remind her of Tommy's dreadful murder, and it would be a mistake for both of them, she thinks, to start on a new life with the shadow of the old one still stretching across it so dark and strange.

He reads the letter through again, then places it back on top of the desk. Beneath the sorrow and disappointment, he feels a measure of relief, as if a burden has been lifted. *Easier,* he tells himself, *simpler this way: no one else to care for or comfort, no other sufferings to tend to but my own.*

The lawyer asks him if the news is discouraging, and he shrugs once, then nods.

"I didn't expect her to wait for me," he says. "Why ever would she?"

"I passed that message on just like you asked me to. I think she understood your good intentions."

"I expect she did."

"I heard her mother died and that's why she had to leave so suddenly. She couldn't stay in that house afterward, couldn't stand it there. Does she mention that in the letter?"

Newly's manner is looser than before, more conversational. He looks at O'Connor with a calm satisfaction, as if he is a difficult problem that has been solved with surprising ease.

O'Connor nods again.

"It says she died in her sleep."

"There are plenty of other women in the world like Rose Flanagan," Newly assures him with a half-smile. "She's not so very special. You have your freedom now, you can walk about and breathe God's air. That's what matters most."

Inside the jail, Newly's complacency was reassuring, a glimpse of normality, but here on the outside it feels boorish and misguided.

"I'm only free because Michael Sullivan is dead," O'Connor says.

Newly looks dismayed by this suggestion.

"Oh no. You should never have been in that jail in the first place; that was just Thompson showing off his powers. If it had ever come to a trial, no reasonable judge or jury would have convicted you. You benefited from the death perhaps, but only in a small way and purely by chance. You have no cause to feel guilty about what happened."

O'Connor looks past Newly to the clock on the mantelpiece behind. He notices there is a small crack in the beveled crystal between the one and the two. The ticking is slow and steady as a heartbeat.

"It's Stephen Doyle I'm thinking of now," he says.

"Stephen Doyle has disappeared for good. Two men from Scotland Yard went over to New York to look for him, but they came back with nothing."

"He's alive somewhere. If they can't find him, then they're looking in the wrong places."

"Maybe so, but it's not a matter you should concern yourself with. Rice and Riley are both in Belle Vue Prison, like I told you before, and they'll hang for their crimes. You should grieve your losses now and let others worry about Stephen Doyle."

O'Connor shakes his head.

"I've had enough of the grieving," he says. "I can't abide it anymore."

Later that day, when he gets to the detective office, they tell him that Thompson is occupied and can't be disturbed, so he settles on a bench in the corridor and waits. One hour passes, then another. He drops asleep for a while, then feels a rough hand on his shoulder shaking him awake. Sanders is standing there, looking down. His expression is bored and disdainful.

"What are you after?" he says. "Why have you come here?"

He looks just the same as before—the long narrow face and damp mustache with threads of gray, the dark, eager eyes full of dull hatred and vague belligerence. O'Connor remembers the holding cell, the truncheon pressed hard against his throat until he couldn't breathe. He feels a tightening in his chest and a burn in his stomach, rage impotent and wordless, like thwarted desire.

"I'm waiting for Thompson," he says. "I need to talk to him again."

"Thompson won't see you. Why would he?"

"I need to speak to him about Stephen Doyle."

"Doyle's long gone; he'll never be caught now. And besides, it's not your business any longer. You should leave here now before you get into any more trouble."

"On the boat coming over here he pretended he was a draper from Harrisburg, Pennsylvania. That's what Michael Sullivan told me. If he's not hiding in New York, then it's most likely he's there, or somewhere close by. He must have lived in Harrisburg or he knows someone who does. Why else would he choose it?"

"Is that your grand idea? Is that really why you came?"

"Tell Thompson to send a man to Harrisburg, Pennsylvania."

"I'll tell him no such thing. The investigation into Michael Sullivan's murder is finished with. The body is buried and we have other, more pressing matters to fill our time."

O'Connor stands up too quickly. His legs are unsteady, and his hips and back still ache from the prison bed. His body feels like something borrowed from an older, weaker man.

"You have a duty," he almost shouts. "A duty to the dead."

Sanders squints and looks at him askew. When he answers, he answers slowly and calmly as if addressing himself to a small child or a dimwit.

"Inspector Thompson won't see you, O'Connor," he says. "Not today and not tomorrow neither. He sent me down here to tell you that. You weren't much before, but you're nothing now. Nothing at all. You should remember that."

"If Thompson won't send a man, then I'll go to Harrisburg myself," O'Connor says. "I'll find Stephen Doyle, and when I find him I'll kill him."

Sanders looks away contemptuously, then turns back again.

"You can go wherever you want to," he says. "You can fly off to the fucking moon if the fancy takes you, O'Connor. Just don't come back here to Manchester again or you'll wish you hadn't, I swear it."

CHAPTER 28

When the ship makes harbor in New York, Doyle is taken by cab to a hotel room on Bleecker Street. The room is clean and well-furnished; there are red velvet drapes at the window, and a bottle of whiskey stands unopened on the mantelpiece. Three men are waiting for him. William Roberts is one, but he doesn't recognize the others. They greet him warmly and tell him he has done a fine job over in England; he has spread the fear of God among the Saxons and that's all anyone could have asked for. The two men he doesn't know introduce themselves as Michael Kerwin and John O'Neill. They shake his hand, point him to a chair, then sit down together on a couch while Roberts stays standing by the fireplace. They smile at him again and nod their approval. The mayor of Manchester would have been a great prize, they all agree, a very great prize indeed, but the policeman and the spies added together are very nearly as good. Roberts reaches into his pocket, hands him a bankroll, and tells him he should find a quiet place to hide himself now, somewhere far away from New York where no one will be likely to come looking. A year at least, he says, maybe longer, all depending. Then they uncork the whiskey bottle and drink a toast in his honor.

When the toast is finished, Doyle announces that he wants to go back to England immediately. He has new plans, he says. He has learned from his mistakes and wants to try it over again. This time he will do it alone, or he will bring someone with him from America who he already knows and can trust. That way there will be no danger of betrayal.

They hear him out in silence, shrugging and rubbing their beards as he explains himself. They share a glance when he is finished talking, and then Roberts tells him that although they admire his bravery and commitment to the cause, they can't possibly fund or permit any second venture.

"You must understand our situation, Stephen," Roberts says, his voice just as calm and steady as you like. "The Brotherhood exists to foment rebellion. That is its sole aim and purpose. Individual acts of daring may assist that purpose on occasion, but they can't replace it."

"A rebellion will never succeed," Doyle says. "You must know that after the last time. There aren't enough men willing to fight and die for it. If we want to win, we have to hurt the English in their homes. Scare them enough so they can't sleep at night and are forever looking over their shoulders in case an Irishman appears with a bomb or a gun in his hand. It won't be easy or quick, I'll grant you that, but if the trouble we cause them is bad enough and lasts for long enough, in the end they'll give it up."

"You'd have us win our liberty through murder and arson," O'Neill says. "Is that your proposal?"

"I'm a soldier. It makes no difference to me if I kill my enemy on a street corner or on a battlefield. The result is just the same."

"The result is the same, but on the field the enemy is armed and has a chance to defend himself at least. There is some measure of honor and decency involved. Your path is the path of barbarism and savagery. If we earned the victory in that way, our freedom would be forever tainted."

"There's nothing honorable or decent about warfare," Doyle answers, "and it does no good to pretend there can be. You sent me to Manchester to get revenge, and I killed four men. Now you tell me I must stop. You want to try another path, but there is no other path. Did the English win their empire with gentleness and gallantry? If we are barbarians and savages, then they are just the same. In the battle every man is equal, and his only duty is to do his worst."

O'Neill sniffs and shakes his head.

"You're confused," he says. "We're on the side of justice and truth, and the enemy are on the side of tyranny and lies. To neglect that difference is to betray our cause."

Doyle is about to reply, when William Roberts interrupts him.

"Let's remember the simple facts," he says. "Every policeman in England will be looking out for you by now. Your name and description will be everywhere. If you go back, however careful you are, and however much you disguise your appearance, you will certainly be arrested and hanged, and what purpose will that serve? Whatever the rights and wrongs of the matter, the proposal you are making is not practical."

O'Neill and Kerwin nod their agreement.

"London is like a labyrinth," Doyle says. "It would be easy enough to conceal myself. I would only venture out at night, under cover of darkness."

"And how would you find lodgings? How would you eat? You would need some assistance; you could not survive entirely alone. And each new acquaintance you make would mean a new possibility of betrayal. Even if we wished to send a man to London, we would not send you. After what has happened, it would make no sense at all."

"I have the experience now," Doyle says. "No one else can match me for that."

"You're not even safe here in New York," Roberts continues. "If the British government presses hard enough, you will quickly find yourself in trouble. That's why we're telling you to leave. The fuss will die away eventually, but for now you are safer elsewhere. You have enough money in your pocket to buy a parcel of land in the west if you wish to."

"I'm a soldier," he says, "not a farmer."

"Something else, then, whatever you prefer. You have done your duty well, you have served the cause with courage and conviction, but it's time to step aside now."

Doyle looks back at him without answering. He knows the argument is lost. Roberts and the others think him a fool, reckless not brave, someone to be rid of quickly so they can move on with their far-fetched plans for revolution. They were soldiers once, he thinks, but now they've grown vain and sentimental. They dream of victory but are afraid to pay the price. He licks his lips and tastes the lingerings of their fine whiskey on his tongue.

"What if I give you back this money?" he says, holding out the bankroll. "What if I say you can keep it and I'll make my own way?"

"There are spies all around us," Roberts reminds him coolly. "We both know that. If you won't accept our help, Stephen, then how can we protect you?"

He stays in the hotel that night, and in the morning he walks to Cortlandt Street and takes the steam ferry over to Hoboken then a train on to Philadelphia. He finds a single room in a boardinghouse in the Northern Liberties and pays the landlord the first month's rent in advance. He has the idea of rejoining the U.S. Army using a different name and an imagined history and going down to Texas to fight the Indian there, but when he gets to the recruiting office

they look at him askance and ask him questions that he
will not answer. After that, he decides to remain where he
is, live off Roberts' money, and wait to see what fate will
offer up. He passes the time walking about or sitting in res-
taurants and hotel lobbies reading the newspapers and
drinking beer. The days are dull and easy and as they slide
past, as though on rails, he feels himself slowly softening,
his soldierly resolve leaking away. He remembers what his
life was like before the war came to his rescue, those faith-
less years of lassitude and drift, and wonders if he will go
back to that again when the Fenian dollars eventually run
dry. Is that what awaits him, he wonders—the old life become new and himself the same again but older?

It is the end of March when he sees Fergus McBride, his
uncle, crossing Franklin Square. He is grayer and more
stooped, but it is him without a doubt. Doyle is seated on
one of the benches by the fountain smoking his pipe. The
day is cloudy and cool. There are pigeons pecking in the dirt
at his feet, and he can hear the rattle of carriage wheels on
cobblestones and the steady splash of water. He has not
thought about Fergus McBride for a long time and is surprised to see him now, looking so solid and real. He is about
to call out a greeting but changes his mind and instead
waits for him to go past, then stands up and follows after.
Fergus walks south on Fifth Street, then turns onto an ad-
joining avenue. After twenty yards, he pauses in front of a
narrow three-story brick house, looks up at the front door,
then climbs the steps to the vestibule and knocks. Doyle
carries on walking to the end, then turns around and comes
back again more slowly. He pauses outside the house that
Fergus has just entered. There's a brass plate by the door
with a man's name and underneath the title ATTORNEY-AT-
LAW. A problem with the farm, Doyle thinks, or some dis-
pute about money. That's the only reason his uncle would
ever need to see a lawyer. He looks at the door again and

checks his watch. He decides that he will wait, and when Fergus comes out, he will make himself known. There is no reason to avoid such a meeting; he has nothing to hide. He will tell him that he fought honorably in the war, then went to Ireland to fight again there. He will ask about Anna and Lazlo and the farm, but he won't bring up the manner of his leaving. He tells himself he is no longer angry or ashamed, that too many years have passed for it to matter anymore, and he has seen and done too many other things. If there is some part of him that still yearns for redress, he thinks, then it is only a minor part and one that is easily brought to heel.

After an hour, the door reopens and Fergus comes out. When he first sees Doyle, he nods and looks away as if he is just another passing stranger, but then, after a moment, he stops and turns and looks at him again.

"*Stephen?*" he says.

"I saw you going in there," Doyle says. "I recognized you straightaway."

Fergus frowns. He looks puzzled and unsure of himself for a moment, but then he holds out his hand and the two of them shake.

"Are you living here in the city now?" he asks.

"I'm visiting. I don't live anywhere. I was in the war, then I went back over to Ireland for a while. I was helping some friends with a piece of business there, but it didn't turn out as well as I'd hoped."

Fergus nods as if the news is unsurprising.

"There's nothing in Ireland for a young fellow now," he says. "You'll be better off here."

"How is the farm?"

"Very well. We grow a lot of rye for the whiskey these days. They opened up a big distillery just down the road past Harper Tavern. They take about as much as we can grow and pay us nicely for it."

"Are Anna and Lazlo still with you?"

"Lazlo is gone. We have another hired man, a Negro fellow named George Nichols."

Doyle points up to the brass plate by the door.

"Are you having some kind of trouble? Is that why you're here?"

Fergus shakes his head.

"Peter Phelps died. Do you remember him? The fellow who owned the farm across the valley. I bought a quarter of his land at auction, but now they say there's a complication with the will. Some distant cousin staking a claim. I can't make any sense of it, but the lawyer fellow in there promises me he can untangle it quickly enough, so long as I pay him, of course."

"It's a long way to come from Harrisburg."

Fergus shrugs.

"I gave a good price for that land," he says. "I'd hate to lose it through some mischance."

"You look just the same, not altered at all."

"I'm not so young as I was, but my health is still good. I'm out working in the fields every day just the same as before."

"And is that top land cleared now? Is the timber all gone from it."

"It's long gone."

Doyle shakes his head at the memory.

"That was about the hardest work I ever did. After I left you, I worked as a navvy on the canals and the railroads, but I was never so weary afterward as I was after a day up in those woods."

"It was too much for a young boy, I see that now. You didn't have the strength for it. That was my mistake."

Doyle looks at him again. His uncle is an inch or so shorter than he was, and the skin around his eyes and mouth is scored and grainy now, but the face still reminds him of his mother's face—the shallow curve of the brow and the angle of the nose. He is like a piece of the past brought back to life, like a dream or memory made half-real again.

"We can all make a mistake," Doyle says. "There's no man is perfect."

Fergus takes off his hat, wipes the nap of it against his sleeve, then puts it back on.

"It's strange to see you here, Stephen," he says, "I must confess. I've thought more than once about what happened between us at the end. And I've wished it could have been different somehow."

"A long time has passed since then," Doyle says. "I don't think of it any longer."

"Well, I'm glad to hear you say so. It doesn't do to hoard up bad memories, better just to forget such things."

Doyle nods his agreement.

"There's something else I should tell you," Fergus says after a pause. "Anna and I are married. We have a child, a boy named Patrick."

Doyle doesn't speak for a moment. He wonders why he is surprised by this news, why this possibility, which, in hindsight, looms so large and obvious, has not occurred to him before.

"So I have a cousin," he says. "How old is the boy now?"

"Nine years old next month. He'd be pleased to meet you, I'm sure. He often complains that our family is too small. All his schoolfriends are surrounded by relations—brothers and sisters, cousins and grandparents—but he only has us two. Everyone else is dead or too far away to matter."

"What have you told him about me?"

"Not much, of course, since we never thought he would get a chance to meet you, but if you ever did make the journey, then the surprise would be a part of the pleasure. I can just imagine the look on his face."

"I'm too much occupied here," Doyle says. "I have my plans in place. You understand."

"I understand, of course. The work must come first. But if you change your mind, then we'd all be pleased to welcome you. I'll tell Anna I saw you anyway. She'll ask me everything you said and what you look like now." He taps his head with his forefinger. "I'll have to be sure to remember it right."

"I get my mail at the post office here," he says. "If she ever wants to write me."

"I'll tell her that."

They shake hands again, and Fergus tips his hat and walks away.

He is pleased to see the back of me, Doyle thinks, *however much he likes to pretend otherwise. He is settled now, content and secure, with a wife and a child, and my sudden, unexpected appearance troubles him. I am the past he would prefer to forget.* He imagines Fergus back at the farm, sitting down at the kitchen table telling the story of his trip to Philadelphia. He is shaking his head at the strangeness of it; the boy is listening and asking questions. Anna is with them; she is standing by the stove. He tries to imagine what she must look like now, her face and her body changed, but how? He knows that the years must have altered her, that no one stays the same, but he cannot picture it. All he can bring back to mind when he tries is the crude image, burned like a brand into the haunch of his memory, of her pale sleeping body, damp in the midnight's heat, the bone-white thighs splayed open and the riven darkness unconcealed.

A week afterward, he goes to the post office on Chestnut Street and finds two letters waiting there for him. One is from William Roberts warning him that the British government has posted a reward for information leading to his capture, and advising him that if he is still in Philadelphia, it would be wise to leave the city immediately and go somewhere more remote where there is less chance of him being recognized and reported. The second is from Anna:

Dear Stephen I am happy to know from Fergus that you are alive and well stil. It is a great blesing that you survived that dredful war when so many others yor age were killed or maimed in it. Fergus told you I think that we are marryed now and have a son Patrick. I am happy and Patrick is a joy. I have thoght of you often and wondered where you were and how you were faring. I know your time is ful and you have importent busnus to conduct but if you are ever able to visit us on the farm even for a single day it would be a plesure to see you again. Your good frend always Anna

He returns directly to the lodging house and packs his bag. He will not stay on the farm for long, he thinks, a week or two. Just time enough to get to know the boy a little and to reacquaint himself with Anna. Then he will move away, farther to the west or south. He doesn't know yet where he will go to or what he will do when he gets there, but it is good to be leaving the city now, he thinks, before its luxuries so soften his bones and water down his blood that he forgets who he is and what he lives for.

CHAPTER 29

The poacher appears from around a bend on the plank road wearing mud-caked boots and tattered surcoat. He is singing loudly in mangled German. His voice is bold and clear, with a frail vibrato added to the higher notes as a sign, or so O'Connor assumes, of his general facetiousness and good humor. When the poacher sees O'Connor, he looks surprised, then smiles and doffs his crumpled hat in antique greeting.

"I always remember a face," the poacher says, "I do, but I don't remember yourn. So I'd say you're a stranger in these parts."

"I'm a traveler."

"And where would you be traveling to?"

"Over to the west," O'Connor says, "to Harrisburg."

"Harrisburg?" The poacher rolls his eyes. "That's too far for any Christian to tramp it. You'll wear out them nice-looking boots before you get much past Allentown."

"I'll get there one way or another. I have to."

"There's a stagecoach runs along here on Tuesdays."

"I don't have the money for any stagecoach."

"How long have you been walking now?"

"Three days, and it'll be three more before I get there."

"I'd say it will. Three days, if you're lucky."

The poacher rubs his chin and gives O'Connor an appraising look.

"My guess is you're an honest man who's fell on hard times," he says.

"You could say that."

"I know a sponger when I see one, but you don't look like no sponger to me."

"I'm not one."

The man nods and smiles again.

"How long since you et?"

"I had something yesterday in the afternoon."

"You can stop at any farm about here and ask for a drink of water. No one will begrudge you a drink of water, and if you're lucky, they'll give you something else besides. Cup of coffee, slice of cornbread, maybe more if they like the looks of you. It's not begging. It's sharing. There's plenty of folk have more than they need for their own selves."

"I can work. I don't ask for any charity."

"Too proud," the poacher says. "I understand."

"What's your line?" O'Connor asks him.

"Me? I do whatever's needed at the time. Ditching, walling, chopping wood. I worked down the mines for a year, but that didn't suit me so much. I done cockling, trawling, trolling. Sold murder ballads at the county fair one year. Bought them for a cent and sold them for a nickel."

"Jack-of-all-trades, then?"

"You could say that, aye."

The poacher looks roundabout and then primps his ragged clothing to pass some more time. Beside them, beyond a stand of leafless trees, cattle graze on the sloping pasture, and there are patches of snow still bright on the high brakes.

"Where will you sleep tonight?" he says. "I'll show you a

good place nearby, if you'd like. A fine, warm place, and I'll show you something else besides."

"What else?"

"Something you might profit by."

"I have to be getting on now," O'Connor says.

"There's nothing else down that way, not even a wall or a hedge to rest your head under, just bare fields and forest. Looks like rain to me and it'll be getting dark before you know it. You'd be better off staying here with me."

"Is this place of yours close by?"

"It's close enough," he says. "You just follow me."

The poacher leads him off through the woods. The ground is black and sodden underfoot, and there is frost in the places the light can't reach. Overhead, the bare branches chatter in the wind like teeth.

The poacher turns around and looks at him.

"Do you have any whiskey in your pockets? I could do with a dram."

O'Connor shakes his head.

"Rum?"

"I've got nothing like that," he says.

Soon, the wood gives way to sheep-bitten grass and a tangle of black haw and chokeberry. There is a line of broken wall, then a log cabin, its sod roof half-collapsed, but the chimney and walls still intact. The two men push open the front door and step inside. There's a cold smell of wet ash, mildew, and fox scat. Thick, gray cobwebs sag like monstrous jowls from the roof beams. Rabbit bones and broken glass brocade the dirt floor.

"Get a fire in the hearth and it warms up quick enough," the poacher says.

"I've seen worse," O'Connor says.

"I'll bet you have."

"Do you sleep here yourself?"

"Sometimes I do. When needs must."

There's a rusty bedstead and two grimy wooden chairs pushed into one corner of the room. O'Connor knocks the dust off one of the chairs and sits down. He picks a bone off the floor, rubs it clean, and looks at it for a long time. He has not taken a drink since the morning four months ago when Fazackerley came to the house on George Street. He still feels the tug of it sometimes, just as strong and deep as ever, but the memory of what happened in Manchester is enough to keep him to the narrow path. While his nephew was being murdered, he was lying in bed a mile away in Diggle's Court drinking gin with Mary Chandler. Of all the lies and cowardice that led to Michael Sullivan's death, that is the part that shames him the worst. He will stay sober long enough to find Stephen Doyle and to kill him if he can. That is the promise he has made to himself. And after that, if he is still alive, he will take his comforts wherever he can find them.

"I use a snare to get the rabbits," the poacher explains. "Length of brass wire, good strong peg rubbed with soil so it can't be seen. If I had a gun I'd use that instead, but I lost my gun in a wager last year."

"Who buys them from you?" O'Connor asks.

"The rabbits? No one around here. Rabbits is just for the pot. It's the fish I can sell. Will you look at this?"

He reaches into a crevice between the roof and the wall and takes out a wooden pole with a large iron hook lashed to one end with thick twine.

"Ever seen one of these before?" he says.

O'Connor shakes his head.

"It's the best thing about. Some men like a net, but a gaff is quicker and easier by far. It takes two good men, though. One to shine a lamp to get their attention and the other to hook 'em when they come a-calling."

He looks at O'Connor and smiles.

"We could do a spell of fishing tonight. It's early in the year, but with a slice of luck we'll get enough to feed ourselves and then some."

"I never used a gaff," O'Connor says. "Nor ever seen one used."

"Then you can hold the lantern. I'll show you how it's done."

O'Connor tosses the rabbit bone aside. Since he left New York he has been living on stream water and wizened turnips filched from the fields. He is tired from walking, and the fish will give him strength.

"I need to eat something," he says.

"I figured that."

"How far's the river?"

"Mile or two away. It's an easy walk. We'll wait here till it gets dark enough, then go along."

O'Connor stretches out on the rusted bedstead while they wait. Harrisburg is only a guess, he knows that, but why would Doyle ever claim he was from Harrisburg if he had no connections to the place? Why that one town out of ten thousand others? He will try the drapers first, he thinks, then the bars and barbershops, and then, if he has no luck at all, he will go back to New York and ask his questions there instead. Doyle will show himself eventually. He must. A man like him is too proud and too bold to stay hidden away forever. It is a matter of waiting as much as searching, he believes, a matter of patience and firm resolve.

The poacher passes the time singing ribald songs and breaking sticks for the hearth. When it's become too dark to see, he gets a lantern from the hiding place and lights it with a match. He holds it up to his cragged face and gurns like a mummer.

"I'm a poacher, me," he says, "and I ain't ashamed of it

neither. This earth and its creatures is a gift from the Lord, and it can't be broke apart and owned, no matter what the rich folk says about it."

"It's the men with the money who make the rules," O'Connor answers him. "It's always been so and always will be."

"Aye, but it's the men like me who break 'em when we wish. I'll be a poacher till the day I die, and if there's poaching in heaven, I'll be the same up there."

O'Connor shakes his head and smiles.

"In heaven every man will have his equal share. All will be held in common. That's the promise leastways. So there'll be no need for poaching there."

The lantern light casts strange, distending shadows across the poacher's face. His eyeballs gleam and his pock-marked features melt like wax, then harden.

"Then if I have to give it up, I will do," he says, "but I'll mourn the loss of it, I swear, since poaching is the thing I love most dear."

They walk across a sheep field, through a wooden gate, and into the woods. The twilight thickens around them, and the only sounds are their own wet footfalls and the scratch and creak of birdsong in the trees above. After a mile, they hear water falling onto rocks, and then a stream appears between the trees, narrow and fast-flowing at its center, the surface brown with shifting flares of white, rib-boned and twisting. In a pool below the stunted falls, three thick-bodied trout hang suspended in a void. Matter inside emptiness, like three thoughts waiting for their thinker. The poacher crouches down at the water's edge, raises his lantern up, and smiles at the sight.

"Give me that gaff now," he whispers to O'Connor.

O'Connor hands him the gaff, and the poacher gives him the lantern and tells him where to stand with it and what to do.

"You watch me," he says. "I've got my eye on that fat one yonder."

He rolls up his trouser legs and steps into the shallow water at the edge of the pool, then lowers the gaff and waits. The fish stay as they are, three long shadows, poised and motionless against the flow. The poacher bends a little at the knees, reaches slowly forward until the gaff is inches from the largest fish's flank, then yanks it up and inward. As the fish curls and thrashes on the barbed point, he tugs again to be sure it's firm, then steps back onto the bank and pulls the gaff toward him. The fish fights against the hook but cannot free itself. O'Connor watches it twist and bend in the fatal air, fast then slower, the hard mouth aghast, the long belly palest gray against the dead bracken.

As they walk back through the woods, the trout dangle, blank-eyed and blood-spotted, on the end of the gaff. The poacher hums a jaunty tune. They pass through the wooden gate and back across the furrowed sheep field. The sky is dark purple in the west and black as ink above the saddle-back. There is a hazy half-moon and a muddle of stars over-head. As they approach the cabin it begins to rain, heavy drops, cold against the face and hands. The poacher pushes the door open with his foot and steps inside. In the light of the lantern, they see a tall man with a shotgun seated by the fireplace, smoking a pipe. He is wearing a leather coat, corduroy trousers, and a slouch hat. When he sees them in the doorway, he stands up and raises the gun to his shoulder.

"I warned you once before," the man says. His voice is strong but steady, as if he is used to issuing commands. "I told you not to come onto this land again. I told you if you did there'd be a consequence to pay. Yet here y'are as if my words meant nothing at all."

"Would you have me starve?" the poacher asks.

"I'd have you feed yourself like other men do, through sweat and honest toil."

"I'm no hireling and I never will be," the poacher answers, unafraid and unabashed. "The man who works for wages is no better than a slave if you ask me."

"So you're proud of your thievery?"

"I ain't ashamed."

"I'd say you won't talk so freely when you stand before the judge. That fish is private property no different from a watch or a purse; poaching is just stealing by another name."

"If that fish is property, he ain't none of yourn," the poacher says.

"I work for the squire."

"I know very well who you work for. You're a bought man and I'm a free man, and that's the difference between us two."

The gamekeeper nods in the direction of O'Connor.

"What's this?"

"A helpmeet. He didn't play no part."

"If he played no part, then why is he holding them fish?"

"I asked him to. He's a traveler on his way to Harrisburg. You don't need to trouble yourself with him."

The gamekeeper lowers the shotgun to his hip and looks at O'Connor.

"What's your name?"

"My name's O'Connor. I'm on my way to Harrisburg. I met this fellow on the road and he promised me a meal if I lent him a hand."

"You don't look stupid, but you must be."

"I held the lamp for him, that's all."

"Do you know that poaching is a crime?"

"I was a constable in Ireland. I know the law."

"You know the law in Ireland mayhaps, but that don't mean you know it hereabouts. The man I work for owns this land, every creek and every blade of grass, and he's grown tired of being robbed of its fruits by scoundrels like

him and thee. He knows Judge Scoresby in Allentown, them
two are firm friends, and Judge Scoresby will make his decision as my master advises in a case such as this. Last
fellow I caught poaching got two years, I believe. He's away
breaking rocks somewhere now."

"I have to get to Harrisburg."

"We'll see about that."

They walk back along the road, the poacher first, still
holding the lantern, the gamekeeper with his gun and
O'Connor in between. They hear the bleating of sheep on
the hillside and the murmurings of wind and rain. When
the road bends to the left, O'Connor sees the big house up
on a rise, dark and square-shouldered. The rutted driveway
is lined with ancient oak trees, their black branches wind-
bent and fantastical. When the gamekeeper knocks, a girl
answers and tells them to go around the back, then she lets
them in and they wait in the basement hallway until the
squire is ready. The poacher tries to make merry with the
girl, but the girl pays him no mind, and the gamekeeper
tells him to be quiet. O'Connor is still holding the gaff with
the dead fish bloody on the end of it. He asks if he can put
it down and the gamekeeper shakes his head.

"It's proof of the crime," he says. "The master will wish to
see that for hisself, I'm sure."

Upstairs, the squire is sitting alone at an empty table,
drinking coffee from a dainty china cup. He is a corpulent
man with a wide red face and a mane of thick gray hair
combed back from the forehead. His skin is scaly and scari-
fied and his eyes are large and pale blue. Every now and
then, when he talks, he has to pause to take in more air
through his nostrils. There is a fire blazing in the hearth
behind him and a liver-colored hound asleep on the flags.
Above the fire is a painting of a fine bay horse standing beside an elm tree with a dark-skinned servant in scarlet livery holding the reins.

"I know that stallion," the poacher says. "I seen him run the steeplechase a time or two."

"That stallion is no business of yourn," the gamekeeper tells him. "You keep your eyes to the front."

The squire looks them over, then asks where the fish has come from, and the gamekeeper explains what he knows.

"A man must eat," the poacher says. "Least that's what it says in the Scriptures."

"Can you read?" the squire asks him.

"Not so well."

"If you cannot read, then how can you claim to know what it says in the Scriptures?"

The gamekeeper chuckles.

"You're fencing with the squire now," he says. "He won't put up with any of your damned nonsense."

"Is this the one that was warned already?" the squire says, stabbing his sausage finger toward the poacher.

"I warned him two months past. I caught him on Johnson's Lane with two dead cottontails, and I told him that next time it would be Judge Scoresby. That's what I told him. But the warnings don't do any good with his kind."

"Two rabbits and now some good-sized trout," the squire says.

"I 'spect he's taken a sight more than that in between times, sir," the gamekeeper says.

"I'd expect he has," the squire says. "I'd expect he's been snatching the good food off my table for a long while now, hasn't he?"

He drains his coffee cup and grimaces at the taste. The poacher twitches and scratches his face but doesn't speak. His usual liveliness has faded and he looks suddenly morose and fearful.

"You take a fish from me today," the squire continues, "but what will you take from me tomorrow? If word gets out

that men like you are safe on my land, then soon enough
it'll be stripped bare."

"I'll move away from here," the poacher says. "Go west."

"Too late for such promises. You had a proper warning.
You'll see Judge Scoresby tomorrow and he'll decide what
you deserve. He's a fair man, and he'll give you a fair hearing, but he don't like poachers much, I'll tell you that. No,
he don't like poachers very much at all."

The squire winks at the gamekeeper, and the gamekeeper
smiles back at him.

"What about this other fellow here?" the squire says.

"Says his name's O'Connor and he's a traveler," the gamekeeper replies. "Says he's on his way to Harrisburg."

"He was the one caught holding the gaff?"

"Yes, sir. But he claims he was only helping."

"Where're you from?" the squire asks.

"From Dublin, but I've lived a while in Manchester. I was
a constable there."

"Manchester?" The squire looks affronted. "From what I
hear, that's a filthy place. The air is full of poison and the
people are like jungle savages."

"They say it's the future," O'Connor answers him calmly.
"They say that all places will be the same as Manchester
one day."

The squire frowns and shakes his head.

"That's a lie," he says. "There's no truth to that at all. The
Lord rained his brimstone down on Sodom, and he'll do the
same to Manchester when he deems the time is right. Are
you a Papist, O'Connor?"

"Yes, sir, I am."

"What does the Holy Father in Rome have to say about
the crime of poaching, I wonder?"

"I couldn't tell you."

"He couldn't tell us." The squire turns to the gamekeeper.

"Do you know about the Catholics, Mr. Brown? Do you know what kind of stuff they believe in?"

"Not so much, sir, but I hear they're a superstitious lot."

"They believe in magic, in the power of toenails and bits of old bone. They make carvings out of wood and plaster, then pretend they're alive. Can you imagine?"

"I hardly can."

"It's a backward, heathenish sort of faith."

They look at O'Connor, but O'Connor doesn't try to argue. The hound gets up slowly from the flags, yawns, rotates, then drops back down.

"I'm on my way up to Harrisburg," he says. "There's a man there I'm looking for. If you give me a warning and let me go, you'll never see me in this place again, I swear it."

"You promise to leave, but why should I believe you? That fellow standing beside you was warned, but it made no difference to him. I'd say a man who is bold and brazen enough to steal the fish from my streams is bold and brazen enough to lie to my face."

"I can take them both to see the judge, sir," the gamekeeper offers. "Two prisoners is as easy as one for me."

"I don't like to trouble Scoresby more than I have to. He's a busy man."

"Or I could whip this one and send him on his way."

The squire considers this for a moment.

"I know what we'll do," he says. "We'll set him to work in the mine for a week. Nothing like a spell of honest labor to purge a man's sins. A week is fair, I'd say."

"What mine?" O'Connor says.

"The lead mine. It's five miles from here, to the east. The other side of the river. I've had men digging there a year, and they've just struck a nice-looking vein."

"That will teach him, right enough, sir," the gamekeeper says, "and pay you back for your losses. It's a fine idea."

"You can't force me to work. It's not right or lawful."

"I'm not forcing," the squire says. "I'm making an offer.
It's the mine or Judge Scoresby. You can decide."

"I'll do it, if he won't," the poacher offers. "I'll work there
a whole month if you'd like me to."

"You can shut your mouth," the gamekeeper says. "We're
already finished with you."

"What will I eat?" O'Connor says.

"You'll have hot food at night and a dry place to sleep. I
have a mine agent by the name of Garnett over there who'll
give directions and keep his eye out in case you're ever
tempted to slacken off."

O'Connor looks about the room, the cracked wood panel-
ing, the brass fireplace tarnished and dull with dust, and
then looks back at the squire's square, ogreish features. He
feels like he has been here before, standing in the same
place, hearing the same words spoken, but he can't remember how or why.

"I can work for a week," he says, "but no more. After that
I have to get to Harrisburg."

"To find this man of yours? What's his name?"

"His name's Doyle. He's a Fenian. He killed my nephew
back in Manchester."

The squire raises his whiskery eyebrows half an inch.

"There's more than one Doyle in Harrisburg, I'll wager. I
hope you get the right one," he says.

"I aim to."

"If you kill this fellow Doyle, even if he did as you claim,
they'll likely hang you for it afterward. You can't kill a fellow in Pennsylvania nowadays and walk away scot free. It's
not like it used to be. You know that, I trust."

"I'll take my chances with the law."

The squire scratches his brow and frowns awhile before
commenting further.

"I killed a man once," he says. "Down in Texas near Fort
Mason. Shot him dead. He deserved it right enough, he was

a thief and a liar with it, but it's weighed on my conscience a time or two since. It was twenty years ago now, but I still wake in the night now and then and see him lying there, a-weeping and begging for his life, a grown man weeping like a little child. That's not something you can quickly forget."

"I don't forget much at all," O'Connor says. "It's not in my nature to do so."

"That's both a blessing and a curse, I'd say."

"I'd say you're right about that."

The squire nods, as if satisfied by this exchange, then coughs and turns to hawk into the fire.

"The two of you can sleep downstairs in the cellar," he says. "Anne, the girl, will find you something to eat if you want it. In the morning, this one here will go to the judge, and you and me will drive over to the mine. I'll explain to Garnett who you are. He'll show you the work. I hope you're better at mining than you are at poaching."

"I'm about the same, I expect."

"A week won't kill you either way. If you like it there, you can stay longer."

That night, in his sleep, as the poacher shifts and snuffles next to him, O'Connor hears the whispering voices of the recent dead. They weep and groan and tell him how much they suffer for his sake. Some become angry, some plead for his intercession. He tries to block his ears against their murmurous din, but the voices only get louder and more insistent. It is as if a dam has been breached inside him, and the torrent of memory is rushing through, sweeping aside all that is solid and real. As if the past is taking its bitter revenge on the present.

In the morning, he is set in the back of a hay wain and driven over the hills to the mine. There is a gray building beside a narrow, fast-moving stream. In front of the building, wooden rails arc unevenly from the mine entrance to the washing floor. A boy is standing by an empty ore tub, breaking rocks with a spalling hammer. When the squire asks for Garnett, the boy tells them he is up in the woods checking the sluice gates but will be back down soon. The squire goes into the mine shop to sit, and O'Connor stands outside by the window listening to the low rush of the stream and the dull echo of the spalling hammer on the knockstone. The damp air is cold against his skin and the sky above is thick with cloud. He looks down at the black earth between his boots and wonders how this will finish and how much more of it he can endure.

CHAPTER 30

They had a pony once, but the pony died of dropsy, so now a man must do that work instead. The ore tubs are five hands high with iron wheels and wooden sides, and the man who trams out the bouse must wear a harness on his shoulders and a broad leather band across his forehead to take the weight. Except for a few weeks in midsummer, there is always water flowing down the level, a foot or more in depth, which keeps the stopings dry but adds to the discomfort. If a man is not used to bending, there is the danger that he may strike his head on the timbers and knock himself cold. That has happened more than once, but after you have been in the mine for a while the bending becomes like second nature. The rails are good oak and they are strong but not always true, so there are places where the wheels will jam and extra force is required. On the best days the miners will fill four or five tubs with the bouse or deads.

It is a mile and a half from the vein to the mine entrance. Once a tub reaches the dressing floor, it must be tipped out and the load shoveled into the grinder. The boy will attend to the grinder himself, but it is the job of the man to shovel. If there is time, he may also help with the hotching tubs or join in breaking rocks with a hammer, but only on a quiet day or if the agent has given express instructions to do so. The boy is lazy and dishonest and will ask for help whether he needs it or not. The empty tub can be left by the dressing floor if there is another already standing at the vein, but, if not, it must be trammed back in and refilled. Compared to a full one, though, an empty tub is easy to move, even on a grade.

Garnett, the agent, explains all this to O'Connor on the first morning after the squire has left. He shows him the harness, the dead piles, and the best way to loosen the catch on the tubs to empty them. He tells the boy that O'Connor will take over the tramming in for this week and when the boy asks why, he tells him to mind his business and get back to his work. Garnett is a narrow man with sharp eyes and a stern expression. He wears a gray mustache and dirty green deerstalker cap. When the boy is gone, he tells O'Connor that he will treat him just the same as the other men, neither better nor worse, except if he tries to slacken off or run away, in which case he will come down hard. O'Connor asks if the squire has sent men here before for poaching, and Garnett says yes he has, although not always for poaching, sometimes for debt or trespass or other, lesser, crimes.

It is an hour's work to tram a full load of bouse from the vein to the mine entrance. The harness cuts into O'Connor's shoulders and strains his back, and his wet feet ache from the cold. Once the noise of the stoping fades, there is no sound in the tunnel but the rasp of his own breath and the soft rush of wheels through the constant runoff. Darkness ahead and darkness behind. He counts his steps and when he gets to a thousand, he stops to rest. Shadows flicker at the edge of his vision; black water drips down from the tunnel roof; the air is cold and there is a soft smell of calcite and turned soil. Every load is the same as the one before. For light, he carries a tallow candle in a tin candleholder hooked to the edge of the tub. If the candle blows out, the blackness is so strong and complete that his body dissolves into it and all that is left for that moment is his paltry soul, shriveled and white as a maggot.

After work is over, the miners eat cabbage fried in pork fat and argue about how much money they have made and who has worked the hardest that day. Mostly they ignore O'Connor, but sometimes, without warning, one of them will ask him a question: How many pigs do you own? Who is the king of Ireland? and when he gives his answer they snigger and shake their heads as if he has said something foolish. They all come from the same township; they have the same mouth and nose, and the same hunched-over walk. Because the boy is from a different township, a mile to the west of theirs, they enjoy making fun of him. They invent cruel nicknames, and if he tries to speak, they pretend they cannot understand what he is saying. The miners sleep together on bunk beds in the upstairs room, and O'Connor sleeps below in what used to be the stable before the pony died. Garnett locks him in at night and lets him out again in the morning.

Late in the afternoon of the third day, O'Connor watches Garnett beating the boy with a leather belt. Garnett is standing by the hotching tubs, and the boy is crouched over on the ground with his arms across his head. He shudders as each blow strikes but makes no attempt to escape or resist. When Garnett has finished, he steps back and gestures to the boy to get up and go back to work. The boy picks up his cap from the floor and wipes blood from his mouth. Garnett watches him for a moment, then puts the belt back around his waist and walks back to the office without looking around. O'Connor pulls the wagon along to the hopper and tips it out as normal. The boy picks up the wheelbarrow and walks across to him. He has fresh bruises on one side of his face and his lip is still bleeding.

"You should run away from here," O'Connor tells him.

"If I run away, they will only catch me and bring me back."

"Not if you run quick and far enough."

The boy picks up the shovel and starts filling the barrow with the bouse. He moves slowly as if dazed or half-asleep. The fresh blood on his lip looks almost black against his pale skin.

"Where would I run to?" he asks.

"There are other places, better than this."

"How would I live when I got there?"

"You could make your own way."

The boy shakes his head.

"I can't run away," he says again. "If I run away, they will only catch me and bring me back."

The miners play rummy after dinner. They hunch over the upturned tea chest like a gang of mud-stained necromancers, hissing and muttering prophecies as each card is discarded or retrieved. Garnett doesn't join them and O'Connor isn't invited. He sits by the window instead and looks out at the shifting darkness of the hills.

Later, before Garnett locks him into the stable, O'Connor asks about the boy.

"That boy's only job is to sort the rock and he does it poorly," Garnett says. "He's slow and stupid. He mixes up the ore and the deads. We lose money every day by his laziness."

"Where are his family?"

"His father is gone away and his mother is too poor to keep him, so he belongs to the squire. He's apprenticed here until he comes of age."

"Let me work beside him tomorrow. Have one of the other men do the tramming instead of me. I can watch him. Make sure he doesn't slacken off."

"It's my business to watch him, not yours."

"Why do you whip him?"

"To improve him."

"And do you find he improves much?"

"Not yet, but he shall."

"Let me help him. Why won't you?"

"You should help yourself, O'Connor. Forget about the boy."

There is no fire or stove in the stable, but he has a wool blanket and a pile of straw to lie on. When he dreams of Rose Flanagan now, he doesn't see her face, just an arm or a hand or the shape of her back as she is walking away. He knows it is her, but when he calls her name she doesn't look around or answer.

The next day, at dusk, when the miners come back up from the stoping, they find the dressing floor deserted and the last wagonload of bouse still standing by the hopper untipped. They assume, at first, that Garnett must have sent the boy off on an errand to the smelting plant or up into the woods to check the sluice gates, but when they go into the lodging shop, they realize that Garnett is missing also, and there is no sign of the thieving Irishman O'Connor either. Garnett's office is unlocked, so they step inside and peer about. They take the books and papers off the shelves and sit in his chair and pretend to give each other orders. They dip his pen into the inkpot and write their names on the blotter for the fun of it. They feel happier and freer without Garnett about, but they miss having the boy to make merry with. After dinner, they play rummy for an hour, then go to sleep as usual. In the morning, they draw straws to decide who will walk across the moors to the squire's house to tell him what has happened. The one with the short straw leaves after breakfast, and the others walk up the hill to the powder hut to get more gunpowder for blasting. As they approach the hut, they hear a voice calling from inside, high and furious, and when they unlock the door they see Garnett kneeling there between the stacked barrels, bound hand and foot with twine, with one eye closed and blackened and one ear torn and caked with blood.

CHAPTER 31

When Doyle reaches the farmhouse, there is only Anna inside. The boy Patrick is still at school and Fergus is up in the woods cutting fenceposts with George Nichols the hired man. For a moment she doesn't recognize him, then, when she does, she gasps and puts her hands up to her mouth. She looks older, he thinks, but not by very much.

"Why are you crying?" he says.

She shakes her head, impatiently, then dabs her eyes on her apron and tells him to take off his coat and sit down at the kitchen table. She puts a pot of coffee on the stove to boil and sits down beside him. Her face is eager and alert and her eyes are bright, as if just the sight of him is a pleasure.

"Tell me where you've been," she says. "Tell me everything."

"I can't remember everything. I've been too long away."

"Then tell me all that you do remember."

He tells her about the war, and then about Ireland. He doesn't mention Manchester or what happened there, but, even so, she looks shocked by what she hears.

"Too much fighting," she says. "You might have been killed."

"It's all over now. I won't go back."

"What will you do instead? Where will you go next?"

"I don't know that yet."

She asks him if he still holds any grudge against Fergus, and he shakes his head as if the question doesn't matter anymore.

"He told me what happened that night," she says. "He said that you were watching me while I slept and it made him angry to see it."

"I was taking a scoop of water, that's all. It was too hot to stay in the barn."

"He said you were watching me for a long time, but I told him even if you were, it didn't matter, you were only a boy then."

"When did you marry him?"

"Not long after you left. He'd made me promises before, but he hadn't kept any of them. After you went away, I told him that was the end of it for me, either we were married or I'd look for a place elsewhere."

"I was fifteen," he says.

"That's right. You were just fifteen when you left us."

She looks up at him again and smiles, and he feels for a moment just as he felt ten years before: prideful and awkward, his clenched body drowning in the turbid confluence of half a dozen nameless urges.

When Patrick gets back from school, Anna gives him a piece of cornbread and a cup of buttermilk, and he sits at the table staring at Doyle, speechless and amazed. Doyle asks him questions, and he nods or shakes his head to answer, but he won't talk unless Anna makes him. He has thick black curls like a ram's fleece and jutting-out ears; he resembles his father much more than his mother. After he has finished off the bread and milk, Anna makes him do his arithmetic out loud and recite some verses of poetry, then tells him he is a clever boy and will grow up to be a great man one day. Doyle gives him a nickel and shakes his hand.

"You're lucky to have such a fine mother," he says. "Don't you see how much she cares about you?"

Patrick nods and smiles back at him, but Doyle can see that the boy doesn't understand what he is saying, that he thinks all mothers are the same, more or less, and that his life on the farm is no better or worse than it should be. Anna kisses him on the top of the head and tells him to run up into the woods and let his father know they have an un-expected guest for supper.

In the daytime, Doyle works alongside George Nichols, plowing the fields for oats or mending fences, and in the evenings, after they have eaten, he talks to Anna and plays games with Patrick in the kitchen, or goes out to the barn to help him with his chores. After a week, Fergus jokes that if this carries on much longer, they will have to start paying him a wage, but as soon as he says it, Anna purses her lips in disapproval and tells Doyle that he is family and is wel-come to stay just as long as he likes.

The next day, as they are walking from the house up to the fields, Doyle tells George Nichols that if he's smart and knows what's good for him, he will leave the farm and go to Philadelphia or New York, where there are other Negroes just like him, and well-paid work is easy to find. *You'd be happier there,* he says, *you'd have a better life.* He tells him that Fergus can't be trusted, that he will cheat him when he gets the chance. *When I was a boy, he beat me so hard he almost killed me,* he says. *Me, his own nephew, think of that.* Nichols is a tall man, quiet and slow-moving. He lis-tens carefully without interrupting; then, when Doyle is finished, he tells him he is content where he is. He has worked outside in the fields all his life, he says, and would not thrive in the city.

That evening, as they sit down to eat supper, Fergus asks Doyle what he means by putting ideas into George Nichols' head.

"He says you told him he should leave me and go look for work in Philadelphia instead."

Doyle takes up a spoonful of the stew from his bowl and blows to cool it before answering.

"He'd do a sight better in Philadelphia if you ask me. There are good opportunities for a Negro there."

"George doesn't need any advice from you. He knows his own mind. He's happy here and we treat him well."

Doyle glances at Anna and then looks back at Fergus.

"Just two men talking to pass the time," he says. "I don't believe there's any law against it."

Fergus scowls and clenches his hand into a fist. White steam rises up from the plates in front of them; the oil lamp suspended from a roof beam casts a steady yellow glow.

"You told him that I can't be trusted," he says, "that I'm a liar and a cheat."

Doyle shakes his head.

"I don't remember saying that. Perhaps he heard it from someone else."

Patrick asks for bread, and Fergus saws off a slice and gives it to him. "Here," he says sharply. Patrick folds the bread in two, dips it in the gravy, then bites off the corner. The boy doesn't know what is going on, Doyle thinks, he's too young to understand, but Anna sees it.

"If you're trying to make trouble for us here, then you should leave," Fergus says.

Doyle waits a minute before answering. He enjoys this feeling of being on the brink, this sense of something held precious about to crack and break apart. There is the sound of the clock ticking on the mantelpiece behind him and of Patrick's pewter spoon tapping and scraping against the bottom of his plate.

"It was your wife who invited me. I'll leave when she wants me to."

"Is it true?" Anna asks him. "Did you really say those things?"

"No, it's not true."

"George Nichols swears to it," Fergus says.

"So who do you believe?" Doyle asks him. "A field-nigger off the Kentucky plantation, or your own flesh and blood?"

"George Nichols is a good man, honest and loyal."

"So what does that make me by your reckoning?"

They stare at each other across the tabletop. Fergus' face is pale and bloodless with dark blotches of color on his temple and across the bridge of his nose.

"You can stay here until Sunday," he says, "but not a day longer."

Doyle puts his elbows on the table and leans forward. When he speaks again, his voice is closer to a whisper.

"Are you angry with me now, Fergus?" he says. "Do you wish you could beat me bloody like you did before? We can try that thing over again if you'd like to."

"You two stop it now," Anna says. "Stop it, please."

Early the following morning, before dawn, Fergus hitches the wagon and drives into Harrisburg to collect a new blade for the plow. When he gets back it is almost dark. Instead of stopping in front of the house to unload, he drives the wagon on past the oat fields to the clearing at the edge of the woods where Doyle is cutting up pole wood for cording. He ties up the horse and walks through the trees, guided by the hollow thud of the ax. When he sees Doyle, he calls out, and Doyle stops and turns to look. Fergus' eyes are bright and he is almost smiling. The bitterness of the previous evening has been replaced by something else, something more like curiosity or pleasure. Doyle wonders what could have happened to cause the sudden alteration. He lodges the ax blade in a stump and swipes the wood chips off his pants leg.

"When I was over in Harrisburg today, I had a talk with Walter Alger," Fergus says, "the old man who owns the feed store on Water Street. He told me something you might want to hear."

"I don't know any Walter Alger."

"He knows you. He says there's a fellow by the name of James O'Connor, going around the town asking everyone he meets if they've heard of Stephen Doyle. He was in the feed store asking Walter the same question just the other day. Walter told him he didn't know any Stephen Doyle, but then afterward he remembered that I once had a nephew by that name who lived with me. He was asking me whatever became of you."

"And what did you tell him?"

"Don't you want to know why this O'Connor's come looking for you? Aren't you curious? Or perhaps you already know the reason?"

Fergus raises his eyebrows and waits for the response, but Doyle doesn't move or make an answer.

"He says you murdered his nephew, killed him in cold blood. He's come all the way from England to seek you out."

He waits again.

"Aren't you going to say something, Stephen? Aren't you going to tell me now that you've never been to England? That you never heard of James O'Connor? That it's all just fucking make-believe?"

"Did you tell Alger I was here?"

Fergus shakes his head.

"I have my own good name to protect. I've earned myself

a reputation in this county and I won't let you steal it from me. I told him you'd left here ten years ago, and I hadn't set eyes on you since."

"You think he believed you?"

"So far as I could tell, he did."

"Where's O'Connor staying in Harrisburg? Did Walter Alger tell you that?"

Fergus stares at him a moment, then looks away again.

"You should leave here now," he says. "Walk away quick before I change my mind and drive right back there."

"I'll leave you in the morning."

"You'll leave me now," he says more firmly. "I don't want you going near my wife or son again."

"I'm a soldier. Whatever I did, I did it for the cause."

Fergus shakes his head in disgust.

"I knew from the start there was a badness in you. I've seen it in your eyes. I tried to help you for your dead mother's sake, but some people can't be helped."

"You worked me half to death, then you beat me until I bled. Is that what you call helping?"

"I took you in when you had nowhere else to go," Fergus answers. "I fed you up and put a roof over your head. Any punishment you ever got from me, you deserved it. If I'd beat you some more, then maybe you would have learned something from it. Maybe you wouldn't be what you are today."

Doyle looks up through the mesh of black branches at the broken grayness of the evening sky.

"I need my belongings before I go," he says. "If you'll get them for me, I'd be obliged."

He watches Fergus turn away and start to walk back toward the wagon. *How long have I waited,* he thinks? *How often have I lived this moment out in dreams or masquerades and now it is arrived at last?* He tugs the ax out of the stump and takes three quick strides forward. The blade is already in motion, arcing brightly through the darkened air, when Fergus, too late, looks around. For an instant, as the chipped steel edge cuts down into neck muscle and spine bone, the two men stand there, in the clearing, weirdly conjoined, the ancient ax and its sweat-stained handle stretched out between them like a blood-black cord.

CHAPTER 32

The boy will not leave his side. Even at night, they must sleep pressed together or else he suffers nightmares and wakes in the early-morning darkness, shouting out or shaking with fear. Whatever is wrong with him will not easily be made right. O'Connor understands that now. He had supposed that once they were away from Garnett and the mine, the boy would improve, if not immediately then soon afterward, but they have been in Harrisburg a month already and nothing has altered. He is stubborn and silent still. When at rest, he sniffs and peers about and scratches at himself like an animal. He is not stupid, certainly, he may even be clever in his own secret ways, but he knows almost nothing—simple arithmetic is a mystery to him, and so are the letters of the alphabet and the months of the year. He should rightly be in a school somewhere, O'Connor thinks, so he can learn to become normal, like other boys, but they have no money for that, and even if they did, he would never agree to go. He asks himself sometimes why he has chosen to add to his troubles in this way, but he already knows the answer: Michael Sullivan is dead, but this boy is still living. He failed once before, and now he has been given another chance.

They live together in a single room in a cheap boarding-house by the railroad yards. They hire out as day laborers when they can, and on days when there is no work to be found, they go fishing in the reservoir or sit in one of the city squares watching the Negroes dance for money and lis-tening to the barrel organs. They have spoken to every Doyle listed in the Harrisburg street directory, and they have visited every draper's shop and every barroom and general store in the city without reward. O'Connor knows he should properly go back to New York and start the search anew, but they are settled here, in their own way, and if they stay another month, or even two, he thinks, what dif-ference will it make? The fury that drove him from Man-chester has lessened, and, in its place, he feels uncertainty and emptiness and occasionally, growing between the two, like a weed between flagstones, a frail and incongruous kind of hope.

One afternoon toward the end of April, as they are walk-ing back to the boardinghouse along Water Street, O'Connor hears the owner of the feed store, a man named Walter Alger, calling out to him through the half-open doorway. They turn to look and Alger beckons them inside.

"I have something you'll want to know about," he says. "There's an old Irish farmer, a fellow named Fergus McBride, who lives about twenty miles from here. He has a nephew who used to live with him on the farm. That was ten years ago and no one's seen him since. I haven't thought of the nephew for years, haven't had any cause to, but when Fergus came in here last week, I remembered right away."

He taps his wide forehead with his finger and winks.

"Remembered what?" O'Connor says.

"The nephew's name was Stephen Doyle. He must have been the sister's boy. *Stephen Doyle*. That's the one you're searching for, ain't it? The very one?"

"You say he left here ten years ago?"

"The two of them had some kind of falling-out, I believe. I don't know what it was all about. Fergus never told me and I never asked."

"Did you tell McBride about me? Did you say I was looking for a fellow with that name?"

"Certainly I did. He told me his nephew was a bad character but not so bad as all that. He doesn't believe he could be any kind of murderer."

"If he hasn't seen him for ten years, how would he know?"

"That's what I thought too, but I didn't like to say it to his face."

"Will he talk to me if I go out there to the farm?"

"He might talk, but I doubt he has much more to say. Even if this nephew's the man you're looking for, Fergus can't tell you where he is now. He could be anywhere at all."

"There might be another relative he could point me to, someone who knows where the nephew's living now."

"That's possible too."

"I'd almost given up," O'Connor says. "I thought it was all finished with."

Alger grins and looks pleased with himself.

"Then I done you a favor, ain't I?" he says. "I put you back in the game."

Later that night, in their boardinghouse room, the boy asks O'Connor what he will do after Stephen Doyle is found. They are sitting side by side on the edge of the metal bedstead, sharing a can of oyster stew. From beyond the dusty window, they can hear the noise of crashing boxcars in the rail yards and the heaves and whistles of the steam engines as they pass by.

"I may go back to Ireland," he says. "I'm not certain yet."

"Will you take me with you?"

"If you want it, I will."

They continue eating slowly, passing a single metal spoon back and forth between them.

"Will we go on a boat?" the boy asks.

"There's no other way to get there."

"I never been on a boat before. I never even seen the sea."

"The sea is something, a thing of wonder."

"What if I drown in it?"

"You won't drown in it."

"But what if I do?"

"Then I'll throw you a rope," he says.

The boy is smiling, which makes a change. O'Connor lets him have the last bite of the stew, then licks the spoon clean and puts it back in his pocket. He wishes, for a moment, that he was someone else, that he had never heard of Stephen Doyle or Michael Sullivan or Tommy Flanagan or any of the others, that the slate was wiped clean and he was free again, but he knows it is a childish way of thinking. It is too late for that now. He is what he is, and he must follow this path to its ending.

Next day, they are up at first light. They boil water for coffee and oatmeal, then wash themselves at the pump in the yard. The air is still cold and the morning light is dim and gray as they cross the railroad tracks and the Pennsylvania Canal, but as they strike the Jonestown Road heading east the cloud cracks and the sun breaks through. The boy walks slowly but steadily; sometimes he whistles a tune. When they stop by a stream to drink and rest, he curls himself into a ball on the damp ground and falls asleep until O'Connor wakes him. It is early afternoon by the time they reach the McBride farmhouse. A tall, gray-haired woman opens the door. Her pale eyes are red-rimmed, and she smells stale and unwashed, as if she has just risen up from a sickbed. There is a child standing just behind her, a boy of

nine or ten with thick black curls and ears that jut out sideways. O'Connor tells the woman his name and explains
they have come to speak to Fergus McBride. The woman
glances away for a moment, then looks back at them again.
She tells him that she is Fergus' wife and her name is Anna
McBride, but that Fergus is dead.

"He was robbed and murdered coming back from Harrisburg," she explains, her voice gruff and strained. "A huck-
ster found his body lying by the side of the road a few miles
away from here. We buried him two days ago in the churchyard yonder."

"Just yesterday I was talking to Walter Alger, the fellow
who owns the feed store on Water Street in Harrisburg,"
O'Connor says. "He told me he spoke to your husband only
last week."

"Then that must have been the very day he was killed,"
she says.

He looks about the yard. The farm is tidy and prosperous-
seeming. He has not heard any talk of the roads hereabouts
being dangerous, and it's an odd piece of misfortune, he
thinks, to be robbed and killed so close to home.

"I'm very sorry," he says. "Can we help you at all? Is there
any work that needs to be done on the farm?"

She shakes her head.

"I thank you," she says, "but I have all the help that I
need here."

She invites them to come inside, and they sit down together at the pine table. The room is cluttered and grimy
and smells of pork fat and ashes. O'Connor can see that the
woman is exhausted by grief. Her thin face is pale, and she
moves with the slowness and imprecision of a sleepwalker.
She gives them a jug of water to drink and they thank her
for it.

"Is this your son?" she asks O'Connor, looking at the boy.

"No, not my son. His father died and his mother is elsewhere. I'm his guardian."

"How did you know my husband? I don't recognize your face."

"I didn't know him, Mrs. McBride, but I'm searching for someone, and I thought your husband might be able to help me."

"Then I'm sorry you made the journey for nothing. You're welcome to rest here for the night if you wish. There's a room above the stables, and I can give you supper too, although it won't be much."

"Perhaps you can answer my questions?"

"I doubt that I can. My husband kept his business mostly to himself."

"They concern your nephew, Stephen Doyle."

She looks surprised.

"If you want to know about Stephen, it's best to talk to him yourself. He's working up in the pasture now, I believe."

There is a silent interval while O'Connor tries to fathom what he has just been told.

"Are you telling me that Stephen Doyle is here on this farm?" he says eventually. "That he's here right now?"

"He's been with us this fortnight since, and it's a great blessing to have him. I'm not sure I could have managed all alone with my sadness. He's been a great comfort to me, to both of us."

She reaches over and touches Patrick on his cheek, but the child flinches away.

"I was told that he left you ten years ago and hadn't been seen or heard of."

"He did leave us once, that's the truth, but lately he returned. Is it Stephen you're looking for?"

The boy begins to speak, but O'Connor gestures for him to keep quiet. He looks back at Anna calmly as if nothing unusual has just happened, as if everything is still just as it should be.

"Was your nephew ever in the war, Mrs. McBride?"

"Certainly he was. They made him a captain by the end of it."

"In the New York Infantry, was it? The Eighty-eighth?"

"That's right."

"And he has two scars on his face from his service? One here and another one here?"

She nods.

"So you know him?" she says. "You're a friend of Stephen's?"

"An acquaintance. I knew him in England. We two had some business dealings there."

"I didn't know Stephen was ever in England. He told us he went back to Ireland once, but he didn't say anything about England."

"The time was brief. It may have slipped from his mind."

"If you'd like, I can send Patrick up to the pasture now to tell Stephen you're here."

"It's better if we go up there ourselves, I think."

She nods again, then frowns.

"Is something the matter?" she says. "Is Stephen in some trouble?"

O'Connor is trying to keep his voice steady now, to betray neither surprise nor alarm.

"No," he says. "At least, none that I know of."

O'Connor glances again at the boy, then stands up from the table.

"We won't keep you any longer," he says. "Thank you for your help."

In the yard, O'Connor takes Garnett's service pistol out of his pocket and checks its readiness, then tips back his head to the sky and screws his face into a scowl. The boy watches him.

"What will you do now?" he asks.

"I'll do what it is I came here to do."

"I can help you."

"No, you can't. You're too young. I would have left you back in Harrisburg if I'd had any notion Stephen Doyle was going to be here."

O'Connor pushes the gun into his belt and presses his hands together in front of his face as though offering up a final, furious prayer. If Doyle is here on the farm and Fergus McBride has been murdered, then he knows there is a chance that Doyle killed his uncle, and the only reason he would do that is to protect himself from discovery. If that's the case—if he suspects that he is being looked for—then there is every chance he will have armed himself. O'Connor is not afraid for his own life, but he wishes the boy was somewhere else entirely. He doesn't want these actions to be witnessed or shared; he wants the dread weight of them to be his alone.

"You stay where you are," he says. "Wait here for me."

"What's a guardian?"

"That's just a word. It's not important."

"But what does the word mean?"

"It means I protect you, until you can protect yourself."

"How long does it last for?"

"A year," he says, "two years, maybe more."

"Let me help you to kill him."

"No, I won't do that. I can't."

He tells the boy again to stay where he is, that he will be back soon enough. As he walks off along the dirt track toward the pasture, he remembers his father in the jail cell in Armagh on that last afternoon before they took him away to Spike Island, how he held each of them in turn and kissed them hard and made them promise they would never forget the evil, thieving bastards who were to blame for all their sufferings. He spoke it like a blessing, when really it was a curse, a way of binding them to him forever. Daniel O'Leary, the man he had murdered, was the son of Charles O'Leary, the bailiff who had evicted O'Connor's grandfather from his farm near Forkhill almost twenty years before. Cherish your bitterest memories, feed them carefully, and let them grow—that was the rule his father had lived by and the rule he wanted his children to live by too. O'Connor has labored all his life to forget the past, to put those years behind him, but he wonders now if his efforts have all been in vain and if the ghost of Paul O'Connor, vexatious and vindictive, has been living inside him all along, hidden away, silent and all-controlling.

He walks another fifty yards along the path as it rises slowly up past the hog pen and the smokehouse, then stops where he is and stands for a minute looking off into the pale distance. The wind is twitching the tops of the elm trees and, in the field behind, the sheep are bleating. He feels his conscience coiled up tight inside him. It is one thing to risk himself for the sake of vengeance, he knows, but the boy is an innocent, he has no part in this, so why should he be sacrificed too? For whose sake? He looks down at his feet for a moment, spits once into the dirt, then turns about and starts walking back the way he came. When he reaches the yard, the boy is still standing there, his boots half sunk down into the mud, motionless and with the same empty look across his face.

"We'll go back to Harrisburg," O'Connor says. "I'll tell the police what we've learned. They can come out here and arrest him."

"I thought you intentioned to kill him yourself."

"So I did, but I changed my mind about that," he says. "This other way is better."

They have been walking for an hour when it starts to rain. Water drips off the bare branches of the trees and collects in

runnels in the plowed fields on either side. Dark clouds drift
across the limestone sky. O'Connor wonders if he has made
yet another mistake, if he has betrayed his own cause yet
again. If they can hitch a ride, it will be three more hours
back to Harrisburg, but with the boy, if they have to walk all
the way, it might be five or six. When Anna McBride tells
him about their visit, Doyle will know it's not safe to remain
on the farm any longer, and by the time O'Connor persuades
the police to come out, he may be ten miles away already,
twenty even. They may never find him again, however hard
or long they look. All this way, all this suffering and trouble,
he thinks, and nothing to show for it. He should feel disappointed or enraged, but he doesn't. He is pleased to be away
from there and glad that the boy is out of danger.

As they walk along, the boy starts singing a song about a
man named McGinty who left one day and never came back
again. His voice is frail but steady, and when he finishes
O'Connor asks him to sing another, but the boy tells him
they should rightly take it in turns.

"You sing the next one," he says, "then I'll go after."

The rain has stopped, but they can see it falling still over
the hills off to the north, the dark lines angling down.
O'Connor hasn't sung a song in he doesn't know how many
years, he hasn't wanted to until now, but when he tries it,
the words and tune come back without any effort, easy and
unbidden, as if they have been lying dormant inside him all
that long time like seeds buried deep in the black earth.

CHAPTER 33

San Francisco, Eight Years Later.

At the crossroads, a young man is preaching. He is lean and hollow-cheeked with deep-set eyes, long black hair, and a ragged beard streaked here and there with premature strands of silver-gray. The sun is high up in the sky. It is the hour before noon, and, as he speaks, dampness glistens on his pulsing throat and drips down from his brow. He preaches death and the end-time and God's promised salvation through the blood of Jesus Christ Our Lord. Some people passing by pause a minute from their daily business to listen. Others, the greater number, scowl or laugh at him or look away. His voice is high and impassioned. He holds a sweat-stained Bible in his right hand, and when he quotes from Scripture he raises it above his head and beats it like a tambourine.

"Hear my story and heed it well," he cries. "For once I was lost as you are. My spirit was sunken in darkness and shriveled by ignorance and I was on the very brink of despair, but God lifted me up. I was born in Pennsylvania into poverty and backwardness. At the age of ten, I was sent to

toil in a mine where every day I was beaten and mocked. A
man named O'Connor saved me. He became my guardian
and we lived together. O'Connor had an enemy somewhere
nearby, a man named Doyle, who had injured him griev-
ously in the past. Wanting revenge, O'Connor looked out for
him every day, but he never did find him. Then, one day, a
day of reckoning, the two of us were walking alone in the
farm country, when Doyle appeared to us suddenly and
without any warning. He was riding on a gray horse and
holding a pistol. Only the moment before we had been singing and laughing together and now death was upon us. Let
that be a lesson to all poor sinners. My guardian had no
time to escape or defend himself. Before he could even draw
his own gun, he was shot through the head.

"He lay dying at my feet, but I had to abandon him and
to flee into the woods to save my own life. I ran just as far
as I could and then I hid, shaking with fear, until night
fell. When morning came, I tried to find my way back to
the road, but whichever way I walked I only returned to
the beginning. I was going around in a great circle—it was
as if I was under some strange spell and there was no way
to break from it. As it is said in the Psalms: *They wan-
dered in the wilderness in a solitary way; they found no
city to dwell in.*

"I was tired and thirsty, and the pain of O'Connor's death
was a fire scorching my heart. I was beginning to give up
hope when I heard a noise, like a whistle or a hum, off in
the far distance. The harder I listened, the more strange
and curious the noise became. I determined to find its
source. I started to walk and soon I arrived at a clearing. In
the center of the clearing was a tent, and from the tent
came the sound of singing. When I went inside, the people
there turned to look. I thought they would scold me, but
instead they greeted me with warmth. It was just as Christ
teaches us: *In my Father's house are many mansions: if it*

*were not so, I would have told you. I go to prepare a place for
you there.*

"When the hymn was finished, the priest called me up to
the altar. He asked me to say my name and then he laid his
hand on my forehead and gave me a blessing. At that moment, as I stood there, weak and desperate and laid low
with grief, the Holy Spirit filled me and all the fear and
anguish fell away. For it is truly written: *God shall wipe
away all tears from their eyes; and there shall be no more
death, neither sorrow nor crying.* That day was the first day
of my second lifetime. My guardian was dead, but I had
found a truer comforter and protector in the Lord Jesus.

"I became the priest's attendant and served him loyally.
He taught me to read and write and I ministered to his
needs. After several years in his household, I experienced a
great vision. I was lying in my bed one evening, sweating
with an ague, when I saw an angel hovering above me. The
angel told me that Christ would come again in the west and
that, on his return, the New Jerusalem would be raised
there also. As soon as I was well enough to walk, I packed
my bag to leave. The journey here was long and frightful,
and my faith was tested many times, but I knew that Christ
was watching over me, so I endured the pains of it for his
sake.

"When I reached the great city of San Francisco, the
angel came down to me again. He told me it was my task to
prepare the people here for what was surely coming. He
revealed to me that very soon this place will burn with furious flames, that the ground beneath it will shake, and that
the Lord will avenge himself upon the wicked and all those
who have aided their wickedness. Soon, sooner than you
think possible, the seven angels will descend from heaven
and the whoremongers and idolaters will be cast into a lake
of fire. That is the true prophecy and I am its humble mes-
senger. That is the word of the Lord. Repent and scrub

yourselves clean of your sin or you will be cast into hell for a thousand years or more. Ignore or insult me at your own peril, for *Behold, the day of the Lord cometh, cruel both with wrath and fierce anger, to lay the land desolate.*"

It took him a year to complete the journey west from Pennsylvania, and many times he thought he would die before he reached the end. He was almost drowned crossing the Missouri River. Near Wichita, he was robbed and beaten and left for dead. In the high mountain passes he nearly froze, and in the deserts he was stung by serpents and burned black by the sun. Despite these privations, his faith never wavered, and when he reached San Francisco, lice-ridden and ragged, with his boots broken apart and his feet blistered and swollen to twice their size, he knew for certain that his long path had reached its promised conclusion, that he had entered Babylon at last. On every side and in every place, in the banks and offices, churches and temples, in the filth-strewn rancorous streets, the signs of sin and false prophecy were plain for him to see. Everywhere he looked, idolatry and avarice. Everywhere he looked, lechery, destitution, corruption, and greed.

It is only a matter of time now, he knows, before God's judgment is meted out. When he imagines the city being razed to the ground and the people being cast into the fire or struck down by a plague, he feels, beyond the pity and horror, a sense of clarity and great purpose. He has seen evil in his life, he has suffered and watched others suffer, but he understands now that all of that was needful. Every pain he has known and every confusion is a part of the same eternal and unalterable plan. Nothing can be left out of the plan, and there is nothing that lies beyond or outside it. What seems strange or past our understanding will all be explained by what comes at the end. What seems false or terrible will be shown in the final days to be what was required by the true and the good. In the last reckoning, there is not a single dollar or cent left uncounted. That is his faith and his surety. That is his satisfaction and his joy.

When he speaks on the street corners and in the marketplace, he is jeered at or ignored, but he is not dismayed because he knows that when the Last Trumpet sounds the iniquitous will be cast down and the righteous will be raised up in glory. James O'Connor is dead and Stephen Doyle is still alive somewhere and at liberty, but when Christ returns their two souls will be weighed in the balance and the true and final verdicts will be rendered. The law of man is weak and corrupted, but the law of God is endless and undefiled.

He is all alone in this place, without friends or trusted companions, because he has found no one whose heart is sufficiently pure or whose character is sufficiently strong to stand beside him. Every day, in every countenance he passes, he sees the marks of the beast writ large. It is only when he looks at himself in the glass that he sees on his own forehead, written in letters made of golden light, the blessed name of the Lord.

At midnight, he goes down to Pacific Street and waits in the alleyway by the deadfall. Men come to him there. Some are still young, like him, but most are like the priest was: old and foul-smelling, with soft wet lips, round protruding bellies, and trembling finger-ends. He understands their desires and knows how to pacify them. Although he touches their flesh and lets himself be touched, although he takes them into his mouth sometimes and swallows their seed, he is never tainted. He takes their money but is not corrupted by it. God is his shield and protection always. Although, at night, he sleeps in the lowest lodging houses, amid filth, beside drunkards and criminals, and in the daytime eats his broken victuals with gamblers and whores, his purity and holiness remain undiminished because he knows the angels are watching over him and guiding him forever. As he lies in his bed in the fetid darkness, he hears the rustling of their great wings in the stale air above his head and listens to the easeful hush of their enormous voices, sonorous, calm, and soothing, like beautiful music playing in a different room.

Author's Note and Acknowledgments

This is a work of fiction rooted in historical fact. It is a fact that three members of the Irish Republican Brotherhood—William Allen, Michael Larkin, and Michael O'Brien (afterward known as the Manchester Martyrs)—were hanged outside the New Bailey Prison in Salford in November 1867 for the murder of Manchester police sergeant Charles Brett, but the events that follow on from that in this novel are all imagined. Although a small number of the characters are loosely based on actual people who were involved in encouraging or suppressing Irish revolutionary activity in England in the 1860s, the majority, including James O'Connor and Stephen Doyle, are my inventions.

I am grateful to John McAuliffe, Judith Murray, Denise Shannon, Suzanne Baboneau, and Gillian Blake for all their assistance and support.

About the Author

IAN MCGUIRE is the author of *The North Water* and *Incredible Bodies*. He is a winner of the Royal Society of Literature's Encore Award and Historical Writer's Association Gold Crown Award. He lives in Manchester, England, where he teaches at the University of Manchester's Centre for New Writing.